Red Labyrinth

RED
LABYRINTH

DOMINIC ADLER

LUME BOOKS
A JOFFE BOOKS COMPANY

LUME BOOKS
A JOFFE BOOKS COMPANY

Lume Books, London
A Joffe Books Company
www.lumebooks.co.uk

First published in Great Britain in 2023 by Lume Books

We love to hear from our readers!
Please email any feedback you have to: feedback@joffebooks.com

Cover design by Imogen Buchanan
Cover images © Shutterstock and Figurestock

ISBN: 978-1-83901-563-2

'To my Son, with love.'

The War in Europe will soon be won, but Peace presents challenges of its own. To meet them, I propose we recruit the best and most ideologically committed young people from every corner of the Socialist world. They will join a special part of our security apparatus and be trained to the highest standards. These 'Spartans' of our Tenth Directorate will be our eyes and ears across the Globe. They will also, where necessary, be our swords.

Colonel-General Sergei Kruglov, NKVD chief and architect of the Spartan programme, December 1946

Chapter 1

March 1947, Surrey, England

'You gonna shoot yourself, Mrs Graham?' asked Tommy, stabbing his shovel into the mud. Earlier, two of the borstal's instructors locked themselves in the staffroom with a bottle of whisky and a Walther. Everyone heard the shots.

Mrs Graham held the title of Matron. As far as the boys were concerned, she was a prison warder. 'Shut up, Fairburn. Reinforcements will come.'

'They said the Germans ran away.'

'Defeatist gossip. Keep digging.'

Tommy shovelled gloopy earth into a sandbag. 'I heard the radio, Miss. They say the Russians do horrible things to prisoners.'

Mrs Graham's hand rested on her holstered pistol. 'I could shoot you right now, Thomas Fairburn. Nobody would care.'

Tommy smiled. 'You won't, though, will you?'

'Why?'

''Cuz you're scared,' the boy replied, knuckles white around the shovel's handle. *How would it feel, to drive the tip into her face?* Then, in the distance, came the sound of guns.

'Boys, follow me,' Mrs Graham ordered, grabbing Tommy's arm. 'Bring sandbags and shovels.'

'Why?' asked one of the children.

'The King's orders are to resist until the last bullet,' she snapped. 'Our soldiers need your help.'

Tommy often eavesdropped on the soldiers stationed at the borstal. When they weren't complaining about their officers, they predicted the Soviets would head straight for Croydon aerodrome. Tommy used to watch RAF fighters flying overhead, but now there were only Russian aircraft. A young lieutenant in battledress appeared, a swagger stick under his arm. 'Mrs Graham? There's transport heading back to London. Wouldn't it be safer if you went too?'

'I'll stay,' the matron insisted.

The lieutenant pointed his stick at the boys. 'What about them?'

'They're the children of traitors, use them to fetch water and supplies. When they die, throw them on the barricades. Just don't give them guns.'

The lieutenant shook his head. 'I take it their re-education was a failure?'

The matron shrugged. 'They were brainwashed by communists. They think the Soviets are coming to liberate them.'

The lieutenant shook his head. 'Well, the little buggers are in for a surprise, aren't they?'

The boys were ordered to drag sandbags to a machine-gun nest overlooking the main road. Tommy only half filled his, hoping Russian bullets would pass through them more easily. The soldiers wore khaki battledress, their helmets covered in netting. 'Want some chocolate?' asked a corporal. Tommy shook his head, remembering what his father told him: *it's better to starve than take food from a fascist*. Tommy's father was a hero. 'Suit yourself,' the corporal replied, wincing as a shell exploded in the woods nearby. A column of boy scouts on bicycles rattled by, Panzerfaust anti-tank rockets strapped across their chests. Dismounting, they disappeared into the trees, led by an elderly scoutmaster wearing a steel helmet.

The lieutenant reappeared, a radio operator at his shoulder. 'B Company are in contact with the enemy,' he announced. 'Only fire on my orders, not before.'

'Yes, sir,' the corporal replied, working the action on his Vickers gun. Crossing the schoolyard, the lieutenant led Mrs Graham inside a bunker next to the bicycle sheds.

'Lads, find cover. Keep your heads down,' a sergeant ordered, pointing at the borstal. Most obeyed, but when he reached the door, Tommy peeled away.

'Where you goin'?' asked one of the boys.

'To watch the Reds kill Mrs Graham,' Tommy replied, scrambling up the wall. Fingers probing gaps in the crumbling brickwork, he hauled himself onto a gable. From his perch he saw soldiers frantically digging shell-scrapes in the fields next to the school, an old Matilda tank half hidden under camouflage netting. A Soviet plane circled overhead and moments later the tank was shrouded in fiery smoke. Artillery pounded the woods like giants stomping across the land, levelling everything with their boots.

When the barrage was over, Tommy heard the unmistakeable sound of tanks. He recognised the noise of steel tracks on tarmac from German military parades in London. A flurry of anti-tank rockets whooshed from the treeline, sparkling and twisting like fireworks. A Russian T-34 clattered to a halt, smoke spewing from its turret, the infantry riding on the deck leaping down to fight. More armour appeared, followed by waves of men in dun-coloured uniforms. They roared – *Urrah!* – machine guns chattering and mortars coughing. As a tank was knocked out, another took its place. Tommy thought about the boy scouts hiding in the trees. Boy scouts were fascists and now they'd be dead.

Soviet infantry charged the machine-gun nest, reinforced by a ragged line of British soldiers with bayonets fixed. Through the smoke, Tommy saw the lieutenant and the matron hurry back to the borstal. Finding a piece of slate on the roof, slimy and cold to the touch, Tommy climbed back down. Teeth gritted, eyes watering from the smoke, he followed them inside. 'Run, Mrs Graham,' the lieutenant begged. He fell against a door, his khaki trouser leg darkened with blood. 'I'm not German. I'm not SS. They'll take me prisoner. But you…'

'No,' the matron snapped. Hearing the crash of boots on concrete, Tommy spun to see Russian soldiers swarm the doorway. They wore camouflage uniforms and carried machine pistols, hard-looking men with dirty faces. Mrs Graham fired, a bullet taking one of the soldiers in the chest. Another Russian appeared, a big man wearing a blue-topped cap, machine pistol shouldered. The matron, grim-faced, aimed again.

Then Tommy was on her.

Gripping the piece of slate like a dagger, he dragged it across the matron's throat. Eyes bulging, she clamped a hand across the wound, her pistol clattering to the floor. Gurgling, she fell.

'*Prekratit' strelyat',*' said the Russian in the blue-topped cap. His men lowered their weapons, watching Mrs Graham's twitching body. Turning to Tommy, the Russian spoke in heavily accented English. 'Kid, are you okay?'

'Through there,' Tommy panted, pointing at the office door. 'There's a fascist inside. He's wounded.'

'Good lad,' the Russian replied. 'Now, stand back.' Pulling the pin from an egg-shaped grenade, he tossed it into the office. There was a small explosion and, with a wink, the Russian stepped into the room. Moments later there was a single gunshot. The Russian reappeared, holstering a pistol. 'It's done. Now, let's talk, eh?'

Tommy and the Russian stood watching the borstal burn. Soldiers stripped the dead of valuables and equipment. Army trucks trundled south, filled with hollow-eyed prisoners. 'What is your name, boy?'

'Thomas Fairburn, sir.'

'How old are you, Thomas Fairburn?'

'I'll be seventeen in December.'

'I am Captain Nikolai Andreyevich Sechkin,' the Russian replied, plucking a cigarette from a bloodstained pack. 'I think you saved my life, Thomas Fairburn who-is-seventeen-in-December. That crazy woman would have shot me.'

'I wanted to kill her.'

'Why?'

'She was a fascist.'

Sechkin chuckled. 'I agree, that's as good a reason as any. Is it the first time you've killed anyone?'

'Yes.'

Sechkin nodded approvingly. 'You were quick. No hesitation.'

The boy shrugged. 'Like I said, she was a fascist.'

You aren't a fascist, then? Isn't Britain a fascist country?'

'The fascists put my mum and dad in a camp, then they sent me here. My parents were Communists.'

'I see. Where did they take your parents?'

'I don't know.'

'Are there many comrades?' asked Sechkin gently, pulling a grubby notebook from his pocket. 'In Britain, I mean? Do you know who they are? Or where they are?'

'They put them in camps with the Jews. People say they're dead.'

Sechkin wrote something down. 'Tell me, Thomas Fairburn, how well do you know this area? Do you know the way to the aerodrome?'

Tommy nodded. 'Yes. I've been all the way to Brixton on my bike and I used to watch the planes at Croydon aerodrome. I know London from day trips, places like the Houses of Parliament and Buckingham Palace.'

'Excellent, *tovarich*. We need a guide. Our maps are old, maybe you can show us the way to Croydon aerodrome?'

Tommy smiled. His father would have approved. 'I'll help.'

Sechkin slapped Tommy on the back. 'Good. Do you like coffee?'

'I've never had coffee.'

'We'll fix that. We'll find sausage and cheese. You can make sandwiches.'

'Can I ask you a question, Captain?'

'Of course, Thomas,' the Russian replied, a smile on his big ruddy face. 'You will call me *Comrade* Captain, though. It is our way.'

'Why is your hat blue, Comrade Captain?' Tommy was intrigued by Sechkin, who wore badges with hammers and sickles pinned to his camouflaged chest. Tommy wanted to know everything about these tough-looking men.

'My hat is blue because I am a political officer of the NKVD,' said Sechkin proudly.

'NKVD?'

'The sword and shield of the Soviet Union. We protect our workers and hunt fascists.' Sechkin smiled. 'I think you will like helping us.'

6

'Will we kill more fascists?' asked Tommy, watching the borstal's roof tumble into the flames.

'Oh yes,' Sechkin replied, stubbing out his cigarette end with his boot. 'You have my word!'

Chapter 2

From: Capt. N.A. Sechkin, 157th NKVD Special Rifle Division
Date: 27th October 1947

Subject: Thomas Henry FAIRBURN (b. 09/12/1930)

Comrade Colonel Turov, Fraternal greetings!

This report concerns Thomas FAIRBURN, a British national my men liberated from a fascist re-education camp. For the past seven months he has become something of a mascot, acting as a scout, interpreter and partisan fighter. On many occasions during our advance into London he displayed bravery and cunning. He shows no hesitation when it comes to fighting fascists.

FAIRBURN has a basic grasp of Marxist-Leninist principles. His parents were members of the British Communist Party (he tells me they were imprisoned by the Gestapo for Resistance activity). He shows promise learning Russian, is intelligent and physically fit. It is worth reiterating the boy's impressive appetite for violence against the Hitlerites. I believe he has the potential to become a useful asset to the Soviet Union.

8

I respectfully hope you do not find my suggestion impertinent, but Major A.T. Balakin (First Main Directorate) recently asked all political officers to identify young British nationals with potential recruitment value. Therefore, I propose this young man for your consideration. Otherwise, I shall place FAIRBURN with the Workers Placement Office for reassignment to our reconstruction efforts.

Very respectfully yours,

Capt. N.A. Sechkin

From: Col. B.N. Turov, 157th NKVD Special Rifle Division
Date: 5th November 1947

Subject: Person of interest — Thomas FAIRBURN

Comrade Captain Sechkin, greetings and congratulations on your diligence and initiative. I have seen nothing but excellent reports concerning your performance, especially during the final offensive on the fascist's London redoubt.

I have spoken with Maj. Balakin, who sends fraternal greetings. He asks that Thomas FAIRBURN is taken to Divisional HQ immediately for evaluation. Please see me when you next visit and we shall toast your success.

Yours,

Col. B.N. Turov

SECRET

OP. SPARTAN FILE NOTE – 31ˢᵗ October 1950

Author: Lt. Col. A.T. BALAKIN (1ˢᵗ Main Directorate, MGB)

Subject: Junior Lieutenant Thomas Henry FAIRBURN

Jr. Lt. FAIRBURN was the most promising student in the first cohort of non-Russians to graduate from the VRSh under the SPARTAN programme. Fifty-seven cadets began the course but only twelve met the required standard. FAIRBURN was the only British candidate.

FAIRBURN'S performance was outstanding in all areas, including political theory, physical and technical surveillance, skill-at-arms, unarmed combat, sabotage, interrogation and agent cultivation and handling. His Russian is fluent and spoken with a pronounced Muscovite accent. Instructors noted only one area where he was found wanting: FAIRBURN can occasionally come across as aloof, especially to those less gifted than himself. This is clearly unacceptable for a covert operative tasked with infiltration operations in hostile countries. When this was explained to him, the officer immediately took action to improve his personal manner. He has now exceeded the required standard.

For his first assignment, the officer requested the First Main Directorate's Special Mobile Group in Poland. This is a paramilitary counter-partisan role with a high attrition rate. At this time, he shows little interest in being deployed to the country of his birth, but understands it is inevitable. In the meanwhile, he lodges in Moscow with Maj. N.A SECHKIN and his wife, who have acted as guardians and sponsors.

I commend Jr. Lt. FAIRBURN, who I believe is a model for future SPARTAN recruitment from nations within our sphere of influence. A cadre of such agents can only strengthen our mission in promoting and protecting the USSR's interests across the globe.

Chapter 3

London, October 1957

Red flags flew over Sloane Square, workers erecting hoardings displaying Soviet warriors slaying Nazi serpents. The serpents' eyes were shaped like swastikas, their fangs painted red, white and blue. It was nearly the tenth anniversary of Britain's liberation from fascism and the end of the Great Patriotic War. To celebrate, a Guards division of the Soviet army would march from Sloane Square to Whitehall. There, the President of the Socialist Republic of Great Britain would award battle honours. He would be joined by Britain's great friend and ally, Nikita Khrushchev, First Secretary of the Communist Party of the Soviet Union. Khrushchev's face adorned thousands of posters across the city, smiling his gap-toothed smile, dressed in an open-necked shirt like a humble factory foreman.

A green-uniformed KGB officer stepped out of the Underground station, a duffle bag slung over his shoulder. His boots were well-polished but worn, his blue-topped cap faded. Passing the Peter Jones – GUM store on the King's Road, he stopped outside Burgess House, headquarters of the British Committee for State Security. 'Your papers, please, Comrade Captain,' asked a sentry wearing a black beret; a Kalashnikov hung across his chest.

The KGB officer produced his *dokumenty*. 'I'm Captain Thomas Fairburn.' He was softly spoken, his accent southern English. 'KGB.'

The sentry cocked his head. 'KGB? You're British?'

'Yes, Comrade,' Fairburn replied.

'Blimey. Are there many British KGB officers?'

'I imagine that's a secret. Now, may I come in?'

'Of course, Comrade.' Returning the sentry's salute, Fairburn stepped inside the former army barracks. He saw a German tank, a war trophy, parked on a corner of the parade square. A burly man leaned against the panzer's hull, smoking a cigarette. 'I remember you blowing one of those up,' said Fairburn in Russian, pointing at the tank. 'Was it a King Tiger?'

'I'm not sure. I was drunk.' The big man shrugged. 'Those were the days, eh, Tommy? How was your flight?'

Fairburn pulled the Russian into a bear hug. He felt Nikolai Sechkin's stubble on his cheek and smiled. 'Too much turbulence, Nikolai Andreyevich.'

'There's always turbulence when you're around.'

'It seems that way. It's good to see you, Comrade Colonel.'

'And you too,' Sechkin replied. Tommy's mentor now worked in the KGB's 2nd Main Directorate – Counter-intelligence. 'You've put on muscle, Tommy,' he said, playfully punching Fairburn's stomach. 'They kept you busy in Budapest, little *Spartan*?'

'And you've got fat,' Fairburn chuckled, jabbing Sechkin's belly. 'Yes, it was busy.'

'Too much paperwork and too many meetings,' Sechkin replied testily, sucking in his gut. 'I polish a chair with my arse all day. English beer doesn't help, either. Luckily, Irina doesn't mind.'

The two men crossed the parade square, female clerks hurrying by. There was a statue of Lenin, of course, gazing east. A pigeon sat on his head, looking the other way. 'It feels strange to be back,' said Fairburn.

Sechkin lit another cigarette. 'Get used to it. Moscow said I can have you for six months.'

'I was only meant to be in Budapest for a week. Look how that turned out.'

'And Cairo?'

Fairburn grimaced. 'Three years.'

'I'm told you did well.'

'I did what was asked.'

Sechkin lit another cigarette. 'And Hungary? I'm told there was plenty of work.'

'Not the sort of work I'm in any hurry to repeat,' Fairburn replied. The uprising in Budapest had been crushed mercilessly. 'It was bad, Nikolai.'

Sechkin rolled his neck and winced. 'I've heard the stories, Tommy. What conclusions do you draw from the affair?'

'I think the Americans orchestrated the whole thing,' said Fairburn. 'The CIA's stink was all over the counter-revolutionary effort.'

'They probably did. If the Hungarians took the bait? Fuck them. A revolt's a revolt. Wreckers and traitors. What else could we do?'

'The Hungarian rebels were brave, Nikolai. They were singing as we marched them in front of the firing squad.'

'Firing squads? There's a place for them, but I've always been a believer in sticks *and* carrots.' Lowering his voice, he added, 'Although there's a bit of a carrot shortage at the moment.'

'I didn't see a single carrot in Budapest,' Fairburn said. He recalled the bodies sprawled in the courtyard of Andrassy Place – the Hungarian secret police headquarters – and sighed. 'I believed if we killed enough wreckers, we could rescue Hungary.'

Sechkin shot his young friend a look. 'And now?'

'As you say, all we have is sticks.'

They approached the old barracks headquarters, a grand-looking Regency building. An elderly man in a black three-piece suit appeared. Despite domestic service being forbidden in the Socialist Republic of Great Britain, he reminded Fairburn of a butler. 'Good morning, comrades,' said the old man. 'The Director will see you presently. Would you care for a drink?'

'Vodka,' Sechkin replied, shaking his head. 'I'll never get used to your English habit of asking obvious questions.'

'Coffee, please,' said Fairburn. 'Black. No sugar.'

The old man nodded and ambled away. After ten minutes, during which time several nervous-looking uniformed CSS officers hurried up and down the stairs, the old man reappeared. 'The Director will see you now,' he announced regally. 'He's been especially looking forward to meeting you, Comrade Captain Fairburn.'

'Then let's get on with it shall we?' Fairburn replied, his boots ringing on the marble steps.

'Be patient with the Director,' Sechkin warned. 'He was playing this game when you were sucking on your mother's tit.'

'Patience? That's a card game, isn't it?' Fairburn smiled. 'I was never much good at cards.'

Two men sat in an office overlooking the parade square. Fairburn immediately recognised the Director of Britain's Committee for State Security. The second was a smartly dressed man with an aquiline nose and wire-rimmed glasses. His hair, bluish-black, was swept back and neatly parted. Fairburn thought he looked Indian. 'Welcome, gentlemen,' said the Director, gesturing towards his colleague. 'This is my Chief Political Officer, Ashim Prasad.'

'Good afternoon, comrades,' said Prasad, squinting as he looked Fairburn up and down. 'Please, I prefer to be called Ash.'

The Director nodded. 'No need for formalities.' The Director of the CSS was a legend in the Soviet intelligence establishment, the only foreigner to hold the honorary rank of Lieutenant-General in the KGB. The red-and-gold Order of Lenin gleamed on the lapel of his baggy tweed jacket. 'Now, where are our drinks?'

'I'm sorry, Comrade Director,' said the old man, appearing in the doorway with a squeaky-wheeled trolley. He put a steel ice bucket on the table containing two bottles of *Stolichnaya*. Then, carefully, he placed a cup of coffee in front of Fairburn.

'Thank you, Howard,' said the Director. 'You may leave.'

'Of course, Comrade Director,' Howard replied, closing the door behind him.

The Director stood and smiled, blue eyes creasing behind heavy-framed glasses. He nodded at the ice bucket. 'Nikolai, would you do the honours old boy?'

'Of course, Kim,' Sechkin replied, reaching for a bottle. 'Tommy, this is Director Harold Philby. He's been a close ally of ours for many years.'

'Since 1934, actually,' Philby added. Then he smiled. 'Please, call me Kim. I can't remember the last time anyone called me Harold.'

'General Serov still does,' Sechkin chuckled, referring to Ivan Serov, Chairman of the recently formed KGB. 'He asked me to mention it's the name written across the top of your file.'

'Tell Ivan Alexandrovich he's an arse.' Philby smiled. 'Remind him of the time we went to dinner in Kyiv with the Turkish foreign minister. That should give him pause for thought.'

Ashim Prasad made a note in the journal resting on his knees. 'Don't worry,' he said lightly. 'I'm not writing about you, Kim.'

'How would I know?' the Director replied. 'I can't read Hindi.'

Prasad raised an eyebrow. 'I prefer Sanskrit if I'm feeling particularly cautious.'

Fairburn took Philby's offered hand. 'The instructors at the Academy spoke of you, Comrade Director. They told us you met Franco.'

Philby nodded. 'Yes, I was covering the civil war as a reporter. I was nearly blown up by Nationalist artillery, so Franco's people decided to give me a medal.' The Spanish dictator remained in power, protected by his American allies. US military bases now ran from Bilbao to Barcelona, then from Casablanca in the west to Istanbul in the east. They called it 'The Truman Line', America's atomic bulwark against Communist expansion.

'Franco? You should've shot the bastard when you had a chance,' said Sechkin sourly. 'You would've saved us a lot of trouble.'

'Quite,' Philby replied, 'although I suspect my career would've been cut tragically short.'

Sechkin poured three glasses of vodka. 'I'm not so sure, Kim. You've outfoxed every fascist you ever met.' He raised his glass. '*Na Zdorovie!*'

Philby studied Fairburn's coffee cup. 'Cheers, old boy. Tell me, Tommy, are you teetotal?'

'No, sir. I just prefer not to drink in the daytime.'

Philby's eyes twinkled. They were very blue. 'After ten years in the KGB? Most commendable, but I find the stuff helps lubricate the mind. Especially on a day like today.'

Prasad sipped his vodka, smiled and made another note. 'Very wise, Comrade Captain. I wish I'd never tasted the stuff. Now? I rather enjoy it.'

Fairburn took a sip of his coffee. It was good. Proper Arabica beans. He'd picked up a taste for decent coffee in Cairo. 'What would you have of me, Comrade Director?'

Philby's smile was warm. 'Nikolai said you were a young man in a hurry.'

Fairburn stiffened in his seat, fists resting on his knees in the approved manner. 'I apologise for any impertinence.'

Philby held up a hand. 'There's no need. You're one of the new breed, Tommy. A *Spartan*. A true socialist, unfettered by my generation's class strictures. If anything, it's I who should apologise to you.'

'Of course not, Comrade Director,' he replied stiffly.

Philby pulled a file from his desk drawer. 'In any case, this assignment will suit a man of your talents. It requires a sense of urgency, utmost discretion and a fresh pair of eyes. I'm told by the Hungarian AVO you were very thorough in Budapest.'

Prasad's eyes remained on his journal. 'Indeed, Kim. We could use a dose of vim and vigour.'

'I like to get things done,' said Fairburn. 'It's how I was trained.'

Philby nodded. 'I see you operated against Polish counter-revolutionary networks.'

'They fought harder than the Hungarians,' Fairburn replied. He'd learned much about irregular warfare in the icy, primeval forests outside Krakow. Terrorists would hide in specially built tunnels. They'd appear in the night, like foxes, to cut Russian throats.

'And Egypt?'

Fairburn didn't conceal the contempt in his voice. 'Cairo was a cesspool of gin-soaked fascists, dreaming of the day their Queen will cross the sea. There's a few ex-Blackshirts too.'

'Yes, Royalty. A particularly British cancer,' Philby replied, prising open the file with a long, sharp fingernail. 'Ash, when were you in Cairo last?'

'1940, I think. Horrible bloody place,' Prasad replied. 'Happily, most of my work was in Rhodesia and South Africa.'

'Ash was a Colonial Office man,' Philby explained. 'He ran the Pretoria Network for our Soviet friends during the war.'

Prasad looked up from his journal and smiled. 'We're not here to talk about me.'

'It's important Tommy knows you've been a field man, not just a commissar,' Philby replied. 'He's being set work by people who've been in his shoes.'

Prasad chuckled. 'A *commissar*? As if anyone could play commissar with you, Kim. I'm an advisor. I simply keep an eye out for bear-traps.'

'Bear-traps indeed,' said Philby, turning his attention to Fairburn. 'The British Politburo's something of a dichotomy, Tommy. They venerate Stalin, yet never displayed any of his… shall we say *gumption*?'

'The newer apparatchiks are lifestylists,' said Prasad, his lip curling. 'They're excellent when it comes to Socialist theory, but completely hopeless in practice.'

Philby finished his vodka. 'We lost many excellent comrades during the war. Those who survived were, frankly, second-rate. They struggle to apply proper Marxist-Leninist principles. Agricultural collectivization? On the verge of collapse. Industrial output? Mediocre. Terrorism's on the rise. One feels the anger on the streets. What conclusions would you draw, Tommy?'

Fairburn put down his coffee cup, back straight. 'These are problems typical of newer Socialist states, not just Britain. You have a lack of political rigour, weak party structures and an indulgence of counter-revolutionary sentiment. Also, Budapest taught me never to underestimate the Americans. They've a special talent for spreading insurrection.'

'I agree,' said Prasad. 'They crave crisis abroad. It deflects from their system's rottenness.'

Philby tapped the file lying on his desk. 'This file contains the names of three high-ranking suspects inside the British Politburo. At least one of them, I'm sure, is working for the CIA. I would like to unmask this traitor. Think of it as a Liberation Day gift to Comrade Chairman Khrushchev.'

'You'd have me interrogate these men? Secure confessions? I mean no offence, but I'm sure you've CSS officers capable of police work.'

Philby cocked his head. Was he surprised by the question? Fairburn wondered. 'This matter requires proof. *Irrefutable* proof. Ironically, such evidence is rarely found by secret policemen.'

Nodding his agreement, Prasad steepled his fingers. 'The situation in London's febrile. We can't afford to take action against senior comrades based on confessions acquired through torture or denunciation.'

'Besides, I want the network around the traitor,' Philby added, reaching for the vodka bottle. 'That's the prize. I want to humiliate the Americans. I want to show the Socialist Republic of Great Britain isn't a soft touch.'

Sechkin nodded at Tommy and smiled. 'Gentlemen, it's no secret Major General Teplyakov has reservations about 10th Directorate support.' Anatoly Teplyakov was the KGB's permanent *Rezident* in London, a Chekist of the old school. 'He's especially sceptical about using a Spartan.'

'I presume that's because the programme wasn't his idea?' said Prasad.

'Heavens forfend, Ash. I respect Major General Teplyakov, of course. However, I can't help but wonder if his preferred methods might make our situation worse.'

'Chairman Serov clearly agrees,' said Prasad, allowing himself a smile. 'Why else would we be here without Teplyakov in the room?'

'Nonetheless, we must act quickly,' Sechkin replied. 'And, of course, make sure Comrade Teplyakov gets his fair share of the credit for any successes.'

'Of course,' Philby replied. 'There you go, Tommy. No pressure eh?'

'I will do my utmost,' Fairburn replied.

Sechkin poured more vodka. 'Gentlemen, it's no secret Moscow's patience with Britain wears thin. There's no British Tito, someone capable of facing us down. And your war debt to the Soviet Union isn't going to pay itself. If you don't turn the situation around, Moscow will let Major General Teplyakov off his leash. It won't be pretty.'

Philby limped towards the window, vodka glass in hand. Outside a company of CSS troops goose-stepped across the parade square, boots crashing on concrete. 'Indeed, Nikolai. I'd rather we had a *British* solution to a British problem. That's partly why I asked for a British Spartan. Do you understand, Comrade Captain Fairburn?'

'Yes, Comrade Director.'

The Director pointed at the file on his desk. 'From now on, you'll deal directly with Colonel Sechkin. However, you are acting expressly on my authority as CSS Chairman. Good luck, Tommy. Liberation Day's in two weeks' time.'

Fairburn stood up and snapped to attention. 'It's an honour to serve,' he replied.

Philby smiled. 'Yes, it is, isn't it?'

21

Chapter 4

The tunnels beneath Burgess House smelled of disinfectant and cigarettes. 'We have a good team,' said Sechkin. 'Twenty hand-picked men, all English speakers, including surveillance operatives. I've also been assigned two CSS officers – a technician and a liaison officer.'

'None of them are General Teplyakov's people?'

'No, Chairman Serov allowed me to choose my own staff. Besides, Teplyakov has enough on his plate with the security arrangements for the Liberation commemorations.'

'What do you think of Prasad?' asked Fairburn. 'I'm surprised Philby tolerates a commissar looking over his shoulder.'

'Prasad's slippery,' said Sechkin, '*suyot svoi nos vo vse dyrythe* – the sort with a finger in every pie. His family were from India. Bourgeois. They moved to Africa to work for the British imperialists.'

'When did he begin working for us?'

'The NKVD recruited Prasad at Oxford in the '30's. It was their idea for him to join the foreign service. His African spy network's still running; he's well liked in Moscow.'

'Philby trusts him?'

'You can never tell with Kim. He's too good an actor. Don't worry about Prasad, Tommy, we've got the measure of him. Besides, if this operation goes wrong? He'll have shit on his shoes.'

Tommy nodded. 'Yes, he seems the sort who keeps his shoes clean. Now, I need time to read the file.'

Sechkin squeezed the younger man's shoulder. 'Of course, Tommy. I've arranged for lodgings nearby. Now, take the afternoon to familiarise yourself with the operation. Later you will join us for dinner. Irina's looking forward to seeing you.'

'How is Irina?'

'She has a job at the embassy,' Sechkin replied. 'Although I think she wants to go back to Russia.' He led Fairburn into a dark, low-ceilinged office. A brawny man sat reading *The Daily Mirror*, a cigarette stuck to his lower lip. Lying on the table in front of him was a half-eaten bacon sandwich, a holstered Tokarev pistol and a truncheon. 'This is Senior Sergeant Ross,' said Sechkin. 'He's our CSS Bureau 5 liaison officer.' Fairburn was familiar with the history. When CSS was established in 1949, Philby merged MI5 – domestic intelligence – with their foreign intelligence counterparts in MI6. The Soviets managed with one overarching intelligence service, so Philby decided the British could too. The distinction, however, remained in Bureaux 5 and 6.

'Good to meet you,' said Fairburn.

Getting up from his chair, Ross brushed the crumbs from his shirt. He reminded Fairburn of the sort of growly old dog one might find chained up at a scrap yard. 'Good morning, comrades,' he said in a husky London accent. He offered a beefy hand, a swallow tattooed between his thumb and forefinger. 'I'm Sidney Ross. Call me Sid.'

'I'm Captain Thomas Fairburn, 10th Directorate.'

'So I'm told. Let me know when you need takin' to your digs, Comrade Captain.'

'Straight away, I think,' Fairburn replied. 'You're Moscow-trained?'

'Yes, Comrade Captain,' Ross replied in passable Russian. 'I passed the Special Activities course at the NKVD school in 1949. I was one of the first Bureau 5 officers.'

'Before that?'

Ross switched back to English. 'I was a copper. I was a sergeant on the Flying Squad.'

'Scotland Yard?'

A nod. 'For my sins.'

'Why didn't you join the Militia?' The existing British police forces were all disbanded in 1948, replaced by a People's Militia on Soviet lines. The old police had collaborated with the Nazis and were despised.

Ross shrugged. 'The Militia don't like me and I don't like the Militia. If you ask me, they're a bunch of fucking clowns.'

Sechkin laughed. 'It's okay, Sidney was a good communist. He spent the war in a camp for his politics.'

'I wouldn't say I was a *good* communist,' Ross replied. 'It was too much like Sunday school. I couldn't be getting on with Marx and Lenin an' all that.'

'Then why join?' asked Fairburn.

'The girls, of course,' Ross laughed. 'There was a fair bit of crumpet in the CPGB.'

Sechkin laughed too, making his eyes disappear into slits. 'Have you forgotten the English sense of humour, Tommy? Nobody takes anything too seriously.'

'That could be a drama when Comrade Stalin was in charge,' Ross added. 'Although I'm told Comrade Khrushchev's a cheery enough fella.'

In Moscow, Fairburn would've counselled anyone using such language in the strongest terms. Sechkin, in particular, should have rebuked him. 'Sergeant, please take me to my lodgings,' he said curtly. 'What time is dinner, Comrade Colonel Sechkin?'

'Eight o'clock, Tommy. Don't be late, Irina will be cross.'

'Whenever you're ready,' said Ross, holstering his pistol and putting on his jacket.

Fairburn put on his peaked cap. 'I'm ready now, Comrade Sergeant. Let's go.'

Fairburn sat in the back of Ross's black GAZ saloon and began reading the file;

```
1. There have been several defections by signif-
   icant cultural figures from the Socialist
   Republic of Great Britain (SRGB) to the
   United States of America. Notable defectors
   include the writers Doris LESSING, George
   ORWELL, Phillip LARKIN and John CONQUEST.


2. The most recent was novelist and former
   Communist Party member Eliza CREWE. It
   is suspected she was in contact with an
   American agent, passing on seditious mate-
   rial intended for publication abroad.


3. Eliza CREWE was educated at Girton College,
   Cambridge. She initially studied Chemistry,
   but soon gave up the subject in favour
   of English Literature. She joined the
   Communist Party of Great Britain in 1934.
```

```
    After graduation, CREWE became part of
    'The Clerkenwell Set' which included the
    writers Claude PURCELL, Anna DE CARTERET
    and Peter DUNSEITH.

4.  CREWE was a dedicated CP member in the 1930s,
    where she became known to a number of influ-
    ential Party figures (see below).
```

Fairburn knew the gaps in an intelligence report were as important as its contents – in this case the lack of information on the 'American agent'. Hadn't Crewe been thoroughly interrogated prior to her defection? If not, why? Were Bureau 5 incompetent?

```
5.  During the war, CREWE worked as a courier
    for the British Resistance. However, after
    the Liberation in 1947 she began to display
    counter-revolutionary tendencies.

6.  In 1952 CREWE received an 18-month sentence
    for sedition after criticising the Party's
    guest worker policies during a radio inter-
    view with the BBC. She claimed the transfer
    of manpower from Britain to Russia was a form
    of punishment for British support for Nazi
    Germany, rather than an act of socialist
    solidarity. Then, in 1955, she released a
    book lampooning aspects of life in the SRGB.
    After being placed under house arrest at her
```

```
home in Hampstead, CREWE absconded on 3rd
December 1956. She subsequently reappeared
in Washington DC, where she gave a televised
press conference denouncing the SRGB.
```

Fairburn knew how important 1956 had been for many dissidents. British communists were especially shaken by Soviet repression of the Hungarian counter-revolution. Some denounced the Party, leading to arrests and imprisonment. Many British communists of previous good standing were sent to labour camps in Russia.

```
7. In the weeks before her defection, intel-
   ligence indicates CREWE communicated with
   three high-ranking members of the Politburo
   in London. These men are now suspects.
```

Fairburn smiled. Crewe most likely had dirt on important figures inside the Politburo. Had an attempt to handle her with kid gloves backfired? He'd seen powerful people compromised in such a manner before.

```
8. The suspects identified by Bureau 5 are:
```

```
Francis Arthur FRAYNE
FRAYNE is Deputy Chairman of the CPGB's Central
Committee. Moscow-trained in 1934, he acted
as conduit between the USSR and the British
Trades Union Congress. When war began, FRAYNE
was imprisoned by the Moseley regime. He is
```

described as politically astute, but bullish and overconfident.

* * *Secret Intelligence* * * Frayne is a stalwart Stalinist and a personal friend of Soviet Deputy Chairman Georgy MALENKOV, who remains unreconciled to Comrade Khrushchev's agenda. MCGROUTHER (see below) is an ally of FRAYNE'S inside the Politburo. Intelligence indicates both spoke to CREWE on several occasions in the weeks leading up to her defection.

What was Frayne's link to Eliza Crewe? Why hadn't Frayne's phone been tapped? His home and office bugged? Perhaps Frayne considered himself untouchable. He should know better; Khrushchev had recently sacked Georgy Malenkov, Deputy Chairman of the Council of Ministers, for agitating against him.

William Henry MCGROUTHER

MCGROUTHER is Deputy Chairman for Public Information. In that capacity he sits on the board of the BBC. During the 1930s, MCGROUTHER was employed by the 'Left Book Club' and was on the periphery of 'The Clerkenwell Set'. He studied English at Cambridge with Eliza CREWE. It is widely believed they were lovers before and during the war.

* * * Secret Intelligence * * * MCGROUTHER is suspected of unauthorised contact with

```
foreigners, especially journalists and 'diplo-
mats'. He is known to have visited CREWE at
her Hampstead apartment after she was placed
under house arrest.
```

Lovers? Of course. Fairburn had seen love make clever people do stupid things.

```
General Gerald Michael SCANLON
Deputy Chairman for Public Protection, General
SCANLON is head of the People's Militia. Along
with Eliza CREWE, he was a member of the influ-
ential Poplar branch of the CPGB. During the
war SCANLON became a senior resistance figure,
personally leading the operation to assassinate
Lord Tavistock (Gauleiter for the East Midlands)
in November 1944. He enjoys a reputation as the
most popular member of the Politburo.

    * * * Secret Intelligence * * * SCANLON is
alleged to have taken a personal and 'intrusive'
level of interest in the security arrange-
ments concerning CREWE'S arrest. CSS officers
submitted reports expressing their concerns,
which SCANLON shrugged off as part of the
rivalry between the Militia and the intelli-
gence service.
```

Scanlon was clearly the most substantial of the three suspects. A Resistance hero and man of the people. As head of the Militia, he would also have the necessary resources to protect himself from scrutiny. He would require careful handling.

9. **Objective: identify and apprehend ALL persons linked to CREWE'S defection as soon as possible and in any case by 29th October 1957.**

Fairburn shook his head. The British Politburo was set to unravel for a *novelist*? 'What a mess,' he sighed.

'What is it, Comrade Captain?' asked Ross, glancing at Fairburn in the rearview mirror.

'This operation, Comrade Sergeant. I said it's a mess.'

'How so?'

'I've been given a sow's ear and asked to make a silk purse.'

'Well, that's about right,' Ross said knowingly. 'It's a typical Bureau 5 job, ain't it?'

'You aren't surprised?'

'Nope.' Ross grinned. 'Shovelling shit is what we do.' He drove the unmarked car along Chelsea Embankment, the Thames the colour of lead and bronze. Buses crawled across Battersea bridge, shrouded in dirty yellow smog. 'How well d'you know London, Comrade Captain?'

'A little. I was last here during the Liberation with Colonel Sechkin.'

'The Colonel told me some of the story, Comrade. It's impressive.'

'I was a child.' Fairburn shrugged. 'Where were you?'

'I was pinched by Special Branch in '42 for being an ex-CP member. They sent me to a concentration camp on Dartmoor. The Red Army took its time reaching Devon.'

'How long?'

'Christmas '47, a few weeks after the Battle of Swindon. We hanged our guards, then liberated a local pub.'

Fairburn studied Ross' meaty face. 'An executioner? Have you been sent to do my dirty work, Sergeant Ross?'

'I'm here to follow orders. If that means a spot of the dark work? No problem. Unless you fancy doin' it yourself, of course. You've got the reputation.'

'Don't believe everything you hear.'

'I do when Colonel Sechkin says you're a Spartan. I've heard the stories.'

'The 10th Directorate doesn't discuss operations,' Fairburn said. 'I'm sure you understand.'

'Sure,' Ross replied, pulling up outside an apartment block in Battersea. The area was nondescript. Unremarkable. Fairburn approved. Ross handed him an envelope. 'You're in number 49, flat D. The key's inside.'

'Thank you, Sergeant,' Fairburn replied, hefting his duffel bag onto his lap.

Ross nodded. 'No problem, Comrade Captain. I'll pick you up at nineteen twenty-five hours.'

'Excellent.'

'Oh, one more thing.'

Fairburn was halfway out of the car. 'Yes, Comrade Sergeant?'

'Lose the uniform,' said Ross. 'Truth be told, Soviets are about as popular in Britain as the Germans were.'

'You seem to specialise in dangerous talk, Comrade.'

Ross smiled a snaggle-toothed smile. 'I'm here to keep you on the straight and narrow.'

'And who gave you that job?'

The secret policeman stubbed out his cigarette and lit another. He shrugged. 'Philby and Sechkin. Sechkin's a good man. Sensible. Not like that fucker Teplyakov.'

'You've had dealings with Teplyakov?' asked Fairburn.

'In a roundabout way. He's a proper bastard,' Ross replied. 'Most of us reckon he'd like London to go the same way as Hungary. Tanks and firing squads.'

Fairburn frowned. 'Those are rumours.'

'Bollocks. We all know what happened. We also know Teplyakov was in Poland. They say he was the one who had Lodz carpet-bombed in '51.'

Fairburn looked out of the car window, one boot on the pavement. 'Sechkin thinks you can protect me from Teplyakov?'

'Me? Fuck off,' Ross laughed. 'You understand the KGB better than I ever will.'

'So how do you plan on keeping me on the *straight and narrow*?'

'Think of me as a rat-catcher, except the rats live in our house.'

'Well, thanks for your advice,' said Fairburn, getting out of the car. Ross drove away, leaving behind a cloud of dirty grey smoke. Before long a crowd had gathered, watching the KGB captain with suspicion. A teenager, pale-faced and angry, swore under his breath.

Welcome home, Tommy.

Chapter 5

The Sechkins lived in the KGB's residential block overlooking Kensington Palace Gardens. 'I've made *golubsty* and *pelmeni*,' said Irina Sechkina, peeling off her apron. She was an unlikely housewife; during the war she'd been a bomber pilot, surviving fifty sorties over Germany. '*Pelmeni* are your favourites, Tommy.'

'Only the way you make them.' Fairburn smiled, handing her a bunch of flowers Sid Ross had brought. He was already beginning to see why the big man was useful. Irina's perfume reminded him of the Sechkin's Moscow apartment. He'd lodged with the couple after leaving the academy, spending the evenings reading Tolstoy and perfecting his Russian.

'You're a smooth talker, Tommy,' Sechkin guffawed. The KGB Colonel wore a cardigan, a pair of tartan slippers on his feet. 'Did they teach you that at Higher Intelligence School?'

'Any charm I possess was probably learned from Irina.'

'See, Nikolai? The boy's silver-tongued,' said Irina, offering her hand for Fairburn to kiss.

Fairburn obliged. 'Of course, smooth-talking only takes you so far in the Białowieża forest. If the terrorists didn't get you, the wolves and bears would.'

'You see? That's why I prefer it here,' said Sechkin, opening a bottle of beer and pouring three glasses. 'No wolves or bears.'

'Beer, Nikolai?' said Fairburn, taking a sip. 'You've definitely been in London too long. Even I prefer vodka.'

Irina disappeared into the kitchen, returning with a casserole dish. 'The irony isn't lost on me either. You get more Russian every time I see you, Tommy, and Nikolai gets more English.' She put the dish on a side table. Ignoring the beer, she poured three glasses of vodka from a carafe.

'What can I say?' Sechkin replied, chasing down his Watney's with Stolichnaya. Sighing happily, he wiped his mouth with the back of his hand. 'I like England. It never gets properly cold, the work is easy and the food is simple.'

Irina shook her head. 'Well, I'm glad *you* like it.'

'Only a year of this posting left, darling,' the KGB Colonel replied. 'I'll ask for a Leningrad next, eh?' Irina was from Volkhov, just east of Russia's second city.

'I'll believe it when I'm dangling my legs in Lake Ladoga,' said Irina.

The smell of food made Fairburn hungry. 'Do you spend most of your time in London, Nikolai?'

'Well, I've responsibilities in East Anglia. It's flat and windy and very boring. My department protects sensitive technical operations. The British have many excellent scientists, you see? We're investing millions of roubles into Cambridge and the other universities.'

'Eat, Tommy, before it gets cold,' said Irina, serving up platefuls of food.

Fairburn wolfed down two platefuls of *golubsty,* cabbage rolls stuffed with minced pork, and *pelmeni* dumplings. Dessert was a large slice of *medovik,* honey cake with autumn berries and sour cream. 'I'm full,' he said finally, pushing his plate away.

'I'll make tea, then leave you boys to talk,' said Irina. 'I think I'll listen to the radio. I like the music on the BBC.'

'Thank you for a delicious dinner,' said Fairburn, dabbing his mouth with a napkin.

'Keep an eye on Nikolai,' Irina replied. 'He'll eat the rest of that medovik if you don't.'

They sat on the balcony overlooking Kensington Palace Gardens. Soviet soldiers patrolled the grounds, rifles slung across their chests. 'So,' said Sechkin, lighting an American cigarette, 'what's your opinion of this bullshit operation?'

Fairburn poured a cup of green tea. 'It's bullshit. Part of me thinks Teplyakov's wise staying out of it.'

'Well observed.'

'I also think the British Politburo's crazy. Three of their top men facing a firing squad for what? A novelist?'

'Yes, the Politburo would like to forget about Eliza Crewe, which is why Philby doesn't. He sees the opportunity for a purge. A small opportunity, but in this game you play the hand you are dealt.'

'But surely Philby sits on the Politburo too?'

'Yes, but he's a clique of one. Philby was never part of the Party machine, he was too busy spying for us. He was above politicking, or at least he thought he was. Now he needs allies in the room, not outside.'

'And what about this Prasad fellow? Where do his loyalties lie?'

'Prasad is Philby's man. He might be a political officer, but ultimately his loyalties lie with CSS.'

'So we find ourselves in the middle of a sordid British turf war? If I didn't know better, I'd think I was being punished.'

Sechkin shook his head. 'No, Tommy, on the contrary. This is an opportunity, especially if the CIA are involved. Even if it's only a people-smuggling network, breaking it up it will reflect well on you.'

Fairburn shrugged. 'The CIA are slippery. I'll probably need to crack a few skulls.'

'Of course, Tommy. Just be careful which skulls.' They paused as an aircraft roared overhead, an Aeroflot Tupolev Tu-104, the world's first jet airliner. Sechkin pointed at the silvery fuselage. 'You see? That makes me proud to be Russian. Technology, Tommy. It's the future. There are many more wonders to come.'

'Not in Britain,' Fairburn replied, realising how little he felt for the country of his birth. 'Nothing of any consequence ever happens here. It's a backwater and the world's a better place for it.'

Sechkin shook his head. 'Britain is very important. Why else would I bring you here?'

Fairburn watched a guard shoo a tramp out of the park. There was housing for all, so why were there tramps? Another mystery. 'If you say so, Nikolai. You said Comrade Philby wants me to be discreet?'

'Yes.'

Fairburn sipped his tea. 'Then I'll gently nudge the nest. Let's see if any hornets pop out for my net. I'll begin with Francis Frayne, I think.'

'Then speak to Senior Sergeant Ross. He has surveillance reports on all of the suspects.'

Finishing his drink, Fairburn walked to the balcony. The breeze smelled faintly of bonfires. In the distance, he heard a gunshot. 'I should get some sleep. I'll begin work early.'

'Very well, but there's one more thing,' Sechkin replied, pulling a crumpled envelope from his pocket. 'The favour you asked?'

Fairburn took the envelope. 'I'm grateful, Nikolai.'

'It's not much,' Nikolai warned. 'The archivists only completed cataloguing the British material recently. So much was destroyed at the end of the war.'

'Still, I'm grateful.'

Sechkin gripped the younger man's shoulder. 'The past is important, Tommy, but don't forget the present.'

Fairburn put his hand on the older man's shoulder. 'I won't let you down, Nikolai. You have my word.'

Sid Ross stood outside the apartment block, chatting with the KGB guards in Russian. Seeing Fairburn, he got in the car and started the engine. 'You had a good evening, Comrade Captain?'

'Yes, thank you,' said Fairburn, settling into the back seat. 'I need a moment to read a report Colonel Sechkin gave me.'

'Then I'll keep me trap shut,' Ross replied, pulling onto Kensington High Street. Fairburn took the envelope from his pocket and opened it, straining to read the letter under the GAZ's flickering internal lights.

> *Dear Tommy,*
> *I wish there were more details. It isn't much, but I hope it*
> *helps you find peace.*
> *Your friend,*
> *Nikolai.*

Attached was a typewritten report:

Subjects: Malcolm and Joanna FAIRBURN

The Tribunal for the 'Examination of Fascist Crimes in Great Britain' has completed its ten-year mission to

examine the surviving records concerning the British concentration camp system (1941–1947). As requested by Colonel N.A. Sechkin (KGB 2nd Directorate), we have searched the archives for any mention of the abovementioned persons.

JOANNA KATHRYN FAIRBURN (dob 03/09/1910) Gestapo / Metropolitan Police special branch indices confirm Joanna FAIRBURN'S arrest in September 1943 for 'Resistance-related activities'. Records detail her incarceration in Pentonville women's prison, before she was transferred to Cadmore End concentration camp, High Wycombe, in November 1943. Cadmore End's fatality returns for January 1946 show a woman called JK FAIRBURY, with an identical date of birth, dying from 'respiratory failure' (a euphemism commonly used for prisoners executed in the gas chambers). It is assumed 'FAIRBURY' is a typographical error, and this person is in fact Joanna FAIRBURN.

MALCOLM ARTHUR FAIRBURN (28/04/1908) was arrested with his wife. The 'comments' section of his charge sheet notes FAIRBURN was 'a Communist agitator of long-standing', suspected of 'industrial sabotage and other resistance activity'. He was sent directly to Dungeness concentration camp in Kent. Most records from Dungeness were destroyed before the Red Army's arrival in early 1947; however, SS casualty returns for November 1946 states all Dungeness inmates

```
were executed by Einsatzgruppe 'F', commanded by
SS-Oberführer und Oberst der Polizei Horst Wiebens.
There is no record of what happened to the bodies
(Nazi practice was to douse them in petrol and burn
them in shallow pits). Red Army war records show
Wiebens and his men were captured and summarily
executed by the NKVD on 27th March 1947.


CONCLUSION: The partial records available suggest
the FAIRBURNS were arrested for resistance activity
in 1943. Both were interred in concentration camps
and subsequently murdered by the fascists in 1946.
Their names have been entered into the register of
British Socialist Heroes.
```

Fairburn read the report twice. Then, a third time. 'Are you alright, Comrade?' said Ross.

'Why do you ask?'

'You look like you saw a ghost.'

'I think I did, Sergeant Ross,' said Fairburn, putting the envelope in his pocket. 'Now, tell me about Francis Frayne.'

Chapter 6

Fairburn rose early and dressed in a singlet, shorts and plimsolls. After a few minutes of stretching exercises, he left the flat and ran towards Battersea bridge. Breathing in cold autumn air, he watched London creak into life like a cobwebby piece of machinery. The city was a place of wheezy buses and plodding workers, the streets potholed and the buildings bullet scarred. Even the trees looked morose, London planes with papery leaves and birch trees with dirty grey bark. A glossy black saloon crawled by. 'Good morning, Comrade Captain Fairburn,' said the driver in Russian.

'Who are you?' asked Fairburn. The exhaust fumes from the car prickled his nose. The driver flashed a red identity card – KGB. 'Please, get in.'

'I'm hardly dressed for work.'

The driver was sharp-featured and handsome, his blonde hair cut short like a soldier's. 'General Teplyakov doesn't stand on ceremony. I'm told you're fairly clever, so get in the car and stop fucking about, eh?'

Fairburn did as he was told, relieved to see there was nobody else inside. The KGB seldom abducted people single-handed. 'You didn't give me your name, Comrade,' he asked.

'No, I didn't,' the driver replied. He drove to a park by the Thames and pulled up next to a bandstand. A tall, slender man wearing a trilby hat stood watching the river.

'That's General Teplyakov?' Fairburn asked.

'Yes. Watch your manners. He doesn't have time for prima donnas.'

'Who says I'm a prima donna?'

The driver smiled. 'You're 10th Directorate, right? A Spartan?'

Fairburn sighed. 'Have a good day, Comrade-whoever-you-are.'

'I'm sure you've memorised the route here. I'm not giving you a lift back.'

Fairburn got out of the car, leaving the rear door open. He knew it would annoy the driver. He walked to the bandstand. 'Captain Thomas Fairburn,' he said, stiffening to attention. 'You wanted to see me, Comrade General Teplyakov?'

The man in the trilby examined Fairburn. Teplyakov was young for a general, with high cheekbones and close-set eyes. Beneath his raincoat he wore a double-breasted suit and a silk tie. Fairburn had spent enough time in Cairo's expatriate gentlemen's clubs to know Saville Row tailoring. 'I'm sorry to interrupt your exercise, Comrade Captain, but nobody thought to formally introduce us,' he said.

'I'm only a captain, Comrade General. I wouldn't have expected one.'

'Bullshit. You've been given a politically sensitive assignment on my territory. Now, that doesn't bother me too much. I've enough on my plate. That doesn't mean I've nothing to say on the matter of missing novelists.' Teplyakov smiled a thin-lipped smile.

'Of course, Comrade General.'

The KGB General lit an American cigarette. An old anti-aircraft gun rusted nearby, its barrel aimed skywards. 'I've had my differences with Director Philby, but I retain a great deal of respect for him. To that end, you have my best wishes in performing the task he's set you.'

A cold wind cut across the river. 'Thank you, Comrade General.'

'Nonetheless, you've been sent on a fool's errand. The British Politburo's beyond salvation. It's riddled with wreckers and bourgeois fools. It needs replacing with alacrity, but I've yet to win that argument with Moscow. In the meantime, you and Sechkin are being played for fools.'

'By whom, Comrade General?'

Teplyakov's lip curled. 'Philby, or whoever's pulling his strings. If your mission fails, the KGB will be blamed for British failures. If it's successful, Philby becomes more powerful in the Politburo. I'm not sure he's the man to sufficiently stiffen their spines.'

'And if I uncover enough to bring all of them down?'

The KGB General flicked his cigarette into the river. 'If that were even remotely possible, d'you really think they'd have asked for you? The reason I'm especially wary is Comrade Khrushchev arrives soon. He's not known for tolerating failure.'

Fairburn waited for the General to continue, but Teplyakov said nothing. Fairburn cleared his throat. 'I'm humbled by your counsel, Comrade General.'

'You are most welcome. Now, two more things before you go.'

'Yes, Comrade?'

'First of all, mention this meeting to Philby and you'll have made an enemy of me. That would be stupid, as I'm told you're a clever young man. I know you'll tell Sechkin, that's fair enough, he'll keep his mouth shut. Secondly, you will update me on your progress.'

'How so?'

Teplyakov nodded at the car. 'My driver, Rogov, will provide you with a telephone number. It's a secure line to the Embassy.'

'Yes, Comrade General.'

The General kept his eyes fixed on the leaden river. 'Goodbye, Captain Fairburn. I would say good luck, but it's a concept I've never set much store by.'

It was noon by the time Fairburn and Ross arrived at the office block near St Pancras railway station. 'Welcome to Harry Pollitt House,' said Ross, sounding like a tour guide as he tucked the car into a side street. 'The Communist Party's head office.'

'I'm surprised they never renamed it,' Fairburn replied. Harry Pollitt, a pioneering British communist, died in a car accident soon after Stalin's death. Many believed Pollitt, who venerated the dictator, was killed on Kim Philby's orders. The eradication of hard-line Stalinists extended far beyond the Kremlin's walls.

'Frankie Frayne was good friends with Pollitt,' Ross replied. 'He insists the Party don't change the name. Frayne even tried to denounce Philby once. He accused him of protecting members of the old aristocracy.'

'What did Philby do?'

'He invited Frayne to a slap-up dinner at White's for a chat,' Ross chuckled. 'Frayne was furious.'

Fairburn straightened his tie. He wore a dark single-breasted suit, his hair slicked with brilliantine. 'Are there microphones inside Frayne's office?'

'There were, but he had the place swept.'

'Get more installed. Russian ones this time.'

'Our technical officer, Comrade Renton, is workin' on it.'

'Tell him to hurry.'

'Yes, Comrade Captain. All of the telephones inside are tapped.'

'Good. And you're sure Frayne leaves his office at 12.15?'

'Like clockwork,' the secret policeman replied, pointing at a clock tower above the railway station. 'We've got watchers up there. Frayne goes for lunch at the same café every day.'

At 12.10, Fairburn got out of the car and checked himself in the wing mirror. He looked older than his twenty-six years. His eyes, especially, were those of an older man: deep-set and red-rimmed. 'Wait here, Sergeant. After I'm done, we'll go for coffee.'

Ross checked his wristwatch. 'A pint, you mean? We can go to the Hibernian club in Fulham, I'll introduce you to some of the Bureau 5 boys.'

'We don't drink on operations.'

'They said you were like a Russian. Russians think beer's a bloody breakfast drink.'

Fairburn's smile was thin. 'I've tried to adopt the most effective traits of our Russian comrades while avoiding their vices.'

Ross raised an eyebrow. 'Effective traits? Like what?'

Fairburn straightened his tie and walked towards the CPGB headquarters. 'Hopefully, Sergeant, you won't find out.'

At 12.15pm Francis Frayne, Deputy Chairman of the Communist Party of Great Britain, stepped onto the pavement outside Harry Pollitt House. Fairburn recognised him from his surveillance photograph: craggy-faced, sixtyish and with neatly cut hair. He wore a navy blue suit and a trilby hat. Carrying a copy of *The Morning Star*, he turned right and walked towards Camley Street. 'Excuse me, Comrade Deputy Chairman?' Fairburn called.

The Deputy Chairman's eyes were dark and watchful. He stopped and smiled. 'How can I help, Comrade?'

Fairburn produced his KGB identity card. 'I'm Captain Thomas Fairburn,' he replied. 'I was wondering if we could talk?'

'KGB? But you're English.'

Fairburn smiled. 'It's a long story.'

'I'd be happy to hear it sometime, but not now. I'm going for lunch.'

'My story is of little consequence, Comrade Deputy Chairman. However, yours certainly is.'

Frayne glanced at his watch. 'How so?'

'I'm investigating Eliza Crewe's defection. A review of the circumstances, if you will. You were friends?'

'You mean you're running a steward's enquiry?' Frayne replied. His smile was startlingly insincere. 'It's an unfortunate business, Comrade Captain Fairburn. Look, I've already provided a full statement about Eliza. We were acquaintances before the war. That's all there is to it.'

'I'm not the CSS,' Fairburn replied, returning the smile. 'Moscow's taken an interest in this matter.'

'I wonder why? It's not as if they haven't got problems of their own. Captain, do you want my honest opinion? I blame the toll the war took on people. Many comrades who fought in the Resistance had breakdowns and such. That's why Eliza fell by the wayside.'

'Not everyone falls by the wayside and into an American submarine, Comrade. I intend to be more thorough than the CSS or the Militia.'

'Very well,' Frayne replied, checking his watch. 'Then make an appointment. I'll make sure my Party legal representative's there too. You see, Moscow might have taken an interest, but this isn't Moscow. Our rules are different and those rules were agreed with Comrade Chairman Khrushchev.'

'Of course your legal representative is welcome,' Fairburn replied.

Frayne reached into his jacket and pulled out a business card. 'Welcome home, Comrade Captain. You've the air of a man who's been away too long.'

'I've been in Hungary. I was busy, as I'm sure you can imagine.'

Frayne locked eyes with the young KGB man. 'Call my secretary. I'm sure she'll find a convenient time for an appointment.'

'Thank you, Comrade Deputy Chairman. Please, enjoy your lunch.'

'I suppose you know where I'm going. It's good to see the KGB's got its priorities sorted.'

'Yes, I think we have,' said Fairburn, pocketing the card. Watching Frayne until he was gone, he returned to the car.

Ross sat reading his newspaper. 'What happened?'

'I got under Frayne's skin. Now, get on the R/T set and tell Renton to monitor his telephone calls.' Frayne could sweep his office for bugs, but telephone exchanges were a different matter. The Deputy Chairman might expect his phone to be tapped, but Fairburn considered the content of the call less important than *who* he contacted.

'Yes, Comrade Captain,' Ross replied. He opened the car's glove compartment, revealing a radio set with a green plastic handset.

'Take me to Burgess House,' said Fairburn. 'We'll leave Comrade Frayne to stew for a bit.'

Ross shook his head. 'Frayne ain't the type who stews. This'll be like water off a duck's back.'

'Even better,' Fairburn replied. 'That means he's more likely to make a mistake.'

Chapter 7

The CSS technical laboratory was on the uppermost floor of Burgess House, its windows overlooking a spiky forest of rooftop antennae. Fairburn and Ross were met by Renton, the CSS engineer. He was a bald, rubbery-faced man, standing protectively in front of a bank of modern-looking teleprinters. 'I'll have the details of Comrade Frayne's telephone calls presently,' he said carefully.

Fairburn scowled. '*Presently*?'

'Within two hours, Comrade Captain.'

'And the new microphones?'

'If your KGB men aren't caught installing the equipment inside Harry Pollitt House, hopefully by the day after tomorrow.'

'Where's the sense of urgency, Comrade? You've got twenty-four hours.'

'Yes, Comrade Captain.'

'Good,' Fairburn replied. 'Sergeant, let's go. We've work to do.'

'I thought we were going to the Hibernian club for a pint?'

'Absolutely not.'

Renton smiled. 'Have a good day, Sid.'

Muttering under his breath, Ross followed his new boss out of the door.

* * *

'According to your surveillance report, William McGrouther attends the BBC Board of Governors meeting every Friday,' said Fairburn. 'He takes a late lunch at a bistro near Broadcasting House. Then his driver takes him to his dacha in Wiltshire.'

'*Dacha*,' said Ross, lip curling. 'Why'd they call it that? It's a fucking *house*.'

'They seek to copy our Russian comrades,' Fairburn sighed. 'I agree, it's an irritating affectation.'

Ross' knuckles whitened on the steering wheel. 'You know what really pisses me off? All the posh arseholes who ran things before the Liberation are still in charge. And they've still got big houses in the country. Don't change fuck all, does it, callin' it a *dacha?*'

Fairburn smiled. 'What would you do?' Ross' criticism might be crudely expressed, but it was a point often made in Moscow of Britain's Party elite.

'I'd purge the lot of 'em,' Ross growled, driving fast along Sloane Street. London buses chuntered by, sending up clouds of dirty smoke. 'Just like 1917.'

Fairburn couldn't help but admire Ross' revolutionary zeal. 'A compelling suggestion, Comrade. Now, tell me about William McGrouther.'

'They say he was Eliza Crewe's fella at Cambridge,' said Ross. 'They were close during the war, if you know what I mean?'

'Quite. Is there anything else?'

'McGrouther liked denouncing people when Stalin was alive. I heard he used to boast to the newspaper editors about who was next for the chop. All he does now, as far as I can make out, is wine and dine foreign reporters. He's a proper wrong un.'

Fairburn wound down his window, filling the car with the odour of diesel fumes and boiled vegetables. Frowning, he wound it up again. 'Comrade McGrouther's responsible for public information. Isn't part of his job dealing with foreign journalists?'

'Sure, but we bugged his suite at the hotel,' said Ross, turning onto Portland Place. 'He's always talking the country down.' The BBC's headquarters, Broadcasting House, was opposite the Party-run Langham Hotel. Ross pulled up outside and held up his ID card for the doorman. The doorman nodded and walked briskly away. 'A lot of foreign reporters use this place, so we wired it with microphones. Most of the staff are on Bureau 5's books.'

'It's a shame we can't say the same of Harry Pollitt House,' said Fairburn sourly.

'Renton might drip but he'll sort it out,' Ross replied. He nodded at Broadcasting House. 'When he leaves, McGrouther usually goes to a bistro called Pascal's.'

'You know this area well?'

'The old Communist Party offices weren't far from here. I went to my first meeting there with my brother, back in the '30s.'

The radio-telephone rang, sounding like a bug trapped in a shoebox. Fairburn tugged the handset free. 'Hello?'

'Comrade Captain? It's Renton.'

'Yes?'

'There was a telephone call to William McGrouther at the BBC. It originated from Frayne's office inside Harry Pollitt House. The message was *lunch is cancelled, I'm feeling a bit peaky*. McGrouther replied *that's a shame, let's try next week*, and thanked the caller.'

'Who made the call?' asked Fairburn.

'We don't know, except it was twenty-five minutes ago. The caller was a young woman. We're trying to identify the number from the CPGB's internal directory.'

'Frayne's secretary, I'd imagine,' said Fairburn. 'Anything else?'

'Yes, Comrade McGrouther immediately telephoned his assistant. He said he'd be unable to take any calls until Monday. He said there was a family emergency.'

'Thank you, Comrade. Call if you hear anything else.' Fairburn turned to Ross. 'I think we might've missed McGrouther. I think Frayne's warned him we're sniffing around.'

'Nah, we're alright.' Ross smiled, nodding at a grey ZIS limousine nosing out of Broadcasting House's car park. 'That's Bill McGrouther over there, sittin' in the back of that limo.'

'These Russian motors are useless for surveillance,' Ross grumbled, tucking the GAZ behind a coal lorry for cover. 'Most people know we use 'em and they only come in black.'

'What happens when they reach the priority lane?' Fairburn asked. Like Moscow, London had lanes reserved for government officials.

'I'll drive faster, won't I?' Ross replied. 'Havin' said that, it's Friday. The fucking Party lane's jam-packed with high-ups knockin' off early.' The limousine swept into the priority exit for the Great West Road. 'I reckon he's going to his sodding *dacha*.'

Fairburn checked his road map. 'McGrouther has a place in a village called Neston in Wiltshire. It's a few hours away, I'd guess.'

'Then they'll spot us sooner or later. I'm gonna overtake, see if I can pick 'em up near Brentford.'

Fairburn shook his head. 'No, stay with him.'

'You're the boss,' the CSS man replied.

Ross turned out to be a good surveillance driver. Every time Fairburn thought they were lagging too far behind the ZIS, he saw its grey coachwork in the distance. They followed the limousine to a quiet residential street near Ealing Common, where it slid into the drive of a mock-Tudor villa.

'Park around the corner,' Fairburn ordered, checking the action on his Makarov. 'I'll go and take a look. RT control and check who lives at this address: *29 Warwick Dene, Ealing.*'

'Yes, Comrade Captain,' Ross replied, reaching for the radio-telephone set.

Fairburn approached the house. The ZIS limousine idled on the drive, engine purring, the driver reading a newspaper. A man stood at the door, dressed in a corduroy suit and a knitted tie, his features matching the photograph in McGrouther's file. He glanced around nervously, like a man waiting to enter a brothel. Fairburn walked casually into a neighbouring garden. Shielded by a privet hedge, he stood and listened. 'Hello, Fran,' said McGrouther, trying to sound calm. 'I'm terribly sorry to turn up unannounced.' His voice, cultured and smooth, was the sort Fairburn associated with the expatriate clubs of Cairo and Alexandria.

'Bill?' A woman's voice. Irate. 'You know the procedure. You should've bloody well called, or at least sent a message.'

'There wasn't time. Look, can I come in?'

'Were you followed? You might have brought them here.'

'I doubt it. I only got the call from Frayne an hour ago. Besides, CSS are always drunk as skunks on a Friday afternoon.'

'What do you want?'

'I need to leave. They're onto us.'

'Leave? That's not your decision to make, Bill.'

'Yes, it is,' McGrouther replied. 'I've done everything you asked. I'm scared, Fran.'

'And what about Frayne?'

'Frankie can make his own decisions. You know what he's like, he probably thinks he can brazen it out.'

'Come inside,' the woman ordered.

Fairburn walked back to the car. 'We're onto something. McGrouther's going on the run.'

Ross held the radio handset to his ear. 'This gets even better. Guess who lives at number 29?'

'Who?'

'A certain Mrs Francesca Mayhew,' Ross replied. 'She gets a mention in Crewe's file. Her brother was briefly engaged to Eliza Crewe in the '30s.'

'Have Colonel Sechkin send men immediately. I want anyone going in or out of this address detained.'

Ross looked surprised. 'We ain't pinching McGrouther now?'

Fairburn shook his head. 'No. I want to see what he does next.'

'Yes, Comrade Captain,' Ross replied, watching the limousine reverse out of the drive. A woman sat in the back of the car next to McGrouther. 'Mayhew's going to Wiltshire?'

Fairburn felt a familiar sense of excitement. The hunt was on. 'They're running,' he said. 'Let's see why.'

They tailed the ZIS, dropping in and out of sight. Fairburn saw Ross mumbling under his breath. 'What are you doing?'

'Speed, time and distance calculation,' Ross replied. 'It lets me back off without losing him. It ain't perfect, but it's better than nothing.'

'I've never seen this technique before. Where did you learn it?'

'Flying Squad,' Ross replied proudly. 'We were the first proper mobile police group. We came up with all sorts of tricks.'

They finally arrived in a tiny village called Neston. It consisted of a cluster of Bath stone cottages, a boarded-up pub, a schoolhouse and a gothic-looking church. The limousine dropped McGrouther and the woman outside an ivy-covered rectory before driving away. Ross held back, parking next to a green overlooking the house. The sky was grey and the trees black; a crow cocked its head as it watched from a nearby fence. 'Well done, Comrade Sergeant,' said Fairburn. He'd radioed Burgess House en route. 'Two of Colonel Sechkin's men will be here within the hour.'

'Why not arrest 'em now?'

'In case someone else is inside or they lead us to another suspect. Besides, two officers aren't enough to raid a house that big.'

'How many would you recommend?' asked Ross, tapping his fingers on the steering wheel.

'At least four. Eight would be better.'

Ross rolled his eyes. 'Where'd you learn that?'

'Poland.'

'Fair enough, but this ain't Poland. It's bloody Wiltshire. The most dangerous thing round 'ere is a bloody cow.'

'I'm sorry you find my caution irksome, Sergeant. I've an idea – why don't *you* attend officer academy? Then you can give the orders.'

'No need to be chopsy, boss. On the Flying Squad we'd just kick the door in.'

Fairburn smiled. 'I'm sure you would, but in Pomerania every farmer has a rifle in his kitchen and a grenade under his bed.'

'I doubt McGrouther's got anything more than a rolling pin.'

'The woman worries me,' Fairburn replied. 'She appears to be in charge. If she's a terrorist, she'll be armed.'

Another GAZ saloon arrived and two hard-faced men got out. The first, a square-shouldered giant, tapped on their car window. 'Good evening, Comrade Captain,' he said in Russian. 'I'm Senior Sergeant Bortnik.'

'Excellent,' said Fairburn, getting out of the car.

The second KGB man nodded. 'Sergeant Yakunin, Comrade Captain.'

'Are you armed?'

Yakunin pulled back his coat to reveal a PPS submachine gun. He smiled. 'Yes, Comrade Captain, I'm armed.'

'It's an important Party figure we're dealing with,' said Fairburn. 'There's a young woman with him. I think she might be the more troublesome of the two.'

'Then let's get on with it, eh?' said Ross, pulling a sledgehammer from the car boot. 'Let's give this bloke a kicking, then we'll get some dinner.'

Fairburn raised an eyebrow. 'I'm happy for you to remind Comrade McGrouther of the gravity of his situation, Sergeant Ross, but I'd like him to walk away unaided.'

Ross nodded at the sledgehammer. 'This is for the door, Comrade Captain.'

'Then let's go. Bortnik, Yakunin, take the back. Sergeant Ross and I will take the front.'

'*Da*,' Yakunin replied, checking the action on his PPS. Bortnik reached into the back of his car and produced a pump-gun. 'Winchester. American. Good for house clearing.'

'This is Wiltshire, Comrade. Not Stalingrad,' Ross replied in Russian. The two KGB men laughed and disappeared around the side of the rectory, weapons ready. Rolling his head like a boxer limbering up for a fight, Ross attacked the front door with the sledgehammer. The first blow bounced off solid oak. The second hit the lock. With a splintering crack, the third swing smashed the door off its hinges. 'CSS!' Ross bawled, dropping the sledgehammer and pulling a truncheon from his pocket. Drawing his Makarov, Fairburn followed him inside. The rectory was low-ceilinged, the sitting room lined with bookshelves. The house was cold, the fire unlit.

McGrouther appeared, grey-faced and trembling. 'Who the hell are you?' he whined .

'You're nicked,' said Ross, smashing his truncheon into McGrouther's ribs. Winded and gasping, the Deputy Chairman fell flat on his backside.

'That's enough,' said Fairburn. With a crash, the back door flew open and the two KGB men appeared. 'Check upstairs,' he ordered.

'Yes, Comrade Captain,' Bortnik replied, shotgun shouldered.

'W-what d'you want?' McGrouther wheezed.

'I'm Captain Thomas Fairburn. I'm from the KGB. You're under arrest for espionage.'

'Did you say KGB? But you're *English*. Who the hell do you think you are?'

Fairburn felt a flush of anger. These British communists – especially those from bourgeois backgrounds – couldn't disguise their arrogance. 'Where's Francesca Mayhew?'

The question was answered by a burst of gunfire. Yakunin appeared on the landing, smoke wafting from the muzzle of his PPS. 'The woman was in the bedroom,' he said.

'You shot her?' asked Fairburn.

'Oh yes, Comrade Captain.' The KGB sergeant pulled a handgun from his pocket. 'The bitch nearly got the drop on me.'

McGrouther's eyes shone with tears. 'I'd no idea Fran had a gun. I swear.'

'Anything else, Yakunin?'

'Hey, Bortnik,' Yakunin called. 'Bring down the woman's bag, will you?'

The KGB men trooped down the stairs, Bortnik carrying a scuffed leather holdall. He dumped the contents on the floor. 'You're definitely onto something here, Comrade Captain,' he said, nodding at the mess of passports, identity cards, driving licences and wodges of banknotes.

'I'd say you were proper fucked, McGrouther,' Ross agreed.

Fairburn looked McGrouther up and down. 'Sergeant Ross has a point, wouldn't you say?'

'What about Fran?' asked McGrouther.

'She's dead,' said Fairburn.

'She'd better be,' said Yakunin cheerfully. 'I gave her half a magazine.'

Fairburn began sorting through the pile of papers. 'Let's see what was worth dying for.'

Chapter 8

Fairburn found identity papers in the name of George Keen, but the photographs were unmistakably those of William McGrouther. He wore a disguise of thick-framed glasses and a stubbly beard, his hair dyed glossy black. 'You were defecting to America, McGrouther?' McGrouther, lips trembling, said nothing.

'Can I have a look at the passport, Comrade Captain?' asked Ross. 'Of course.'

Ross examined the document, rubbing his finger against the ink and flexing the passport's spine. 'Blimey, this ain't counterfeit. It's real. Fresh from the passport office.'

'Which suggests the involvement of others. Actually, McGrouther, this might work to your advantage.'

McGrouther's eyes were fixed on the floor, his shoulders slumped. Fairburn thought he couldn't look any guiltier. 'How?'

'You're looking at a firing squad, but who knows? Give up your co-conspirators and maybe you'll get five years in a gulag. I'm sure someone well connected like you will end up with a job in the kitchen. Or even the library.'

'Gimme the kitchens any day,' said Ross. 'You can't eat books. Trust me, I tried it back in the winter of '46.'

'I'm still a Deputy Chairman of the Communist Party of Great Britain,' said McGrouther indignantly. 'I'm a member of the bloody

Politburo. I'm entitled to see my Party legal officer. In fact, I bloody well insist.'

Fairburn cocked his head. 'Sergeant, we'll search the house. In the meantime, would you show Comrade McGrouther exactly what he's entitled to?'

Ross smiled. 'Of course, Comrade Captain.'

Upstairs, the KGB men found Francesca Mayhew's body curled in the doorway to the master bedroom. 'Cover her up, Sergeant Bortnik,' said Fairburn.

'Yes, Comrade Captain,' Bortnik replied, tugging a blanket from the bed and tossing it over the body. They searched the upstairs rooms, ransacking the place like drunken burglars in the KGB style. They'd found what they'd come for – the search was theatre designed to warn others. The only other incriminating material was a selection of forbidden literature. 'This one's illegal, ain't it?' said Bortnik, holding up a copy of *Robinson Crusoe.*

'He'll get away with that by virtue of his work,' Fairburn replied in his Moscow-accented Russian. 'Is there anything else?'

'These,' Bortnik replied, holding a shoebox. 'This was hidden in the bathroom.'

'Let me see,' said Fairburn. Inside the box was a set of first edition Eliza Crewe novels, signed by the author *to my dearest Billy.* They looked brand new, except for one called *The Bridge of Sighs.* It was well thumbed, notes pencilled in the margins. 'If it was important enough to hide, it's important enough to examine. Put it with the rest of the evidence, Bortnik.'

'Yes, Comrade Captain.'

When they returned downstairs, they saw a figure stood in the doorway – an elderly militia constable. 'There ain't no need to point guns all over the bleeding place,' the old man grumbled, eyes fixed on Yakunin's machine pistol. 'Someone reported shooting. I knew it was you lot. Big cars and tommy guns? Who else would it be?'

'Al Capone?' Ross chuckled, standing next to a bruised-looking McGrouther.

'Stop bothering us,' said Bortnik in English. 'Fuck off, *starik*.'

'There's no need to be rude,' said the militiaman. 'You're Russian? Who's in charge?'

'I'm sorry, Comrade,' Fairburn replied in English. 'We're KGB. We had to shoot a terrorist. The body's upstairs.'

The constable rubbed his stubbly chin. 'A terrorist? Comrade McGrouther, are you alright?'

'Speak to *me*, Officer,' said Fairburn. 'McGrouther's under arrest.'

The constable licked his teeth, trying not to meet McGrouther's eye. 'Well, my superintendent says anythin' concerning the Deputy Chairman's residence is reported to HQ straight away.'

'He receives additional security measures?' asked Fairburn. He remembered the third suspect in Philby's report – Gerry Scanlon – was head of the Militia.

'All Politburo members do,' the constable replied, pulling a dog-eared policeman's notebook from his tunic. 'Anyhow, I'll need to be callin' the coroner.'

'We'll make the necessary arrangements,' Fairburn replied.

'That ain't normal, is it? My bosses'll be wanting your details, Comrade Captain.'

'I'm Captain Thomas Fairburn of the KGB. Oh, and tell your superintendent my work's far from finished. He might want to pass that message up your chain of command. Right to the top, perhaps?'

Once the constable finished writing, he gave Fairburn a half-hearted salute. 'I better get back to the station.'

'Thank you. I'll mention your diligence in my report.'

The constable raised an eyebrow. 'Er, much obliged, Comrade.'

When he was gone, Bortnik closed the door. 'Why were you so nice to that *musor*?'

'You must remember, the English are islanders,' Fairburn replied. 'They're stubborn by nature. But tickle their tummies? They're easily managed.'

'If you say so,' the KGB man sniffed.

'Tickles are cheaper than bullets.' Fairburn shrugged.

'You didn't tickle McGrouther, Comrade Captain,' said Yakunin, studying Fairburn with hard yellow eyes. 'Your man just beat the shit out of him.'

Fairburn pulled on a pair of leather gloves and made for the door. 'Good point, Comrade, but did you ever meet a senior Party man you wanted to tickle?'

The two KGB men were poker-faced. Then, finally, they laughed.

It was the small hours in an interrogation room beneath Burgess House. A glum McGrouther sat slumped in a chair next to Ross. The secret policeman wore shirtsleeves, a truncheon lying on the table in front of him. Fairburn sat opposite, slowly eating an apple. 'I'll get to the point,' he said, spitting a seed into a bin. 'We knew you were involved in Eliza Crewe's defection. But guns? Terrorism? That changes things.'

McGrouther was sullen. 'Fran wasn't a terrorist. I'm sure the gun was for self-defence. She didn't deserve to die.'

'She tried to shoot a KGB officer,' said Fairburn. 'Sergeant Ross, strike the prisoner for lying.'

Ross rapped the truncheon against McGrouther's kneecaps. Howling, he tumbled out of his chair. 'Get up, you soft cunt,' the secret policeman growled. 'It was only a tap.'

Fairburn nodded. 'You need to develop a thicker skin, I think, McGrouther. I see your file mentions you were a conscientious objector during the Great Patriotic War.'

'Yes,' McGrouther whimpered, climbing back into his seat. 'I'd have been conscripted into the army otherwise. I didn't want to fight for the fascists.'

'Were you active in the Resistance?'

'I published propaganda leaflets. I didn't cut throats or blow up railway tracks, but I did my bit.'

'I agree, propaganda is important. Ideas are like bullets if used properly. You took risks for the struggle,' said Fairburn gently. 'So how did it end up like this? When did you decide to betray the Party to the Americans?'

'Americans?'

'Don't insult my intelligence.'

'Comrade Captain, I doubt you understand the delicacies of the political situation. No offence intended, of course, but we're all men of our time and upbringing. I imagine you were very young during the war.'

'None taken,' Fairburn replied. 'Please, enlighten me. I've no desire to put you in front of a firing squad. Not if there are more significant traitors to be found.'

'The sort who cut throats and blow up railway tracks,' Ross added.

'Quite. Would you arrange for some coffee, Sergeant Ross?'

'Yes, Comrade Captain,' Ross replied, heading for the door.

Fairburn took another bite of his apple. 'Please, McGrouther, carry on.'

'Eliza and I were lovers, many years ago. That's why I risked everything, I suppose. I still love her.'

'Really?' Fairburn smiled. '*Love*? I think you'll need to do better than that.'

McGrouther shook his head. 'Comrade Captain, you've obviously never been in love.'

'Perhaps you're right.'

'What guarantees do I have about my treatment?'

'Only one,' said Fairburn.

'Which is?'

Fairburn made a lazy shrug, tilting his head and gently rolling his shoulders. He'd met an Egyptian arms dealer who made the gesture when considering a deal. It combined insouciance with a touch of menace. 'I've plenty of evidence. Sooner or later, I'll arrest the others involved in your network. One of them will offer you up in return for their safety. Then you'll face a firing squad.'

'What do you mean?'

Fairburn tried not to look surprised. How had McGrouther survived the Stalin years? Britain really was soft. 'Think of it as a bidding war. Who can offer the most information? You? Francis Frayne? His secretary, perhaps? Who can best help CSS combat counter-revolutionary activity? Who is of most service to the State?'

McGrouther looked at his feet. He wore no shoes or socks, his toes bloody from where Ross had stamped on them. 'You've arrested Francis Frayne?'

Fairburn nodded. 'Of course. Just after midnight. Who knows what he's saying about you?'

McGrouther looked as if he were about to burst into tears. 'What happens now?'

'It depends on Comrade Director Philby.'

'Philby wants blood,' McGrouther hissed, his sudden ferocity taking Fairburn by surprise. 'He hates us. He thinks the CSS should run the Politburo.'

'Then you should bid higher than Frayne, don't you think?'

When McGrouther looked up at Fairburn, he was crying. 'Yes, Comrade Captain,' he said. 'I suppose I should.'

Chapter 9

'You don't waste any time do you?' said Philby. His smile was warm, his eyes bright with excitement.

Nikolai Sechkin nodded. 'Well done, Tommy. That was solid work, even by your standards. Fast. Decisive. And a dead terrorist too?'

'Kick the hornet's nest and have a net ready.' Fairburn replied. 'McGrouther was the weakest link. To be fair, most of the credit belongs to Senior Sergeant Ross. He has a wealth of common sense and his surveillance skills are outstanding.'

Philby sipped tea from a china cup. 'He's a solid chap. If only I had a hundred more like him.'

'Indeed,' Fairburn said. 'I see why you chose him.'

'What of our third suspect?' said Philby. 'Gerry Scanlon's involved, I feel it in my bones. I'm sure you can beat something incriminating out of McGrouther to prove it?'

Ash Prasad sat in a corner, fiddling with his cufflinks. 'Bill McGrouther's still a Deputy Chairman, Kim. And he's beginning to cooperate.'

'I'm open to alternative views. Tommy?'

Fairburn, freshly shaved and smelling of cologne, folded his hands in his lap. 'I agree with Comrade Prasad. I'd rather present McGrouther to a tribunal in one piece. Let's see if Scanlon makes a move, just like Frayne. We'll be waiting when he does.'

For a moment, the only sounds in the room were the ticking of a clock and the scrape of the Director's teacup against its saucer. Finally, Philby smiled. 'Of course, Tommy. Nikolai, any thoughts?'

Sechkin shrugged. 'If a tactic works, reinforce it. If it fails, try something else. That's the KGB way. At the moment? The tactics are working.'

'Very well,' the Director replied. 'What do you suggest we tell General Teplyakov?'

Sechkin's meaty face was expressionless. 'That we're making progress, but nothing specific. He might overreact, Kim.'

'Your counsel's always welcome, Nikolai,' Philby replied. 'However, we're dealing with CIA infiltration at senior Party level. Who knows what else the Politburo are planning? Comrade Chairman Khrushchev arrives soon. This affair must not cast a shadow over his visit.'

Sechkin nodded. 'Of course, Comrade Director. Will you let me speak with General Teplyakov?'

'Please do, Nikolai.'

Fairburn stood and cleared his throat. 'Director, with your permission, may I return to my duties? I must check the telephone monitoring records. We'll need to move quickly if Scanlon breaks cover.'

'Of course, Tommy. Nikolai, Ash and I will chew the fat while you do all the work,' Philby chuckled. Prasad smiled too, the open journal on his lap blank.

Fairburn put on his cap, stood to attention and saluted. 'Of course, comrades. I shall be in touch soonest.'

'One last thing,' said Philby.

'Sir?'

'Ash and I have agreed you'll leave Francis Frayne for my officers to interrogate. We'll let you know what he says, of course.'

Fairburn pulled a face. Prasad cocked his head. 'You disapprove, Tommy?'

'I think it would be better for Sergeant Ross and I to interrogate all of the prisoners. I think consistency is important in this type of investigation.'

Prasad smiled. 'Usually I'd agree, but I've the best interrogator in Bureau 6 at my disposal. I think a woman might make better progress with Frayne. Softy-softly, eh?'

'Comrade Captain King is outstanding,' said Philby. 'I'm confident she'll do an excellent job.'

'As you wish, Comrade Director,' said Fairburn. Saluting, he turned on his heel and left the room.

Sechkin stood by the tank on the parade square, smoking a cigarette. 'What is it, Tommy? You've got a face like a slapped arse.'

'I didn't have time to tell you, Nikolai. I saw Teplyakov yesterday.'

'I'm surprised it took so long. I suppose he wants you to report back?'

'Yes. He thinks we've been sent on a fool's errand.'

Sechkin frowned. 'Teplyakov is pissed off because he's not in charge of our operation. It's dick-swinging. Just tell him the bare minimum and show him respect. You'll be fine.'

Fairburn looked at the grey London sky. He couldn't remember the last time he'd seen the sun. 'He really does want another Budapest. I saw it in his eyes.'

'Which is why you need to focus on the mission.'

'Teplyakov said he knew I'd speak to you about this.'

'When all is said and done, he's my boss too. He leaves me alone because I'm friends with Serov, and because I'm without ambition. I've seen off more dangerous dogs.'

'Very well, Nikolai,' said Tommy. 'Best I get back to work.'

'You do that,' Sechkin replied. 'Just remember to keep a spare pair of eyes in the back of your head.'

'Sign these,' said Fairburn, pushing a sheaf of papers in front of McGrouther. 'Before you do, are you sure Gerald Scanlon has no involvement in this affair?'

McGrouther sat in a metal chair, back straight, his sandy hair matted with blood. 'Not that I know of, Comrade Captain. I only see Comrade General Scanlon at Politburo meetings. We don't mix in the same social circles. My work seldom brings me into contact with the Militia.'

'Very well. Read the main points of your confession for the tape recorder. Sergeant Ross?'

Ross switched on a wooden-cased recorder, a CSS-issued Loewe Optaphon. 'Yes, Comrade Captain. The tape's running,' he said.

McGrouther cleared his throat. 'I give this statement freely,' he began, licking his split lip. 'I, William McGrouther, member of the Social Republic of Great Britain's Central Committee and Deputy Chairman for Public Information, am guilty of counter-revolutionary activity by assisting Eliza Crewe's defection to America. This was because of a personal relationship between us, one predating the Great Patriotic War. It was a sentimental decision, based on reckless emotion. I was misguided and wrong.'

'Please, continue, Comrade,' said Fairburn. Now McGrouther was cooperative, he could be addressed as *Comrade* once more. He'd serve five years in a gulag on the Isle of Sheppey. McGrouther would never again enjoy a dacha or a ZIS limousine, but he'd live to contemplate his disgrace.

'Francis Frayne, Deputy Chairman of the CPGB Central Committee, used his influence to help me obtain forged identity documents,' McGrouther continued. 'I asked if he could arrange this as a personal favour. He agreed.'

'Why would a man of his stature take such a risk?'

McGrouther fixed his eyes on Fairburn's and the KGB man knew he was telling the truth. 'Frayne once said, *I don't want to end up like Harry Pollitt.* If he felt under threat, which occasionally he did, he wanted the option to defect. A card to play. Frayne knew Eliza had friends who could make the necessary arrangements.'

'*Friends?*'

'Yes, American friends. Bourgeois so-called Democrats.'

'Thank you for your candour, Comrade. Is there anything else you'd like to add?' asked Fairburn, nudging the script towards his prisoner.

'I was offered the chance to defect by a woman called Francesca Mayhew. She had links to the American CIA. I was considering my position when I was arrested. Mayhew was a terrorist, she threatened KGB officers with a pistol and was shot.'

Fairburn's voice was gentle. 'During your interview, you mentioned some of the things Comrade Frayne told you. Would you repeat them for us?'

'Yes, of course,' McGrouther replied, tracing the words on the page with a bloody finger. 'Deputy Chairman Francis Frayne frequently expressed disillusionment with the Soviet Union, especially about the special military operation in Hungary. He was especially scathing about Comrade Khrushchev. Rather than report these doubts, I naively thought I could persuade him to change his mind. For that, I am deeply sorry.'

'Thank you, Comrade McGrouther,' said Fairburn, signalling for Ross to turn off the tape recorder.

'Well done, Bill,' said Ross, slapping McGrouther on the back. 'I'll get you a cuppa and a sandwich, eh?'

'Thank you, Comrade Sergeant,' McGrouther whispered. 'May I have some sugar in my tea, please?'

'Yes, mate, course you can.'

Fairburn watched Ross button up his grey CSS uniform, piped in green metallic thread. 'You look very smart, Comrade.'

Ross buckled a brown leather belt over his gut and put on his cap. 'I hate uniforms. My old inspector used to say I looked like a sack of spuds tied up in the middle.'

'One should look professional for court appearances,' Fairburn replied, plucking a piece of lint from his tunic.

'The Tribunal for State Justice ain't much of a court, is it?' Ross guffawed as he ran a cloth over his jackboots. 'I mean, courts find people innocent now and then.'

'As opposed to the old system? A bourgeois pantomime, played by rich men in wigs?' Fairburn replied. 'Now, are you ready?'

Reaching into his locker, Ross pulled out a Winchester shotgun. 'I'm ready,' he said, thumbing shells into the pump-gun's breech. They strode through the tunnels beneath Burgess House and into a subterranean car park. The armoured truck parked on a ramp contained William McGrouther, due to be tried, found guilty and sentenced at 14.00. Ross opened the door of his black GAZ saloon and the two secret policemen climbed inside. Behind them, in another GAZ, were KGB sergeants Bortnik and Yakunin. Both wore long leather coats over their uniforms, like Chekists of old.

'Let's go,' said Fairburn, slapping the dashboard with a gloved hand.

'Yes, Comrade Captain,' Ross replied, motoring up a ramp and onto the King's Road. They were followed by the armoured truck, Bortnik and Yakunin bringing up the rear. Ross flicked a switch on the dashboard and a claxon screamed. 'Let people know we're busy, eh? It keeps 'em on their toes.'

Fairburn arched an eyebrow. 'You mean they feel reassured the State's protecting them?'

'I reckon we're saying the same thing, Comrade, just differently.'

The convoy sped along Chelsea Embankment and Millbank, cars parting as they approached. They followed the Thames to Westminster, passing the recently completed People's Assembly. Designed by Soviet architect Dmitry Chechulin, the Assembly resembled two giant concrete shoeboxes, one balanced on top of the other. Big Ben had been replaced by a gleaming steel tower, five hundred feet high, tipped with a golden hammer and sickle. They skirted Assembly Square and Victoria Embankment, passing ministry buildings decorated with red banners. Finally, they reached The Strand and the People's Courts of Justice. The gothic-looking complex had survived the war with minimal damage, the hulks of decommissioned Soviet tanks mounted on plinths either side of the entrance. 'I remember the first time I saw a Stalin tank,' said Fairburn. 'It was the biggest armoured vehicle I'd ever seen.'

'In London?'

'Yes, back in 1947.'

'What was it like?'

'There's an opera called *Götterdämmerung*, about a war between mythical Gods at the end of the world. I suppose it felt like that.' Fairburn remembered crouching in the ruins of St. Thomas' Hospital with two of Sechkin's snipers. They watched Red Army shock troops swarm across Westminster Bridge, wave after wave braving tempests of machine-gun fire. 'The SS and the British fascists turned Parliament into a fortress, what the Germans called a *festung*. They say General Zhukov had five thousand guns and rocket trucks lined up along the Thames. They levelled Parliament.'

Ross whistled through his teeth. 'Fuck me. That's proper history, ain't it?'

Fairburn nodded. 'I was sixteen. I'd never seen anything like it.'

'Next time it'll be Washington DC?'

'The only people who'll see Washington turned to dust will be our bomber crews,' Fairburn replied. 'I've seen how many planes the Americans have at their bases in North Africa. If it ever happens, Yankee pilots will watch Moscow burn too.'

They drove inside the tribunal's car park. As the armoured truck reversed into a parking space, two bored-looking Justice Ministry troops appeared. 'I'll take McGrouther to the cells myself,' said Ross, stepping out of the car. 'I don't trust these ministry clowns.' Fairburn followed, straightening his tunic and putting on his cap. Bortnik and Yakunin, weapons ready, joined them by the rear of the truck. The doors swung open and McGrouther appeared, scrunching up his face against the milky daylight. The Deputy Chairman for Information wore a woollen blanket around his shoulders, his face bruised and his hair plastered to his skull. Taking his elbow, Ross helped him down from the back of the vehicle.

Then, the whip-crack of a rifle shot.

McGrouther jolted as if electrocuted, his head snapping back as a second shot took him in the cheek. Yakunin jumped from the truck's tailgate, scanning the rooftops with his machine pistol. Ross, throwing himself onto his belly, crawled for cover behind the nearest car. Fairburn joined him, pistol drawn. He studied likely vantage points – the shooter could be hiding in any number of tall buildings within five hundred yards. He intuited McGrouther was the marksman's only target, as the sniper could have shot them all. 'Bortnik,' he called, getting to his feet and dusting off his breeches. 'Call the Militia and tell them to cordon off the area. Every direction, for five hundred metres. And find me some bloody witnesses.'

'Yes, Comrade Captain,' Bortnik replied, nudging McGrouther's body with his boot. 'What do you want the witnesses to say?'

'Whatever they saw, Bortnik,' Fairburn sighed. 'Anything suspicious. Someone running away.'

Ross appeared at Fairburn's shoulder, scratching his chin with a dirty fingernail. He seemed indifferent to the reddish-grey flecks of brain plastered across his shoulder. 'I'd say the marksman was to the east,' he said, pointing at a church. Its belltower was clad in scaffolding, tarpaulins flapping like tatty flags. 'That's St. Dunstan's, on Fleet Street. It's high enough, ain't it?'

'Yakunin, get on the R/T,' Fairburn ordered. 'I want a company of CSS troops here now. Block all the main routes out of the city, especially the bridges.'

'Yes, Comrade Captain!' the KGB sergeant replied, hurrying back to his car.

'Inform Colonel Sechkin. Tell him to double the security on Francis Frayne. Now, give me your shotgun.'

'Where are you going?' asked Bortnik, handing over his weapon.

'To church, of course.'

Chapter 10

Fairburn and Ross ran along the Strand, pedestrians scurrying out of their way. 'It's here, Captain,' Ross panted as they reached St. Dunstan's. The church was built from ivory-coloured stone, pock-marked with wartime bullet holes. Since Stalin's death there'd been a rapprochement between the Church and Communist governments across Europe, and the door of St. Dunstan's was open.

'Have you seen anyone leave the church?' Fairburn asked a man at a bus stop. When he saw the two secret policemen, he raised his newspaper like a shield.

'No, Comrade,' he replied. 'I did hear a noise. Maybe a car backfiring?'

'Move along, it's not safe,' Fairburn ordered. Ross darted inside the church, turning right. Fairburn went left, taking cover behind a row of pews. The smell of the church took Fairburn back to his childhood – incense and damp. A white-robed figure lay in front of the altar, open-eyed. A priest.

'Is he dead?' asked Ross.

Fairburn checked the priest. His clerical collar was askew, his throat mottled and mauve. 'He's been strangled,' said Fairburn.

'Strange,' Ross whispered. 'It ain't like the Resistance to kill priests. And why didn't the marksman shoot us earlier?'

'We never saw the sniper's face, but the priest did,' Fairburn replied. 'Let's check the tower.'

'Lead on, Captain,' said Ross, picking up a silver collection plate from the altar.

'What's that for?'

'You'll see.' They crept up the stairs, weapons ready. Sacks of plaster and gypsum lay stacked nearby, a cat's cradle of scaffolding visible through the windows. 'See that?' Ross whispered, pointing at the dusty staircase leading to the tower.

'Yes,' said Fairburn. 'The boot prints only go one way – up.'

Ross lay a hand on Fairburn's shoulder. 'I'll go first.'

'No, *I'll* go first.'

'Just listen for a bloody change,' Ross hissed. Polishing the silver collection plate on the cuff of his tunic, he held it into the doorway. 'See? It's clear,' he said, pointing at his improvised mirror.

Fairburn headed for the east-facing window. 'The sniper must've escaped down the scaffolding,' he said, seeing a ladder lashed to the side of the belltower. He nodded at a set of marks on the dusty floor. 'He was kneeling there when he opened fire.'

'There's no spent brass either,' said Ross, lowering his pistol and pushing his cap onto the back of his head. 'This fella's squared away.'

Fairburn's eyes swept the greyish London streets. He watched militiamen cordon off the street, bellowing orders at passers-by. 'Sergeant, in your experience how professional are the fascist terrorists in Britain?'

'Well, the most effective were the Monarchists. Most had military experience, you see, but they all fucked off to Canada or Egypt. The Soviets rooted out the rest, although we still get letter bombs and the odd arson. Then you've got the *British Action Front*. Ex-Blackshirts and former British SS men. They're a proper bunch of sadistic arseholes.'

'And the last time you encountered a sniper?'

'A while back, up in Scotland. They were Ulster Loyalists. But you're thinking the same as me, ain't you?'

'Yes,' said Fairburn. 'I think our sniper is a professional. Even Militia or CSS.'

'CSS?' Ross replied.

'My recommendation is to suspect everyone, Comrade Sergeant. That way you're seldom surprised.'

Fairburn met Nikolai Sechkin at Tower Wharf, in the shadow of Traitor's Gate. A Soviet gunboat chugged down the Thames, sailors standing on deck taking photographs of the Tower of London. Sechkin studied the tip of his cigarette, dark circles under his eyes. 'Sleeping badly, Nikolai?' asked Fairburn.

'Irina has terrible nightmares. She wakes me up.'

'Nightmares?'

The Russian frowned. 'She has dreams about when her bomber was shot-up over Berlin. Her co-pilot and navigator were killed.'

'Irina's a heroine, Nikolai.'

'She is, but heroism comes with a price.' Nikolai replied, shaking his head. 'The braver the deed, the more it takes.'

Fairburn put a hand on Sechkin's shoulder. 'I'm sorry, Nikolai.'

'She's alive and for that I am grateful. Now, let's concentrate on our work.'

'Of course.'

'Do you really think McGrouther's death was an inside job? Moscow is furious.'

'Quite possibly. The killer seemed professional and he clearly knew our schedule.'

'CIA?'

Fairburn made a so-so gesture with his hand. 'Possibly. Or are the British fighting a civil war? Politburo versus Philby?'

'Well, there's about to be another casualty,' Sechkin replied. 'Philby tells me Frayne's confessed to working for the Americans. Unless he's very lucky, he's going in front of a firing squad.'

'I doubt he was a CIA mole,' Fairburn replied. 'Especially if the confession was beaten out of him.'

'The interrogator was a young woman. Captain King. I've seen her at Burgess House, she's about five feet tall. That would be doubly humiliating for Frayne, don't you think?'

'Scanlon's name didn't come up during the interrogation?'

'No, but in any case, Philby needs more than a denunciation to take Scanlon down. Scanlon's popular and powerful. A resistance hero.'

'I agree. I'd treat him with caution.'

'Anyway, aren't you due to give Teplyakov a call? He'll be delighted about the McGrouther killing. It's more evidence the British aren't up to the job.'

'I'll call the General soon,' said Fairburn, checking his watch. 'Then I've got a murder to solve. I've ordered CSS to take over the McGrouther investigation from the Militia.'

Nikolai scratched his nose, as flat as a boxer's, and sighed. 'Then find the killer quickly, Tommy. Moscow wants answers, before this dung heap grows.'

'And what will Moscow do when the dung heap gets too big?'

Sechkin pulled up his collar. 'Teplyakov will douse it in petrol and set light to it. He wants to install a new British central committee. The British Politburo will protest, people will take to the streets and we'll send in our tanks. Just like we did in Budapest. And all the work we've done since the Liberation? Wasted.'

'The arc of history's on our side, Nikolai.'

'Oh to be young again,' Sechkin chuckled, shoulders hunched against the wind. 'Those of us who carry the Motherland's sword and shield must, on occasion, say the unsayable.'

Fairburn raised an eyebrow. Nikolai was a pragmatist and a patriot. Any criticism of Russia, from his lips, had to be heartfelt. 'The unsayable?'

'The Motherland has over-extended herself, Tommy. Do you know how many people we lost during the war? More than forty million.'

'*Forty?*'

'Yes, and still we garrison Europe. It's why we have manpower shortages in our factories and farms. And if Britain goes up in flames, where next? Meanwhile the Americans build more airfields in Spain and North Africa. Iceland and Scandinavia. They seek to hem us in.'

Fairburn had seen rows of gleaming American B52 bombers in Libya. 'You think there'll be another war?'

'Who knows? Maybe the Americans think they can win.'

Fairburn slapped his old friend on the back. 'I say there's a lot resting on the shoulders of a defecting novelist, Nikolai.'

'When you put it like that, I suppose there is. Forgive me for being so gloomy, Tommy. Now, tell me your thoughts about Sergeant Ross. Is he performing well?'

'Ross is a man of experience and action. He's also overly fond of his privilege to – how did you put it? – *say the unsayable.*'

'He's Philby's hound, and Philby's no fool. Still, I need your opinion.'

Fairburn waited for a smart-looking woman walking a dog to pass. 'Why?'

'I've been thinking about Scanlon. The English would describe him as "old school". A tricky target, wouldn't you agree?'

'I would say so. He's working-class, a decorated resistance hero and a star graduate of the Lenin School. Scanlon is easily the most impressive of our suspects.'

'Then we'll need old-school people to catch him. You don't get to the top in politics without making enemies. I'm sure Scanlon has many. Go and do some digging.'

'I will,' Fairburn replied. 'I can't imagine questioning the man will yield much.'

'You met Scanlon in Moscow once, didn't you?' said Sechkin. 'What did you make of the man?'

Fairburn walked to the river's edge, watching trash floating in the murky water. 'Comrade Scanlon gave a lecture at the MGB school on irregular warfare. It was 1949, I think. One of our instructors tried to correct him on Marxist dialectics. Scanlon demolished the argument – he'd obviously memorised Stalin's *Marxism and the National Question.*'

Sechkin rolled his eyes. 'Just what we need, another Stalinist.'

'Now, Comrade Colonel Sechkin, you doubt the wisdom of the Marxist Dialectic?' Fairburn teased.

'Cheeky little shit,' Sechkin laughed. It was getting cold in the tower's shadow and the big Russian pulled up his collar. 'Now, Tommy, find a stick to poke Comrade Scanlon with. A sharp one!'

Fairburn accepted Nikolai's hug. 'It will be sharp,' he said. 'I'll ask Sergeant Ross to make sure of that. He strikes me as old school, wouldn't you say?'

Chapter 11

It was just after 06.00 when Fairburn dialled General Teplyakov's number from a telephone kiosk. 'Yes?' said a voice. Fairburn recognised it as Rogov's, the KGB General's smug driver.

'Hello, Rogov. I'd like to speak to the General.'

'It's early.'

'I'm a busy man.'

'I'll see if he's free.'

A few moments later, Teplyakov's voice came on the line. 'Why didn't you call yesterday? Why did I have to wait for the British to inform me of McGrouther's death?'

'My apologies, Comrade General. It's been hectic.'

A sigh. Fairburn thought it was a tad forced. 'Go on, Fairburn. I hope you've something useful to report.'

'I'm told Frayne's confessed to spying for the Americans. From my interrogation of McGrouther, I don't think that's likely. I suspect Frayne was doing McGrouther a favour to cover his back in case he wanted to leave Britain, not because he was a CIA asset.'

'And what of General Scanlon?'

'McGrouther insisted he'd no reason to think he was involved. Interestingly, Frayne didn't implicate him either. They used their best interrogator. She could easily have put the words in his mouth.'

'Philby's scared, I think,' Teplyakov replied. 'Scanlon's his equal.

Besides, the Militia has more troops than the CSS. And the British Army isn't big enough to win a bar fight.'

'I'm tasked to find more evidence on Scanlon, Comrade General,' said Fairburn.

'And?'

'I'm going to dig up some dirt. *Kompromat*, maybe. I want to know if Scanlon's a genuine suspect, or if Philby's playing games.'

'Of course Philby's playing games,' Teplyakov scoffed. 'Why else do you think I have to rely on a lowly 10th Directorate officer to keep me informed? He takes advantage of the goodwill he enjoys in Moscow.'

'Quite so, Comrade General.'

'Is there anything else?'

'No, Comrade General.'

'Keep me updated. One more thing.'

'Yes?'

'I agree Scanlon's a suspect in the Crewe affair, but from now on I want you to keep an eye on Philby too. Report back on his decision-making. Any weaknesses, that sort of thing.'

'Comrade General…'

'That's an order, Fairburn,' said Teplyakov smoothly. 'I assure you I make a better friend than an enemy. Am I understood?'

'Absolutely, Comrade General.'

The CSS archives were housed in an old armoury. Now they contained a different sort of ammunition. Protected by a locked steel door, signs in English and Russian warned of grave penalties for unauthorised entry. 'You're sure this person is completely trust-worthy?' Fairburn asked.

'Agnes Muir's a bleedin' legend,' Ross replied, pressing a buzzer. 'She's forgotten more secrets than we'll ever know.'

The door swung open, revealing a tall, dark-haired woman. She wore a high-collared blouse and a neat cardigan, spectacles hanging from a chain around her neck. There was something about her that reminded Fairburn of a schoolmistress. 'Comrade Captain Fairburn? Good afternoon.' Her accent was Scottish. 'I'm Major Agnes Muir, CSS Collator-in-Chief.'

Fairburn snapped to attention. 'A pleasure, Comrade Major.'

Muir studied Fairburn's uniform. 'Well there's a thing, an English KGB officer? The English get everywhere, I swear.' She ushered Fairburn and Ross into a room lined with bookshelves. Young women moved silently along rows of shelves, plucking files from boxes and placing them on trolleys. They wore white cotton gloves and brown aprons, their rubber-soled shoes squeaking gently on the linoleum floor.

'How long have you worked for CSS, Comrade Major?' asked Fairburn.

'Since we were established in 1948. Before that I was a Party member in Edinburgh for many years.'

'Comrade Muir was head librarian at Edinburgh University,' said Ross.

'I was also an intelligence officer in the Resistance,' the collator added proudly, touching the gold partisan pin on her cardigan. Many CSS officers were ex-resistance operatives or Communist Party members – the majority of MI5 and MI6 staff had been executed or imprisoned for collaborating with the Nazis. 'Comrade Director Philby himself chose me for this job. I like to think I run a tight ship.'

81

'I'm sure you do. May I ask what happened to the pre-Liberation records?'

'A significant amount of material was salvaged by the MGB after the war. We hold most of the old MI5 and MI6 records, along with police Special Branch reports and national Court registers. We've only a limited selection of Abwehr and Gestapo material though. The fascists destroyed most of it when the Red Army liberated London. Since 1950, we've also held military service records and those of political parties, including any British national involved with the fascist government between 1940 and 1947.'

Fairburn nodded. 'I'm looking for a suspect with military or resistance experience, most likely an expert rifle shot. This person may have Party connections and links to the CSS or Militia.'

Agnes Muir put on her glasses. 'Militia? We hold *some* material, but they keep their own archives. They're quite particular about their independence, we'd have to make a formal request.'

'I'd prefer not to involve the Militia. This is a sensitive matter.'

Muir gave Fairburn a sharp look. 'Sensitive? How many times a day do you think I hear that, Comrade?'

Fairburn jutted his chin. Muir might technically outrank him, but he was a KGB officer. 'I must reiterate the point, Comrade Major. I wish to cross-reference any suspect with Deputy Chairman Scanlon and the dissident, Eliza Crewe.'

Muir arched an eyebrow. 'Really? Then I shall do the research personally. Be assured, nobody else will know.'

'How long will it take, Agnes?' asked Ross, playing with a packet of cigarettes. A sign on the wall in English and Russian said NO SMOKING.

Fairburn answered the question. 'I expect something by first thing tomorrow morning, Comrade Major. It's what I'd expect from the KGB records section in Lubyanka. I see no reason why London should be any different.'

Muir pursed her lips. 'Of course, Comrade Captain.'

'Excellent. Now, Sergeant Ross, we've some field work to do.'

Ross pulled a face. 'Field work? I'm a city boy, Captain. I don't like fields.'

'You'll do, I suppose,' said Ross. The two men stood in the car park beneath Burgess House, where CSS officers lurked in shadowy corners. They were gossiping and smoking, like sinister schoolboys bunking off class.

'Thank you, Comrade Sergeant. I don't look like a KGB officer?'

'No, you look like a CSS officer.'

'Very amusing,' Fairburn replied. He wore a cheap grey suit, a mauve sweater and heavy lace-up shoes. No tie. 'In which case, so do you, Comrade Sergeant.'

Ross shrugged. He was similarly dressed. 'Don't matter, does it? Every fucker knows Sid Ross. I might as well be wearing my bloody uniform.'

'From your days as a policeman, or with the CSS?'

Ross got in the car. 'Both, but mainly from when I was a copper. We're going to the docks. The place attracts villains like flies to a freshly laid turd.'

'Socialism has eradicated common crime,' Fairburn replied, buttoning up his jacket. 'People are supposed to have what they need if the government is doing its job properly. Why would they steal?'

'Sometimes, Comrade Captain, I wonder if you're serious or taking the piss.'

'Why?'

'You've seen the food queues, ain't you? Even spuds an' carrots are rationed nowadays. People are hungry.'

Fairburn had scored highly in Criminology at the MGB academy. 'People are hungry as a result of crimes of thought and action, the work of wreckers and saboteurs. If we eradicate those, we eradicate hunger too.'

They got in the car. Ross drove up a ramp, the GAZ's engine growling. 'See? That's part of the problem.'

'What?'

'Clever people like you, talking so much shit.'

'Choose your next words carefully, Comrade Sergeant.'

Ross braked suddenly, sending Fairburn slamming into the dashboard. 'Oh I will. You see, we need to come to an understandin' *Comrade.*'

'Such as?'

'Well, you could stop talkin' bollocks for starters. 'Cuz if you don't wise up, the next sniper's bullet might get *me.* In case you ain't noticed, there ain't no onion domes round here. This is London, not Moscow. Different manor, different rules.'

'I know you're trusted by Director Philby, but we've a system to serve. It isn't perfect, not yet, but serve it we must.'

Ross shook his head as he drove up the ramp. A sentry jumped out of the way as he screeched onto the King's Road. 'If you can keep schtum about politics for ten minutes, I'll show you a thing or two they didn't teach at your precious Academy. Deal?'

'Very well,' he replied. 'Today we do things your way.'

'Good,' said Ross. 'In which case, let's go for a bloody drink.'

The Falcon was a Victorian pub on the East India Dock Road, the sort Fairburn's father would have called a 'Gin Palace'. The ceiling was yellowish-brown from a century's worth of tobacco smoke, its wood-panelled walls covered in posters warning of the dangers of alcohol and cigarettes. Someone had scrawled a crude cock and balls on each. Grimy-faced dockers sat drinking, smoking and playing Gin Rummy. Ross spread a handful of coins across the bar. 'Hello, John, two pints of ordinary please,' he called. 'How are you?'

'Oh, I'm makin' a living, Sid,' the landlord replied. He was brawny and red-cheeked, forearms swathed in a bluish scribble of tattoos. 'I ain't seen you for a while.'

'Been busy, John. Protecting the country from villainy an' such.'

John laughed as he pumped watery beer into pint glasses. 'I s'pose so,' he said. He nodded at Fairburn. 'Is this the new boy?'

Ross smiled. 'Yeah, he's called Tommy. I'm breaking him in gently.'

'Well, I ain't sure this is the right boozer. The morning shift will be knocking off soon. It'll get rowdy, especially if they see you.'

'Fighting with drunkards? Militia work,' said Fairburn, sipping his beer. It tasted terrible. 'We're not militia. Anyway, cheers, Comrade.'

'You've got a bit of an accent,' said John. 'Where are you from?'

'Kenley,' Fairburn replied.

'A Surrey boy? Ah, that explains it.'

Ross finished half his pint in a gulp and wiped his mouth. 'I'm lookin' for Danny Groom. Seen him lately?'

'Why?'

'Don't worry, he ain't in trouble. Matter of fact, I've got a bit of time for the fella.'

John began pouring a second pint, eyebrow raised. 'Really?'

Ross raised an eyebrow back. 'Yeah, really.'

'He should be in soon,' John replied, nodding towards the other end of the bar. 'He usually sits over there.'

Ross lowered his voice. 'Danny Groom was a big union man. You know what union men are like, always fightin' like rats in a sack. He had a fallin' out with Gerry Scanlon back in the day.'

Fairburn took another sip of his beer. 'And?'

'Gerry denounced him. Danny did a two-stretch in Pentonville for anti-social activities.'

Fairburn sipped his beer. 'Only two years? He's lucky. Anyway, how can Groom help us?'

'Before the war he was a member of the Poplar Branch of the Communist Party, along with Eliza Crewe and Gerry Scanlon.'

'How did you find that out?'

Ross' smile reminded Fairburn of a crocodile he'd once seen in Moscow Zoo. 'I know, Tommy, because I've spent years sitting in pubs talking to people. Sadly, it's a dyin' art. Your generation's too busy listening to speeches, bugging bedrooms and talkin' shit.'

'Your "wise old man" act is beginning to grate. I've worked the expatriate clubs in Cairo doing exactly the same thing.'

'Drinking gin and tonic while the officer class chinwag about the Queen?' said Ross, draining his glass. He grinned. 'Chin-chin old boy!'

'I suggest you spend some time undercover. There's more to it than drinking cocktails.'

'If you say so, pretty boy,' Ross replied, turning to the landlord. 'John, time for some vodka I reckon.'

'Of course, Sid.'

Fairburn watched a stooped-looking man take a seat at the bar, his face a study in disappointment. He was in his fifties, dressed in dirty overalls. 'That's our man?'

'Yeah. How d'you know?'

'All that gin and tonic must have sharpened my senses.'

Ross waved. 'Hello, Danny. Fancy a pint?'

'I'm fine, Comrade Sergeant.'

'Come and have a fuckin' drink then, or we'll take a trip to Burgess House. You won't get any beer there.'

'Even the coffee's terrible,' Fairburn added.

Groom folded his copy of *The Daily Mirror* and tucked it under his arm. Ordering his own pint, he joined the two secret policemen. 'What d'you want, Sid?'

Ross finished his vodka and smacked his lips. 'This is my new boss, Captain Fairburn.'

'Captain? He's just a kid.'

'Nah, Danny, we're just getting older.'

'John? Four vodkas please ,' said Fairburn. 'You might as well have one yourself, Comrade.'

'That's very generous,' John replied, reaching for a dusty bottle of *Shustov* on the top shelf. 'I've got some decent stuff here.'

When drinks were poured, Fairburn raised his glass. 'Let's drink to the anniversary of the Liberation.'

'That's as good a reason as any,' Groom replied, draining his glass. 'To the Liberation.'

Finishing his vodka, Fairburn motioned for another round. And another toast; '*Za vstrechu,*' he said – *for our meeting.*

'Are you Russian?' asked Groom. 'I thought your accent was funny.'

'Nah, he's from Surrey,' said John.

Sid Ross slapped the table and laughed. 'Fuck it, get us another drink.'

Danny Groom studied his empty vodka glass. 'What do you want, Sid?'

'It's about Eliza Crewe,' said Fairburn.

Groom smiled. 'It's a bit late, ain't it? I've heard she's in America. Not that I approve of defecting, of course.'

'Let me rephrase the question. What can you tell me about Crewe's relationship with Gerry Scanlon? I know you were comrades before the war.'

Groom shrugged. 'Well, that's no secret. Poplar was a well-known branch, especially after Cable Street. Gerry was local, but Eliza was from Hampstead. She'd graduated from Cambridge, a posh girl. Fair play, she wanted to fight fascists, not just talk about it. So she came down to Poplar.'

'Unlike the rest of her friends,' said Fairburn, remembering the pen-picture of Crewe in Philby's dossier. 'The Clerkenwell Set?'

'Never met any of 'em. I didn't even know she was much of a writer back then. I thought she was a boffin-type.'

'How so?'

'I always remember Eliza was good at maths and crosswords. Funny, ain't it, the stuff you remember about people?'

Ross rolled his eyes. 'Was Scanlon fucking her?'

Groom shook his head. 'I doubt it, Gerry was devoted to his missus. If you ask me, he just liked sniffing round well-to-do types. He was always a social climber, and Eliza knew lots of high-ups.'

'And after the war?' Fairburn asked.

'By then Gerry was a proper Resistance hero. Fair play, some of the stuff he got up to was crazy. He put on a German uniform and blew up Abwehr HQ on Grosvenor Square with a truck bomb. He was a legend, none of us were surprised when he shot up the Party ranks. Besides, most of the competition was dead by then. Phil Piratin? Palmer Dutt? Willie Gallacher? The Blackshirts did for the lot of 'em.'

Fairburn ordered more drinks. 'I take it you didn't shoot up the ranks?'

Groom looked sour. 'I thought me and Gerry were friends. I had his back a few times during the war. Anyway, I told him I had doubts about the number of workers we were sending to Russia. I thought he'd respect my views.'

'Now tell me, where did that get you?' Ross chuckled.

'Pentonville. Turns out he had one of his boys lined up for my job in the Union. He wanted me out of the way.'

Fairburn considered Groom lucky. In Stalin's Russia he'd be sent to a gulag for fifteen years. Or executed. 'What about Eliza Crewe? Scanlon never denounced her. I presume they remained friends?'

'That's none of my business,' said Groom, glancing at the door. Other drinkers were taking an interest in their conversation. 'I've gotta go, before these fellas think I'm a grass.'

'It's quite alright,' said Fairburn easily. 'When we're done talking, Sergeant Ross will take you outside and punch you on the nose. I'm sure honour will be restored.'

Groom rolled his eyes. 'That's modern Britain for you, eh? Helping the State earns you a punch in the face.'

Ross guffawed. 'Look on the bright side. You might help fuck Gerry Scanlon over. Now, carry on.'

Groom's eyes were fixed on his vodka glass, his voice a near-whisper. 'After the war, all of us saw Eliza sail close to the wind. She hated Stalin and told anyone who asked. People began to talk, but Gerry told them to shut up. Look, I don't like Scanlon, but talking to you don't sit right.'

'It's your patriotic duty,' said Fairburn. 'Besides, you owe Scanlon nothing. He owes *you* two years of your life.'

'He's right,' said Ross, jabbing the bar with his finger. 'If someone fucked me over like that? I'd give 'em double helpings back.'

Groom sighed. 'I know Scanlon distanced himself from Eliza officially but they kept in touch. A mutual friend would pass messages, even after she was arrested. He's a captain in the Militia. I think Eliza might have introduced him to Gerry before the Moseley coup. He used to work in the publishing business.'

Fairburn nodded slowly. 'Who told you about this captain?'

A shrug. 'The Poplar Branch people are tight. Besides, I keep an ear to the ground where Gerry Scanlon's concerned. Now that's what I know. Take it or leave it.'

'What's this captain's name?'

'Ray Goldman.'

'Where does Goldman work now?'

'Last I heard, he was at Militia HQ.'

'I'm grateful for your assistance, Comrade,' Fairburn replied, pushing his half-finished drink away.

'And if you'd care to step outside,' said Ross, pulling a pair of handcuffs from his pocket, 'I'll give you the punch on the nose you were promised.'

'I suppose we should get on with it then,' Groom sighed. '*Comrades.*'

Chapter 12

The secret policemen sat in the car, beery and black-eyed. Ross studied his grazed knuckles. 'Fair play, Tommy, you're handy with your fists.'

Fairburn dabbed his split lip with a handkerchief. 'I was taught unarmed combat by a Czech Jew.'

'Where?'

'Palestine.'

'Nothing's straightforward with you, is it? Well, it worked. I thought that Irish fella was gonna stab you.'

Fairburn shrugged. His assailant's knife skills were mediocre and he'd been easily disarmed. 'You shouldn't have made such a meal of punching Groom,' he replied. Seeing Ross lay into the ex-union man, a scrum of dockers had piled out of the pub looking for a scrap.

Ross nudged his nose and winced. 'It had to look proper, didn't it?'

'Tell me, do people around here often brawl with CSS officers?'

'Mate, the average Eastender will have a tear-up with *anyone*. Even the Gestapo were careful around these parts.'

The car's radio-telephone set chirruped. Fairburn took the call, his notebook balanced on his knee.

'Who was it?' asked Ross.

'Comrade Major Muir. She checked Ray Goldman's file. He's a Lieutenant-Colonel nowadays, he runs the Militia's political relations directorate.'

'Millbank HQ? Another shiny-arse.'

'That might work in our favour. I assume Goldman's job involves liaison with other government departments.'

Ross lit a cigarette and took a deep drag. 'What were you thinking?'

'I call Goldman's office and arrange a meeting. I'll tell him it's a sensitive matter.'

'For when?'

'Tomorrow morning. Now, go home, Sid.'

Ross eyed his boss with suspicion. 'Really?'

'Yes, Sergeant. Besides, you're half drunk.'

'I've done some of my best work pissed. Where you goin'?'

'Personal business,' Fairburn replied, getting out of the car. 'I'll see you at Burgess House tomorrow, 08.00 sharp.'

'Anything else?'

'Yes, go to the property store. Find the books we found at McGrouther's place.'

Ross gave Fairburn a quizzical look. 'Books?'

'Yes, Sid. Books. The ones written by Eliza Crewe.'

Fairburn hailed a black London taxi. 'Stockwell, please.'

The cabbie wore a Red Star Arsenal scarf and a row of Liberation medals. Most cab drivers were resistance veterans, a cartel created to reward old fighters. 'Right you are, Comrade,' he said. 'I'll warn you now, there's bloody roadblocks all over the place. It might take a while.' They crossed Tower Bridge into Bermondsey, the cabbie threading through building sites and shabby housing blocks. 'It's a liberty, that's what it is,' he sighed, exercising every taxi driver's inviolable right to moan. 'The other side of Vauxhall's still a bleedin' bomb site. So's Kennington. Don't even get me started on Southwark.'

'There's a manpower shortage,' said Fairburn. 'It's the same on the Continent.'

'Too right there is. A fella down my local said thirty-odd thousand British labourers were sent to Russia last year.'

Fairburn bit his lip. Like everyone else in Britain, the cabbie seemed more interested in complaining rather than acknowledging socialism's successes. 'Have faith, Comrade. It'll be put right soon.'

The cabbie laughed. 'They said that in 1950.'

They slowed as they approached Kennington Park, a gloomy place of skeletal trees and bramble bushes. Soviet troop carriers were parked outside Oval Underground station, next to a truck marked with the sword and shield insignia of the CSS. Workmen with brushes scrubbed the station's walls, cleaning away the letters 'BAF', *British Action Front.* Uniformed CSS troops with machine pistols searched vehicles and pedestrians supervised by a Russian officer. 'Here we go,' the cabbie sighed. 'You'll need your papers.'

'They bring out armoured cars for graffiti?'

'They're looking for fascists.'

Fairburn sighed at the heavy-handedness of it all. A checkpoint would achieve nothing, except to inconvenience law-abiding workers. The CSS men would be better employed in observation posts to catch the wreckers in the act. Intelligence and prevention trumped violence. 'Do you often see Russian soldiers on the streets?'

'Not really,' the cabbie replied. 'The cheeky fuckers put their headquarters in Buckingham Palace, but their main barracks is over in Woolwich. You ain't from London?'

'No, Comrade. Surrey.'

'Thought you had a funny accent. Nice down there.' The cab pulled up next to one of the armoured cars, a six-wheeler with a machine gun on the roof. A bored-looking Russian sat in a hatch above the driver's seat. A soldier rapped on the taxi's window with a leather-gloved hand. 'Papers,' he ordered in English. 'Quickly!'

Fairburn pulled out his red-backed identity card. 'KGB. Direct my driver to the priority lane.'

The soldier snapped to attention. 'Yes, Comrade Captain. Let this vehicle through immediately! *Scheveli zhopoi!*'

'KGB?' the driver grumbled. 'That's me out of pocket, I suppose. You lot never pay.'

Fairburn nodded at the soldier as the cabbie drove into the Party lane. 'Don't worry, Comrade, I'll pay my fare.'

'No offence meant. And those things I said earlier, Comrade…'

'Honest workers are entitled to let off steam, especially a man with a chest full of Liberation medals.'

'Thank you, Comrade Captain.'

The cabbie dropped Fairburn outside a shabby block of flats. On a neatly swept second floor balcony, he knocked on a door. 'Who is it?' said a woman's voice.

'Auntie Maggie? It's Tommy. Malcolm and Joanna's boy.'

The door was opened by a small, pale woman wearing a flowery housecoat. 'Tommy? I never thought my letter would reach you.'

Fairburn wiped his feet on the coconut mat outside the door. 'It did eventually. Can I come in?' The letter had arrived in Budapest shortly before Tommy left for Britain, asking him to call. Aunt Maggie led him inside her tiny flat. It smelled of cigarettes and boiled vegetables, a wireless tuned to the BBC. The living room window overlooked a muddy playground where boys chased a ball.

'Have you been fighting, Tommy?' she said, pointing at his lip.

'I slipped leaving the pub,' he replied.

'I can smell it on you. It's a bit early for drinking, isn't it?'

Fairburn felt like a small boy. 'I suppose it is.'

'I should make tea,' Aunt Maggie replied. 'I've got biscuits some-where too.'

'That would be lovely. Are you well?'

Maggie pursed her lips. 'I'm getting by. How long's it been since you left? Ten years?'

'Nearly.'

'And how's Russia?' said Maggie, disappearing into the kitchen.

'They looked after me,' Fairburn called. There was music on the radio, an operetta. Then, an announcement: *Your local Party representative will inform you of your role in the forthcoming Liberation celebrations…*

'The Russians haven't looked after *us*, have they?' said Maggie, reappearing with a tray of cups and saucers.

Fairburn's temple throbbed with an early hangover. 'Were the Germans good to us? Were the Blackshirts? Or the Capitalists before them?'

Tut-tutting, Maggie lay out cups, saucers and a small plate of biscuits. 'That's all we do nowadays, isn't it? Talk about politics. Oh, and where you might find a few ounces of butter, or a pork chop. They even shoot people for putting up posters.'

'People putting up posters are wreckers,' Tommy replied. 'It starts with posters, but it ends up with—'

'I've got eyes, Thomas Fairburn,' Maggie interrupted. 'I've got a belly, too. I'm hungry, just like everyone else.'

Fairburn's cheeks burned. 'I'm sorry,' he said, pulling out his wallet. He counted out ten pounds and a week's worth of Party ration coupons. 'Here, take these.'

Maggie got up and put the money and coupons behind the

mantlepiece clock. 'I'm glad you're doing well for yourself,' she muttered. The kettle whistled, and she disappeared back into the kitchen.

Fairburn saw the family photos on the walls. 'How's Uncle Kenny? And the boys?'

Maggie returned with a teapot and a tiny jug of milk. She put them on the table and motioned for Tommy to sit. 'Your Uncle Kenneth died of cancer five years ago,' she said matter-of-factly, lowering herself into a saggy armchair. 'Both of your nephews are in Russia now. I suppose it's one of the reasons I wrote to you.'

'Robert and Clive? What happened?'

'Robbie was denounced at work. Half his department were, too. Not long afterwards, Clive was found with red diesel in his van. They said he stole it. They sent them away four years ago next month.'

Fairburn's cousin Robbie was a civil servant, Clive a plumber. 'I'm sorry about Uncle Kenny. I'll check on Robbie and Clive too. I'm sure they're fine.'

'You'll ask your Russian friends?'

'Yes.'

'I'm sure your father would be proud,' Maggie replied sourly. 'He worshipped the bloody Russians.'

His aunt had always been bitter. Fairburn refused to rise to the bait. 'And my mother?'

Maggie dribbled tea into a cup and added a dash of milk. 'Joanna was only political because of your father. I warned her nothing good could come of it, especially after they made Moseley Prime Minister.'

'Nobody *made* Moseley Prime Minister,' said Tommy. His voice was sharp. 'His thugs stormed Parliament. The King and the aristocrats backed him. It was a coup.'

'Does it matter now?' Maggie replied, nibbling carefully on a biscuit. 'Moseley's dead. The King's dead. His American floozy's dead. They're *all* bloody well dead.'

Fairburn wasn't listening. He was thinking of the morning his parents were arrested by men in leather overcoats, their smell of tobacco and sweat. A woman in black put Tommy in her car, still in his pyjamas, and drove him to the borstal. 'Mum and Dad were heroes,' he said.

Maggie dunked a biscuit in her tea. Then she shook her head. 'It was a terrible shame, you know.'

'What?'

'How the Germans caught your mum and dad.'

Sechkin's report about his parents' fate was folded inside his notebook. He pulled it from his pocket and lay it on the table. 'I know a little about where they were imprisoned, but not how they were caught. What happened?'

Maggie glanced suspiciously at the piece of paper. 'Well that's no good, it's written in Russian. Why don't they know?'

'Most of the records were destroyed after the war. All of the witnesses are dead.'

Maggie pursed her lips. 'Well, the way I heard it, your father was betrayed by one of his so-called Party comrades.'

'Why?' said Fairburn.

'Money, I'd imagine. Or jealousy? Malcolm was a popular man. Well thought of.'

Fairburn clenched his fists in his lap. 'Who betrayed him?'

'I don't know, Tommy. I never wanted to know, either.'

'Why?'

'What you don't know can't hurt you, can it?'

'Who told you this? I want to talk to them.'

Maggie studied the red-and-gold Communist Party pin on Fairburn's lapel. 'I shouldn't say, Tommy. No good can come of it.'

'Why?'

'He's a local man. A good person, but he's made mistakes.'

'What sort of mistakes?'

The old woman lowered her voice to a whisper. 'He was in the Free Corps. Your lot would execute him if they knew.' The British Free Corps volunteered to fight for the Germans, made up largely of ex-Blackshirts from the British Union of Fascists. The Nazis put them in a special SS division. The few who returned were either hanged or sent to Russia as slave labour.

Fairburn felt his guts churn. 'You're friends with an ex-*SS man*? Why?'

'We've all got feet of clay, Tommy. It says so in the Bible. Your lot would do well to remember that, or have you forgotten how the Reds behaved after the Liberation? All those women and girls they raped?'

Fairburn balled his fists on his knees. 'I was here during the Liberation. I never saw anything like that. It's fascist propaganda.'

'*Propaganda*? Tell that to the Russians who liberated this estate, if liberation's the right word!' Maggie replied, her tear-filled eyes fixed on the rug beneath her feet. She got up and took the ration voucher from behind the clock. Tearing it in half, she threw the pieces at Fairburn. 'You lot are no different from the bloody Gestapo.'

'Auntie…'

'It's probably time for you to leave, Tommy. I'm sure you can let yourself out.'

Fairburn picked up the scraps of the ration vouchers. They could be repaired with tape, he supposed. He put them on the tray with the tea things. 'I'm sorry,' he said.

Maggie hugged herself, unable to meet Fairburn's eye. 'I think I've said everything I wanted to say. If you could check on your cousins, I'd be grateful.'

'I'll do my best. I'll see you soon.'

'Maybe,' she replied.

'Family is important,' Fairburn replied, kissing Maggie's cheek. Leaving the estate, he waited for a moment before finding cover at a bus stop. His training and experience made him suspicious; there was something suspect in Maggie's behaviour. Why would she confess to knowing a former SS man? Not reporting such a person to the authorities was itself an offence. A few minutes later Maggie appeared, dressed in an overcoat and a woollen hat. Using the building line for cover, he tailed his aunt to a nearby parade of shops. The old woman stopped at a red telephone box, pausing to look around, then went inside to make a call. It lasted, Fairburn noted, exactly ten seconds. When she'd gone, Fairburn checked the kiosk, writing the time of the call and the telephone number in his pocketbook. Then, hands in pockets, he waited for another taxi.

Now properly hungover, his face aching, he watched the clouds bubble overhead. Greasy rain spitter-spattering on his face, Fairburn realised he hated this decaying city. Why hadn't they dropped an atom bomb on the place, like they did with Berlin? He rubbed his throbbing head. *Damn, all I want is the bloody truth!* Not the official version, the post-mortem prose of propaganda. Nor gossip whispered into an old woman's ear. He craved the real *truth*. Something he could frame and put on a shelf, like a photograph.

Even though Captain Thomas Fairburn, Spartan of the 10th Directorate of the KGB, knew such truths were the most dangerous of all.

Chapter 13

Major Agnes Muir, CSS Collator-in-Chief, stood in front of a cork-board covered in photographs and index cards. They were connected by pieces of coloured string, red and yellow and green. She spoke to Fairburn like a teacher instructing a reasonably promising pupil. 'You see, the problem with analysis is spotting the difference between synchronicity, coincidence and conspiracy,' she explained. 'There's a lot of chaff.'

'Like panning for gold?'

'Actually, it's more like rooting through a rubbish bin.'

'I'll take your word for it, Comrade Major,' Fairburn replied, sipping his coffee. He'd slept badly, pondering the puzzle that was Aunt Maggie. 'Have you found anything in this bin of yours? Any leads?'

Muir tapped a passport photograph at the centre of the corkboard. It showed a dour-looking man with deep-set eyes and thinning, swept-back hair. 'Perhaps I have. This fellow's Michael Nolan, born in Dublin in 1913. His family moved to London after the Great War. As of January 1954, he was a senior lieutenant of the Militia. Luckily, we have a partial copy of his service record.'

'I thought the Militia kept their records separate.'

Muir nodded approvingly. 'You were paying attention, Comrade. Good. Nolan was briefly attached to CSS in 1953, so we opened our own file. We like files.'

'Very prudent, I agree. What sort of attachment?'

Muir ran a finger along the length of string linking Nolan's photograph to an index card. 'The CSS wanted a marksmanship instructor for our paramilitary troops. Nolan was recommended because of his war record. As a resistance fighter, he reportedly sniped and killed upwards of fifty fascists. After the war, like many partisans, he joined the Militia.'

Fairburn frowned. 'An expert marksman? Isn't he too obvious a suspect?'

'Oh, absolutely,' said Muir, pushing her glasses back up her nose. 'What do you think? Synchronicity, coincidence or conspiracy?'

'I was hoping you'd tell me, Comrade Major.'

'What if I told you Michael Nolan died in March 1955. Allegedly.'

'*Allegedly?*'

She tapped another index card. 'Nolan was a keen sea fisherman. He reportedly drowned off the coast near Penzance. His body was never recovered.'

'Our suspect's a ghost?' Fairburn replied, finishing his coffee. It was bitter but masked the sourness of yesterday's booze. 'Please, Comrade, continue. I'm intrigued.'

Muir opened a file with pale, spidery fingers. 'This is the ballistics report for the bullets retrieved from William McGrouther's body. He was shot with two 7.92x57mm cartridges, almost certainly from a Mauser '98.'

'A German rifle,' Fairburn replied. He'd killed his first German with a Mauser back in 1947. 'I'm sure thousands of Mausers were captured during the Liberation.'

'Precisely, Comrade Captain. Who knows how many are rattling about in lofts and basements all over Britain? I preferred the G43 myself, but that's another story. Anyway, we checked our pre-war records for any mention of Nolan. It's not an uncommon name, but my ladies worked on the problem all night.'

'They're to be commended.'

A shrug. 'Service is its own reward, Comrade, especially when you get a result. A result I believe points towards conspiracy.' The Collator plucked a card from the corkboard, smiled, and passed it to Fairburn. 'I think you'll agree, Comrade Captain.'

Fairburn read aloud from the type-written card. '*Michael Nolan was arrested by the Metropolitan Police in Poplar on October 4th, 1936.*'

'Yes, the date of the Battle of Cable Street. Moseley and his fascists were routed by Jews and Communists.'

'I'm aware of the significance, my father spoke of it often,' said Fairburn, reading the information on the card. 'This says Nolan was arrested for hitting a Blackshirt over the head with a bottle. The fascist was knocked unconscious. Nolan was convicted of assault and served six months in Brixton prison.'

'Yet there's no trace of Nolan being a member of the pre-war Communist Party or any other political group. My theory is Nolan was simply on the streets looking for a fight.'

Fairburn smiled. 'Comrade Major, may I call you Agnes?'

'It's unorthodox, but I'm told 10th Directorate officers usually are,' she replied carefully. 'Am I to call you Thomas?'

'Tommy, please. Tell me, where did Nolan live in 1936?'

'Ah, you've got there, haven't you... *Tommy*?' Muir smiled, turned to a map of London pinned to the wall and placed her finger on the East End. 'His family lived in Grundy Street, Poplar.'

'And where did our other hero of Cable Street, Gerry Scanlon, live?'

'Plimsoll Close. It's less than a hundred yards away from Grundy Street.'

Fairburn rubbed his chin. 'In a close-knit proletarian community like Poplar, what are the chances they *didn't* know each other?'

'I'm not a Londoner, of course, but I imagine it's slim.'

Fairburn stood and straightened his tie. 'This is all very well, Agnes. Intriguing, even, but it doesn't change the fact Nolan's dead.'

'Or is he? After Moseley's coup d'état, Communist Party sympathisers inside the civil service took to faking death certificates for many comrades. It helped them disappear or adopt new identities. Who's to say Scanlon didn't replicate the technique for his tame killer? He's even more powerful now he's in charge of the Militia. Besides, look at the cache you found at McGrouther's dacha. We've seen how easily our plotters can obtain false identity papers.'

Fairburn was impressed, but would it be enough for Philby? 'Please, keep working on Nolan. You're doing an excellent job, Agnes. I think you might even have exceeded the Lubyanka.'

The collator's back straightened. 'Thank you, Tommy.'

'Now I've got something else I need to check.'

'Anything I can help with?'

Fairburn shook his head. 'Maybe later, Agnes. Unless you're an expert on telephone boxes?'

'No, I'm certainly not.'

'That's fine,' Fairburn replied. 'I think there's one upstairs.'

'Comrade Renton, a moment please?'

'Of course,' the technician replied, putting down a metal box covered in dials and switches. His desk looked like a stall at a jumble sale. 'How can I help?'

Fairburn passed Renton a page from his notebook. 'These are the details for a telephone kiosk in Stockwell. I want to know the number called at precisely 1456 hours yesterday afternoon – call duration ten seconds. I want the receiving number traced.'

'I'll have to speak to the post office security people,' Renton replied, putting on his wire-rimmed glasses. 'We don't have the resources to monitor every callbox, so it's done on a rota basis. A bit hit and miss, I know, but it's better than nothing.'

'There was a security sweep in south London yesterday,' Fairburn replied, remembering the checkpoint at Kennington Park. 'Perhaps someone had the foresight to put the wider area on the rota?'

Renton nodded. 'Yes, you'd have thought so, wouldn't you?'

'Would you check?'

'Of course, Comrade Captain. I suppose this is on the hurry-up?'

'You've read my mind,' said Fairburn. 'Do you have a machine for that too? I think the KGB would find it especially useful.'

An hour later, Fairburn and Ross marched up the steps of Militia headquarters. It was a smart building on Millbank, almost decadently American in design. Both men wore their service dress with boots, caps and cross-belts. Ross, cap worn at an angle and two pistols on his belt, somehow reminded Fairburn of a pirate. 'Why two pistols?' he asked.

'The Tokarev's service issue,' Ross replied. 'The Walther came from the Jerry camp commandant I hanged on Dartmoor.'

'Two sidearms? It's hardly regulation.'

'Regulations can go and fuck 'emselves. That's why I'm wearing 'em. I know it'll wind the militiamen up. Besides, you can never have too many guns in this line of work.'

'A fair point.'

'Anyway, I hate this place,' the big Londoner grumbled, nodding at the HQ's modern-looking revolving doors.

'Why, Comrade?' asked Fairburn, returning the militia sentry's salute.

'This ain't a proper police force,' he said, loud enough for the sentry to hear. 'And their investigative department? They couldn't detect a turd in a fruit salad.'

'The Militia protects workers in a manner specific to the unique requirements of a Socialist society.'

Ross pulled a face. 'You mean someone's gotta hassle Teddy Boys and check identity papers? Scrub graffiti off the walls an' confiscate books?'

'Crime evolves,' Fairburn replied.

'Bollocks,' said Ross, glaring at the pristine-looking militiaman standing by the receptionist's desk. 'The Militia's just the Party's private army.'

Fairburn thought Ross would be flapping his gums the day they marched him in front of a firing squad. 'Tell me, where does that leave the CSS?'

Ross shrugged. 'I reckon we protect the Party from itself.'

'You're incorrigible, Sid.'

'You've been paying attention then?'

Fairburn smiled. 'I've realised Socialism's practiced rather differently in Britain.'

'I suppose that's one way of putting it.'

A female sergeant wearing a smart blue uniform approached, her shoulder boards piped in silver thread. 'I'm Senior Sergeant Fletcher. Comrade Colonel Goldman's expecting you,' she said. They followed Fletcher into a lift. She pressed a button and, with a purring sound, they sped smoothly towards the top of the building.

'This is an impressive headquarters,' said Fairburn, noticing the American-made elevator had a carpeted floor.

'Millbank is a state-of-the-art facility,' Fletcher replied proudly, as if reading from a script. 'Comrade Deputy Chairman Scanlon says respectable working conditions are every worker's right.'

'Comrade Scanlon sounds like an inspiring figure,' Fairburn replied.

'He leads by example.'

'Does he visit HQ often?'

'Yes, Comrade Captain. He often eats in the canteen with the militiamen and women.' As Ross rolled his eyes, the lift doors whispered open. Fletcher ushered them along a wood-panelled corridor decorated with photographs of senior officers. 'This is Comrade Colonel Goldman's office,' she said, knocking on a door.

'Is that the KGB chap?' said a cheery voice from inside. 'I thought they kicked down doors, not knocked on 'em.'

'Funny fucker, eh?' Ross whispered.

'Keep quiet, Sergeant.'

'Your visitors have arrived, Comrade Colonel,' said Fletcher, shooting Ross a look. Then, smiling icily, she opened the door before sashaying away. Lieutenant Colonel Raymond Goldman sat behind a brushed-steel desk, his office walls decorated with pre-war Soviet movie posters. His blue-grey uniform was well tailored, his dark hair neatly parted.

'Gentlemen, take a pew,' he said smoothly. 'Would you like a cup of tea? Or vodka, perhaps?'

'Vodka, sir,' said Ross before Fairburn could refuse.

'I'd prefer coffee, Comrade Colonel,' said Fairburn, peeling off his leather gloves. 'I'm Captain Thomas Fairburn of the 10th Directorate of the KGB. This is my CSS liaison, Senior Sergeant Ross from Bureau 5.'

Goldman stroked his pencil moustache, head cocked. 'Excuse the pun just then, Comrade Captain. It's just when they told me there was an *English* KGB officer in town, I couldn't help myself.'

'Who are *they*?'

'I'm sorry?'

'The people who told you there was an English KGB officer in town.'

'The passport office is part of the Militia. So is the customs service. Oh, and the people who protect the airports and railway stations too,' Goldman replied smoothly. 'It would be strange if I didn't know.'

'I see,' Fairburn replied, pulling his notebook from his pocket. He wrote something in pencil and held it up so Goldman could see. It read TURN OFF ANY RECORDING EQUIPMENT. NOW.

'I'm sorry?' said Goldman.

'You mentioned vodka, Comrade Colonel?' said Ross, laying a hand on one of the pistols on his belt.

The militia Colonel opened his desk drawer and Fairburn heard a plasticky clicking noise. Goldman put a spool of tape on the desk with a flourish. '*Voila*,' he said. 'I've switched it off. The recordings are a routine measure. I'm sure you understand.'

'Naturally,' Fairburn replied. 'Although I'd add we're not recording anything for *your* benefit, Comrade, not ours.'

Goldman crossed one leg over the other, revealing a pair of well polished riding boots. 'An interesting opening gambit. I'll look on the bright side, at least I'm not in the cells beneath Burgess House. What do you want, gentlemen?'

'I was investigating the Eliza Crewe affair when someone rudely murdered my suspect. I was wondering if you might be able to help?'

Goldman smiled. 'I believe CSS took over the McGrouther case, old chap. Have a word with Director Philby.'

'I'm asking for your assistance.'

'Well, liaison is what I do,' said Goldman brightly. 'How can the Militia assist the esteemed Committee for State Security?'

'I think you've missed my point, *Ray*. May I call you Ray?'

Goldman raised an eyebrow. 'Well, I don't want to be an arse, but I'm a lieutenant-colonel and you're only a captain…'

'Pulling rank, Comrade? How fucking bourgeois,' Ross growled. 'Besides, he's a captain in the KGB. That must outrank a pretend copper like you.'

Fairburn stood and picked up the telephone on Goldman's desk. 'Comrade Sergeant Fletcher? This is Captain Fairburn, would you bring coffee and a bottle of vodka. Oh, and cancel Colonel Goldman's appointments for the rest of the day.' Yanking the telephone cord from its socket, he sat back down. 'We know you passed messages between Eliza Crewe and Gerry Scanlon. If they were legitimate, why did Comrade Scanlon require an intermediary?'

'Let's not get ahead of ourselves,' Goldman replied. 'May I see these so-called messages?'

'You think I'd bluff?' said Fairburn, although he'd no evidence beyond Groom's word. 'I'm here to resolve this in a civilised manner. Please don't take advantage of my goodwill.'

Goldman shrugged. 'Nonetheless, I'd like to see the basis for these allegations. My legal representative certainly will.'

'You've heard of me, ain't you?' said Ross matter-of-factly.

'Yes, Sergeant Ross, I have. You enjoy something of a reputation.'

'Then you'll know I ain't given to bullshit. If it was down to me, we'd be at Burgess House right now, pulling out your fingernails you fucking ponce. We've got the grounds, but Captain Fairburn wanted to give you a chance.'

'Yes, I did,' Fairburn added. 'Perhaps I was mistaken?'

There was a knock on the door. Sergeant Fletcher walked in with a tray of drinks. 'Coffee and vodka, Comrade Colonel,' she said, raising an eyebrow.

'Many thanks, Susan,' Goldman replied smoothly. 'Please, return to your duties.'

'Yes, Comrade Colonel.'

Ross took the sweating bottle of vodka from an ice bucket, filled a glass and drank it. Then he poured another. 'I don't think we'll bother with toasts today, comrades.'

'I agree,' said Fairburn. 'Would you like coffee, Ray?'

'I'll stick with vodka, I think.'

Fairburn smiled. 'Please, have a drink. I'm really in no hurry.'

'That makes a change,' said Ross, pouring himself another glass.

'What do you want?' said Goldman quietly. There was no bonhomie in his voice now.

'I want you, Comrade Colonel.'

'I'm sorry?'

'As of now, you work for me.'

Goldman grimaced. 'You mean Kim Philby? No, I don't think so.'

'Director Philby's CSS, not KGB. My boss is Colonel Nikolai Sechkin, who answers directly to First Chairman Serov in Moscow. Or perhaps you'd like me to refer the matter to General Teplyakov? I can arrange that easily.'

'Teplyakov?' Goldman replied, pulling a face. 'What's the alternative?'

Fairburn added cream to his coffee and stirred gently. 'If the allegations against Scanlon are true, his behaviour is likely to see Britain go the way of Hungary, especially if Teplyakov hears of it. Unless you want to see Soviet tanks on London's streets, of course.'

Ross chuckled. 'I think, Comrade Captain, Colonel Goldman was talkin' about the alternative for him *personally*.'

Fairburn shrugged. 'If you decline my offer, we'll charge you with espionage for aiding and abetting a defector. Whether you implicate Scanlon or not is a matter for you. Director Philby will decide what happens next.'

'Very well, let's talk,' said Goldman.

Fairburn pulled an envelope from his pocket and laid it carefully on Goldman's desk. 'Inside you'll find the details of an ex-militia officer called Michael Nolan. He's meant to be dead, but I'm not so sure. I want everything you have on him – and I mean *everything*.'

Goldman took the envelope. 'I don't know the name,' he said quietly. 'Besides, I'm rather busy at the moment.'

'Why?'

'Comrade General Scanlon's hosting a gala for Resistance veterans and our Russian friends at Harry Pollitt House. It's an official part of the Liberation celebrations.'

Fairburn raised an eyebrow. 'Your duties include arranging parties?'

'It's a liaison function,' Goldman sniffed. 'I'm a liaison officer.'

'When is this *liaison function*?' asked Fairburn.

'Thursday evening.'

Fairburn stood, straightened his tunic and put on his cap. 'Excellent, Comrade Colonel. Now, there's another favour I need to ask.'

Goldman pulled a face. 'Such as?'

'I shall honour the heroes of the Resistance by attending your gala. Please, have my invitation sent to Burgess House immediately.'

Chapter 14

'I think Scanlon's up to his neck in this,' said Philby. They strolled across Wimbledon Common, a troop of bodyguards following at a respectful distance. Philby walked with a limp, using a long black umbrella as a walking stick. 'I've seen your report, Tommy. It's promising stuff. Especially the information about this Nolan fellow.'

'It's a start, Comrade Director. It's just a shame Frayne wasn't more forthcoming.'

Philby nodded. 'Well, Francis Frayne's a different beast from McGrouther. We had to handle him with kid gloves.'

'How so?'

'He has clout in the Politburo. McGrouther was a gadfly by comparison. It's why we used King to interrogate Frayne. She got a confession of sorts, but not the *coup de grâce* I was hoping for.'

'Do you really think Frayne was working for the Americans?'

Philby swiped the head off a flower with the tip of his umbrella. 'Well, even if he wasn't directly reporting to the CIA, he was linked to the network responsible for Crewe's defection. He's a traitor.'

Fairburn walked close to the older man, his shoulder brushing Philby's. 'I hope to have more on Nolan soon. He's our most promising lead.'

'A *dead* marksman? That was actually very clever. Bravo, Gerry.'

'I owe that breakthrough to Comrade Major Muir.'

'Hiring Agnes Muir was one of my more inspired decisions,' said Philby. 'D'you know why?'

'No, Comrade Director.'

'Not only does Agnes have no friends, but she prefers it that way. It makes her a formidable keeper of secrets.'

'How so?'

The CSS Director stopped near an old windmill, the sails creaking in the wind. Shoulders hunched, he lit a cigarette. 'When I first joined MI6, I made it my business to befriend the fellow in charge of the records section. He was a drunk, so I'd take him to the pub. Before you knew it, I was going home every evening with a briefcase full of secret files. The poor chap thought I was his friend, when friends are the biggest single security risk for anyone in our line of work.'

'I understand the principle. No friends, no risk. Yet how much can you achieve on your own?'

'A fair point, Tommy. Of course, relationships are at the heart of our business,' Philby replied. 'I'm told you prefer your own company, but happily tolerate others. It was why you were successful in Cairo.'

'You've spoken to Moscow?'

'Of course I have. Comrade Director Serov speaks highly of you.'

'I've never met Comrade Serov,' said Fairburn. He'd only seen the KGB chief on a podium at speeches and awards ceremonies.

'Ivan Serov listens to Sechkin. Each has the other's respect.'

Fairburn blushed. 'Nikolai's biased, he thinks I saved his life during the war.'

'Yes, he told me the story. The boy who cut his schoolmistress's throat? Bloodthirsty little blighter.'

'She had a gun.'

'You killed her because she was a fascist.'

Fairburn shrugged. 'We were talking about Gerry Scanlon, Comrade Director?'

Philby studied the younger man, smoke curling from his nose. He smiled. 'Tell me, Tommy, what's your next move?'

'I've secured myself an invitation to a drinks reception at Harry Pollitt House. I'll introduce myself to Scanlon and pique his interest in my investigation. In the meantime, Nikolai's men will plant a microphone inside Scanlon's car.'

'That easily?'

'Comrade Sergeant Ross assures me it's possible.'

Philby nodded. 'Well, Sid Ross is a man happy to be judged on results.'

'He's very efficient,' Fairburn replied.

'Ross knows who and what he is. He's made his peace with it too.'

'In any case, we'll record anything Scanlon says.'

'So your conversation with Scanlon's a trigger? said Philby.

'Yes. Goldman tells me Scanlon always travels with a staff officer he trusts implicitly. A man called Brady. His driver's an old resistance comrade, completely loyal too. Scanlon might expect his office to be bugged, but not his car.'

Philby dropped his cigarette to the ground and stubbed it out with his shoe. 'Be careful, Tommy. What worked with a fool like Frayne and a blusterer like McGrouther won't work with Scanlon. He's an altogether wilier beast. He spent years fighting the Nazis. Running networks. *Killing*. He thinks like us.'

'My instinct's to be direct with the man,' Fairburn replied. 'Perhaps it will bruise his ego if he's challenged by a younger man of lesser status.'

'Yes, I imagine it will,' Philby chuckled. 'You're a precocious talent, Tommy. Get up the man's nose. Now, let me know if there's anything else you require.'

'There was something.'

'Name it.'

'It isn't about the operation, Comrade Director.'

'I told you to call me Kim. What is it?'

'I'm trying to discover what happened to my parents during the war. They were in the camps. Records Nikolai found give some idea, but I'd like something more…'

'Conclusive?' said Philby, finishing the sentence. The Director smelled of tobacco and hair tonic, his hand resting on Tommy's shoulder. 'The Tribunal for the Examination of Fascist Crimes in Great Britain was never going to unearth the full details. Nikolai told me your parents were Socialist heroes. Of course I'll help.'

'You will?'

'Consider it a personal favour.'

Fairburn felt a strange sensation. Affection. He tried to compose himself, but found his eyes pricked with tears. 'You have my gratitude, Kim.'

'Then let's go back to my office and have a drink,' Philby replied, waving to the bodyguards. He shivered. 'It's a bit parky for October, wouldn't you say?'

'Are you ready?' asked Fairburn, buttoning up his uniform tunic and straightening his tie.

'Nearly, Comrade,' Ross replied, rifling through a tool bag. Eight other men stood in the warehouse near King's Cross station: Sechkin, Renton and six KGB watchers. The surveillance men checked their radios, hipflask-shaped sets compact enough to hide in harnesses worn beneath their coats.

'These are good,' said Renton, looking admiringly at one of the radio sets. 'Are they new? They're better than anything we've got.'

'NEVA S-20 radio,' Sechkin said, nodding. 'They're top secret, KGB only. So keep your lips buttoned.'

'Of course, Comrade Colonel,' Renton replied, patting a grey plastic box on his lap, slightly larger than a cigarette case. 'I'm just grateful for the chance to see one of these. It must have cost a pretty penny.'

'It did,' Sechkin sighed. 'Please don't break it.'

Renton studied the box. 'Protona Minifon Mi-51 micro-recorder. State-of-the-art,' he said. 'Of course, I've tweaked it slightly. The sound quality will be better.'

'Don't *tweak* anything,' Sechkin growled. 'That cost three hundred US dollars.'

'Too late.' Renton grinned.

'How long does it record for?' asked Fairburn.

'Three hours, although sound quality depends on where Sid hides the device,' Renton replied. 'Generally speaking, motor cars are good for recording. They're designed to be insulated from external noise, but if the mic's too close to something rattling or buzzing? Or a wireless set? Then we've got a problem.'

Ross turned to the sedan parked in a corner of the warehouse. 'Scanlon's official motor is a Mercedes-Benz 300, exactly the same as this. I've had a good root around, getting used to the interior and whatnot.'

Fairburn studied the gleaming German automobile. 'Isn't it rather luxurious?'

'Only the best for Comrade Scanlon,' Ross chuckled. 'Lovely piece of Jerry engineering. It's a three-litre straight-six, this'll do 95 mph on the straight.'

'Where'd you find it?'

'Didn't Marx say *property is theft*, Comrade?' Ross chuckled. 'I liberated these wheels from a Party car park in Whitehall. It's okay, I'll put it back once we're finished.'

Sechkin shook his head. 'Marx never said that. It was Pierre-Joseph Proudhon.'

'And Proudhon was an anarchist,' Fairburn added. 'You really weren't paying attention during party meetings, were you, Sid?'

'The girls were pretty though,' the big policeman replied. The KGB watchers all laughed, until Sechkin shot them a look.

Fairburn peered inside the Mercedes. 'Where are you going to hide the recording device?'

Ross opened the rear door and wriggled his bulk inside. The seats were covered with green velveteen divided by a padded armrest. 'Your surveillance boys tell me Scanlon's car has identical coverings inside, so we'll take out the armrest and swap it with this.' Gently pulling the armrest free, he prised it open to reveal a space big enough to hide the Mi-51.

Fairburn peered inside the car. 'Very well. How will you get inside Scanlon's car?'

The big CSS pointed at a bearded, scruffily dressed KGB man. 'The Party drivers all park behind the railway station during functions at Harry Pollitt House. There's a kiosk there selling tea and sandwiches. Well, it's a rough old place around there, full of tramps an' beggars. So when Scanlon's driver goes for a piss, Sergei here's gonna try an' mug him. While he's busy, I'll get in the car and swap the armrest over.'

'I promise to be gentle, Comrade,' said Sergei. He certainly looked like a tramp, dressed in muddy boots and a moth-eaten donkey jacket. 'No biting or stabbing this time.'

'That's all very well, Sid, but you've still got to retrieve the device afterwards,' said Renton, the recording device still on his lap. He looked like a child with a rabbit at a petting zoo.

Ross nodded at the Russians. 'These KGB fellas can get inside a motor faster than a shithouse rat. Then, once Scanlon's driver drops his man home in Hampstead, he drives all the way back to Millbank HQ.'

'Millbank? Why?' asked Sechkin.

'Car bombs. The British Action Front planted three pounds of plastic explosive under a senior militia officer's ZIL last year. It didn't go off, but they ordered all official cars had to be parked in secure locations. Scanlon follows the rules to set an example.'

'I see,' Sechkin replied. 'Please, Sid, carry on.'

'When the driver gets to Millbank, Colonel Goldman will let us inside via the secure parking garage. We'll remove the recorder and put the old armrest back. Hey presto, job done.'

'This is a good plan,' Sechkin replied. 'Tommy, do you trust Goldman?'

'No more than any other informer, but Goldman's more scared of the KGB than Scanlon,' said Fairburn.

'As well he should be,' Sechkin chuckled. 'Well done, Comrade Sergeant Ross.'

'You can gimme me a pat on the back if it works,' Ross replied, accepting one of Sechkin's cigarettes. 'All we need now is for Captain Fairburn to scare the shit out of Gerry Scanlon.'

Fairburn put on his blue-topped officer's cap and smiled. 'Well, Sid,' he replied, 'if I've learned one thing in the KGB, it's how to scare the shit out of people.'

The men were still laughing when Fairburn stepped out of the warehouse into the blue-black London night.

Chapter 15

Searchlights painted Harry Pollitt House silver; a jackbooted honour guard lined the steps outside. Fairburn studied the smartly uniformed militiamen as he approached. 'Very smart,' he said to their commander. 'These lads are as good as anything you'd see on Red Square.'

'High praise indeed,' said a militia lieutenant waiting by the door. 'Comrade Captain Fairburn, isn't it?'

'Yes, I'm Fairburn.'

The lieutenant was Fairburn's age and well spoken, a Party sports league achievement badge the only decoration on his tunic. 'I'm Hurst, from the Deputy Chairman's secretariat. Comrade Deputy Director Scanlon asked for me to greet you.'

'Why?'

Hurst's eyes settled on Fairburn's rack of medals. 'You were the boy-soldier who led the NKVD through fascist lines? Of course General Scanlon wanted to meet you.'

'I was a child. A mascot, really.'

'I'm sure you're being modest, Comrade. Now, let's find you a drink.' Hurst led Fairburn into a high-ceilinged room lit by chandeliers, the walls decorated with portraits of prominent British communists. A string quartet played on a podium while stewards served drinks. There were few women and only a handful of Russians present – mainly uniformed military officers and sober-suited officials.

118

A steward appeared, carrying a silver tray with a champagne bucket and two glasses. 'For you, Comrade Captain,' he said.

Fairburn took off his hat and tucked it under his arm. 'Champagne?'

A wiry man with a pockmarked face stepped from the crowd, arms open. 'Of course, Comrade. It's the proper French stuff too. Only the best for the workers, eh?'

Lieutenant Hurst snapped to attention. 'Comrade General, may I present Comrade Captain Thomas Fairburn of the KGB.'

Fairburn took a sip of champagne and smiled. 'Comrade General Scanlon? It's an honour to meet you again.'

'*Again?*' Scanlon replied, cocking his head like a lizard spying a fly. The Deputy Chairman for Public Safety wore a smart blue suit and a dark tie, the red-and-gold Order of Lenin sparkling on his lapel. Three rows of medals jangled across his breast pocket. 'I'm afraid I don't remember the occasion.'

'Moscow in '49. You lectured my class at the MGB school.'

'And how was I?'

'Inspirational, Comrade.'

'That's very fucking decent of you to say so.' Scanlon grinned, revealing a mouthful of crooked yellow teeth. 'Hurst?'

'Yes, Comrade General?'

'Fuck off, will you? I'd like to talk with Captain Fairburn alone.'

'Of course.' Hurst nodded, turning on his heel and vanishing into the crowd.

Fairburn raised his glass. 'Perhaps we should make our toasts before we speak, Comrade?'

'Toasts? That's more of a Russian thing, ain't it?' Scanlon replied, finishing his champagne and summoning the waiter for more. 'We might be Communists, but we're British Communists. It's an important distinction. So let's settle for *cheers*, eh?'

'Then *cheers* it is, Comrade, but Socialism has no borders.'

'Tell that to the people of Teesside or Glasgow or Hackney,' Scanlon declared, jutting his chin. 'They need time for Socialism to find its feet, not more... *reform*. They certainly don't need lectures from Moscow.'

'This isn't the first time I've heard such sentiments here, Comrade. I appreciate they're meant in good faith, but I wonder if they suggest a lack of political rigour?'

Scanlon smiled. 'They said you were clever, Fairburn.'

'How so?'

'You've just given a Deputy Chairman of the Communist Party of Great Britain a gentle bollocking. You didn't even raise your voice.'

'There was no criticism intended.' Fairburn smiled. He noticed Lieutenant Hurst loitering nearby, watching the exchange. 'I'm still familiarising myself with the tone of debate in British circles. Tell me, what elements of Comrade Khrushchev's reforms concern you?'

'Well, I reckon that's something me and Nikita will discuss between ourselves. You know, some people say I'm like Tito: a pain in the arse, but they can't get rid of me.' Scanlon puffed out his chest, his breath smelling of booze.

You're no Tito, my friend. 'You are held in high esteem in Moscow.'

'Of course. My men fought the fascists hard as anyone,' Scanlon replied, his finger straying to the Order of Lenin pinned to his lapel. 'Perhaps Comrade Khrushchev should remember the only part of the Bible I ever saw any sense in.'

'Which is, Comrade Deputy Chairman?'

'Matthew, 22:15. *Therefore render to Caesar the things that are Caesar's, and to God the things that are God's.*'

'And in this scenario, who's God?'

'Well, Khrushchev's the one with the hydrogen bomb.' Scanlon guffawed. 'Anyhow, let's hope his so-called reforms don't lead to another Hungary. Speaking of which, where's General Teplyakov?'

'Was he invited?'

'He goes where he likes, that one.'

Fairburn smiled politely. 'Any process of change carries an element of risk. They create opportunities for our enemies to exploit.'

'I'm glad you see it that way too, Comrade Captain,' said Scanlon, taking a moment to squeeze a passer-by's hand. 'So tell me, Tommy... you don't mind if I call you Tommy, do you?'

'Of course not, Comrade General.'

Scanlon lowered his voice to a growly rasp. 'What exactly is Kim Philby up to? Or was it Ash Prasad who sent you? I know you're part of their little purge.'

The musicians began playing Tchaikovsky's *String quartet Number 1 in D,* which was one of Fairburn's favourite pieces. 'Director Philby asked the KGB to review the Eliza Crewe affair. Mistakes were made. William McGrouther's murder complicates things, of course.'

'Bill McGrouther was a fucking idiot. He abused his position and paid the price. Case closed, eh?'

'Nonetheless, Crewe's defection was facilitated by at least two senior Politburo members. Francis Frayne's still under arrest. I hope you agree that falls under Director Philby's purview?'

'I suppose it does. Although I'm surprised Frankie got himself involved. I thought he was cleverer.'

'And you, Comrade? You knew Eliza Crewe well.'

Scanlon seemed untroubled. 'We stood shoulder to shoulder at Cable Street. I watched her stab a Blackshirt with a kitchen knife. We were comrades and I'll never deny it. It's just a shame Eliza lost her way.'

'Of course,' said Fairburn. 'I like to think we've moved beyond mere guilt by association, don't you?'

Fairburn licked his teeth. 'Tell me, is anyone else involved? Do you have other suspects?'

'Actually, the evidence suggests a leak somewhere inside the Militia.'

Scanlon leaned closer, his breath hot on Fairburn's cheek. 'What sort of leak?'

Fairburn felt like a fisherman, watching ripples on a lake. Now it was time to cast his line. 'I think the marksman who shot McGrouther may have served in the Militia. It's a complex matter. Quite sensitive.'

Scanlon stepped back a fraction, poker-faced. 'Interesting. Anything you can tell me now? I might be able to help.'

'Very soon, Comrade Deputy Chairman. I wouldn't want to trouble you with an incomplete theory.'

'Well, if you need assistance, come directly to me. No fucking middlemen, you understand?'

'Of course, Comrade.'

'While we're at it, I understand you saw Colonel Goldman. Why?'

'A simple liaison matter,' Fairburn replied. 'He is a *liaison* officer, isn't he?'

'That's what it says on his office door. Was he helpful?'

Fairburn declined another glass of champagne from a passing waiter. 'Comrade Goldman did the bare minimum, to the point of obstructiveness. If I may be candid, I'm disappointed by the lack of coordination between the Militia and CSS.'

'The answer to that problem lies inside Burgess House,' Scanlon growled. 'Ask Philby, or that smarmy bastard Ash Prasad. He's got his hand up Philby's arse like a fella running a Punch and Judy show.'

Despite himself, Fairburn laughed. 'I'll be sure to pass on your greetings, Comrade.'

Scanlon seemed pleased. 'Please do. Now enjoy yourself, Tommy. The Red Army choir's on next, then the speeches. You know how much we love a fucking speech.' Scanlon looked Fairburn up and down, winked, and strode away.

Fairburn checked his watch – it was 19.05. The reception finished at 21.00. Leaving Harry Pollitt House, he walked to a telephone kiosk and made a call. 'Renton?'

'Yes,' the technician replied. 'What's the buffet like? Do they have sausage rolls? They always have decent scoff at Harry Pollitt House.'

'I haven't paid much attention to the catering arrangements, Renton. Tell Ross to plant the device in the next hour. Got it?' If the listening device was planted around 20.00, it would record until 23.00 – adequate time to capture any conversation in Scanlon's Mercedes.

'Yes, Comrade Captain,' the technical officer replied.

Returning to the reception, Fairburn made small talk with the Soviet officers. They were wary of an Englishman in KGB uniform, but after they saw his medals and heard him tell a salty joke in fluent Russian, they relaxed a little.

'The bullshit right now is incredible,' said a senior captain from a Guards regiment. 'The Liberation celebrations will see more of our infantry in London than we had in '47!'

'I know,' another officer laughed. 'They've got my men polishing dustbins. As if Comrade Khrushchev will set foot in Woolwich Barracks.'

The Guards captain turned to Fairburn. 'Have the commemorations been keeping you busy, Comrade?'

'Yes, I've been attached to the CSS. They're not polishing dustbins, but they've emptied a few. You'd be amazed what you find.' The army officers paused for a moment, then laughed.

'Ah, the choir,' the captain announced, raising his glass as a troupe of soldiers in Great Patriotic War-era uniforms marched into the hall. 'This will make me homesick.'

'Let's get drunk,' said another.

'Just don't sing, eh?' said Fairburn. 'Leave it to the professionals.'

The Alexandrov Ensemble – colloquially known as the Red Army Choir – lustily performed 'Kalinka', 'Dark Eyes', 'The Partisan's Song' and a newer piece called 'Let's Go!' Then, in honour of their English hosts, a young woman sang 'We'll Meet Again', a ballad adopted by the British Resistance in the early 1940s. Even Fairburn found himself tapping his foot to finale of 'The Internationale' and 'The Red Flag'. The British Resistance veterans sang along, their jackets sagging beneath the weight of their medals. 'Best choir in the world,' the Red Army captain declared.

'Here,' said a fellow officer, passing his friend a bottle of vodka. 'The fun's over. You'll need this for the speeches, Dima.'

Gerry Scanlon shot his cuffs as he bounded onto a podium, holding up his hands to quieten the booming applause. His medals flashed under the electric lights, a jingling display of silver and gold. 'You aren't staying, Comrade?' asked the Soviet officer.

'No,' Fairburn replied, making for the door. 'I suspect I've heard this one before.'

Chapter 16

The streets smelled of bonfires started by the tramps living on the bomb sites surrounding the railway station. Seeing Fairburn's KGB uniform they scurried away, drunkenly whooping and shouting. He walked a counter-surveillance route, stopping at a kiosk to buy a cup of coffee, before hailing a taxi and returning to Burgess House. If he'd been followed, Scanlon's watchers were good. With several hours before the KGB team retrieved the recorder from the Militia General's car, Fairburn headed for his office. Taking off his tunic, he entered the combination into a safe and retrieved the books seized from William McGrouther's house. Fairburn picked out *Bridge of Sighs* by Eliza Crewe, scanning the notes scribbled in the margins. Familiar with cryptography, Fairburn suspected they weren't codes or ciphers, but personal prompts unique to McGrouther. One note read, *just like that day in St. Ives!*

The cipher to this code, he feared, *was* McGrouther.

Bridge of Sighs, according to the description on the back cover, concerned a young woman's political awakening after a love affair with an older man. Yawning, Fairburn poured stewed coffee from a flask. Flipping through the pages, he found something tucked firmly into the flyleaf at the back of the book, secured with a yellowed piece of tape – a photograph showing three people standing by a river. The first was a young Eliza Crewe, dark-eyed and gangly, dressed in black. With her was William McGrouther, smiling directly into the camera, eyes half hidden behind a floppy fringe. The last was an awkward-looking young man with glasses and a babyish face, looking down as if inspecting his feet. Written on the back of the photograph was *Eliza, Bill and Sandy, St. John's, November 1934.* Putting the photograph to one side, notebook ready, Fairburn began to read.

It was nearly 02.00 when Ross appeared with Renton and Sechkin. *Bridge of Sighs* was very dull and Fairburn was unable to glean any clues. 'Any problems?' he asked, closing the book.

'Well, the KGB fella who mugged Scanlon's driver got his nose busted,' Ross chuckled. 'The chauffeur chased Sergei for half a mile before he gave up. At least we got time to plant the recorder.'

Fairburn poured coffee into three cups. 'And Goldman?'

'He did what he was told.' Ross took a cup and nodded his thanks.

'I have the measure of Goldman,' Sechkin declared. 'He is like a lizard on a rock. He is fine as long as he feels the sun on his back.'

Clearing his throat, Renton put the mini recorder on the table. 'Right, let's see if Sid actually recorded anything, shall we?'

Ross scowled. 'Unless you fucked it up when you were fiddling round with it?'

'Shut up the pair of you,' Sechkin snapped. 'You are like old women with your bickering. Just play the tape, Renton.'

'Yes, Comrade Colonel,' Renton replied sheepishly, plugging a speaker into the Minifon recorder.

'And make notes,' said Sechkin, lighting a cigarette. 'Must I instruct you on every minor detail, Renton?'

'Yes, Comrade Colonel,' the technician replied, pressing a button. After a few moments of tinny feedback, they heard voices. The first was the gravelly voiced Scanlon. He called the second person in the car, a younger-sounding man with a northern accent, *Brady*.

'Major Brady is Scanlon's Staff Officer,' said Sechkin. They listened to the two men making small talk, Brady complimenting Scanlon on the quality of his speech. Scanlon said little, agreeing noncommittally with Brady's bitchy observations about people at the reception. Then they joshed with the driver about being mugged by a tramp. Finally, Brady said something interesting. 'I saw you speaking with the English KGB officer. Why did they let him join?'

'The Russians set up a project after the war called *Spartan*,' Scanlon replied. 'They recruited young communists from across Europe and trained 'em as special action types. Commandos. They say Fairburn was one of the best. He fought the Poles, then worked undercover in Egypt. After that they sent him to Budapest. A ruthless fucker, so I'm told.'

'He looked arrogant. What did he have to say for himself?'

'I straight-up asked what Philby wanted or if that stuck-up prick Prasad was involved.'

'That was bold, Comrade General.'

'If you don't approve, Brady, just fucking well say so.'

'I reckon Prasad's the more dangerous of the two. You know I think Philby's yesterday's man. In any case, I don't think we should be talking to the KGB *or* the CSS.'

'You're a clever lad, but not that fucking clever. If I didn't talk to Fairburn, I wouldn't know they're onto McGrouther's killer, would I?'

Brady guffawed. 'Fairburn told you that? Why?'

'It's a trigger, of course. He must think I was born yesterday. They'll be watching us even more than usual, mark my words. Be careful on the telephone. Have your office and apartment swept.'

'I do. Anyway, I'm sure they were watching us before,' Brady replied.

'The CSS maybe, but not the bloody KGB. And I doubt this is Teplyakov's doing, either. It's too subtle. Philby thinks his arse is covered because he's mates with Ivan Serov. Well, we can all play that game. I've got allies in Moscow too.'

'*Do* you know who shot McGrouther?' asked Brady carefully.

Scanlon's voice was inaudible, the recorder making a hissing noise. Then, when his voice returned, it was a near-whisper. The secret policemen all drew closer to the recorder, their heads almost touching. 'I did someone a favour a few years ago. An old comrade from the Resistance. Someone I trusted. And this is how he repays me?'

'A favour?'

'This friend of mine got himself into a spot of bother.'

'What sort of bother?'

'Taking a man for a walk in the woods and shooting him in the back sort of bother. He needed to disappear, so I made it happen. I got him new *dokumenty*. Passport, driving licence, the works.'

'You're too loyal to the old guard, Comrade.'

'Fuck off, Brady,' Scanlon growled. 'This fella saved my life once. He was a good soldier.'

The staff officer's voice softened. 'I'm sorry, Gerry. Why'd he shoot McGrouther?'

'Mick Nolan's a triggerman, not political. I imagine someone paid him. For all I know, he'll do Frayne next.'

'Who'd hire him?'

'How do I fucking well know? The British Action Front? The Americans? Kim-fucking-Philby?'

'And now the KGB are onto your man? Damn it!'

'Nolan ain't my man. I just helped him out of a tight spot once.'

'Of course, Comrade General.'

'Fuck it, I'm gonna get drunk. Cancel my appointments for tomorrow. Lionel?'

'Yes, Comrade?' said a third voice – the driver.

'Take me home. And put your toe down, before another tramp punches you on the nose.'

Ross shook his big bald head. 'So Scanlon didn't order McGrouther's murder?

I don't get it.'

'This is why evidence gathering is a fool's game,' Sechkin sniffed. 'It just leads us down another rabbit hole! It would have been easier to just execute *all* of the suspects. One of them has to be guilty and the rest are implicated anyway.'

Fairburn chuckled. 'Spoken like a true *Chekist*, Comrade Colonel.'

'The Chekists got the job done.'

'Killing all of the suspects wouldn't help us identify the CIA network,' Fairburn replied.

'Tommy's got a point,' Ross agreed, pulling an envelope from his coat pocket. 'This might help.'

'What is it?' asked Fairburn.

'The stuff you asked Goldman to find about Nolan. He handed it over when we retrieved the recorder from Scanlon's car.'

'Have you read it?'

'It's taped up.' Ross smiled. 'I think it's for your eyes, not mine.'

Fairburn pulled out his pocketknife and carefully slit open the envelope. Inside was a single sheet of paper. 'It's a page from Michael Nolan's service record.'

'And?' said Sechkin, folding his beefy arms across his chest.

Fairburn shook his head. 'His last assignment before he supposedly died is interesting. In February 1955 he was posted to Scanlon's private office.'

'Doing what?' asked Sechkin.

'It says *special assignment*.'

'I bet it was,' Ross chuckled. 'Pretending to fall off the back of a fishing boat? That's special, ain't it? Still, it's circumstantial.'

'It corroborates everything else we know,' said Fairburn. 'This and the recording is enough to put Scanlon in front of a firing squad.'

'So why don't we?' asked Sechkin.

'You'd need to put Scanlon on trial,' said Ross, shaking his head. 'You can see how it will play out with the man on the street. He's a national hero who made a mistake when he put his neck out for a brave resistance comrade. If you marched him in front of a firing squad, there'd be rioting.'

'He's right,' said Fairburn. 'We need more. Enough to force a confession. I'm sure there's a deal to be done. Scanlon strikes me as a pragmatist. For now we should concentrate on Nolan. He's the key.'

Ross rubbed his chin. 'How do we find the fella?'

'Round up the assassin's friends and family. Anyone dear to him,' Sechkin replied. 'Put them in prison. Threaten them. The rat will soon scurry from his hole.'

Fairburn took a mouthful of coffee. It was cold. 'Yes, that might work. However, I've another idea.'

'Go on,' said Sechkin.

'We need to speak to Director Philby and Comrade Prasad, first thing.'

'Why?'

'I need the Director to transfer Frankie Frayne to KGB custody.'

'Why?'

Fairburn stood and straightened his tunic. 'I think Nolan's work isn't done, just like Scanlon said. If Nolan killed McGrouther, who's to say he hasn't been tasked to kill Frayne too? Let's use him as bait.'

Ross slapped Fairburn on the back. 'You ruthless bastard. Now, I need a drink.'

Sechkin nodded. 'That's the best idea I've heard all night.'

Chapter 17

'It's Teplyakov. Enlighten me, Comrade Captain, on your investigation. I take it you are making good progress?'

Fairburn stood in a telephone box, a bead of sweat tickling the small of his back. He was a good liar. Good enough, he hoped, to dupe a KGB General. 'The operation against Scanlon was inconclusive. We bugged his car, but the conversation's open to interpretation.'

'How so?'

'We know an old friend of Scanlon's is the suspect for McGrouther's murder.'

'Then bring him in for questioning. I'm sure he'll fill in the gaps after a night or two of gentle persuasion by my men.'

'Comrade General, I suggest more compelling evidence is required. We still haven't properly confirmed the identity of the man who shot McGrouther. If it isn't who we think it is, the KGB will look foolish. The British will use it against us.'

Fairburn heard Teplyakov whistling through his teeth. 'I suppose you have a point. Then discover the murderer's identity. That's an order.'

'Yes, Comrade General. I'm working on it now.'

'Your plan?'

Fairburn put another coin in the call box. The metallic rattle sounded like the action of a gun. 'It's audacious and risky, Comrade General. It could go either way.'

Teplyakov's voice was matter of fact. 'Call me if it works. If it doesn't, I'll formally request Comrade Director Serov puts me in command of Sechkin's operations in Britain. This pantomime has gone on for too long.'

'Of course.'

'Goodbye, Comrade Captain.'

'Goodbye, Comrade General.'

Kim Philby passed Fairburn a copy of *The Times*. 'I spoke with the editor this morning. He couldn't believe his luck when I said he could publish the story with my approval.'

Ash Prasad nodded approvingly. 'A bold move, Kim. The Politburo will see it as a provocation, of course. We're washing dirty laundry in public.'

Fairburn read a mocked-up copy of the next day's newspaper. The headline read FRANCIS FRAYNE CHARGED WITH ESPIONAGE. 'This will make waves,' he said. The photograph showed Frayne in handcuffs, being led inside Burgess House by two uniformed CSS men.

'You asked for bait,' Philby replied, limping to the window overlooking the parade square. In the distance, Party flags fluttered over the Peter Jones – GUM store. 'How did you get on with the Justice Ministry, Ash?' he asked, lighting a cigarette and taking a long drag.

'My people had words with Frayne's lawyer. When Captain King suggested Frayne plead guilty to espionage in exchange for a non-capital sentence, his lawyer agreed it was a fair deal. The hearing will be at the Richmond Assizes, as Tommy requested.' He turned to Fairburn. 'I take it you chose Richmond for a reason?'

'Actually, it was Sergeant Ross' suggestion. The court is surrounded by wooded parkland. Ideal terrain for a sniper.'

Philby's brow creased. 'Now, if you think Scanlon *isn't* involved, why would this Nolan fellow want to kill Frayne?'

'Let's assume Scanlon's link to Nolan *is* coincidental,' Fairburn replied. 'If there's CIA involvement in this affair, they'd eliminate any loose ends threatening their network. What if Nolan's freelancing for the Americans? Scanlon himself mentioned the possibility to his staff officer.'

Prasad looked up from his journal like a man contemplating a crossword. 'I'm going to be generous; if Tommy's right – and it's a big *if* – not only do we bag the CIA network, but we also get rid of the Politburo's dead wood.'

'Frayne has sponsors in Moscow,' said Philby. 'Maybe King needs to question him again in light of the new information we've received. What if he's stalling for time?'

Prasad shook his head. 'Sponsors? Malenkov, you mean? He's out of play, he's crossed Khrushchev once too often.'

Philby stubbed out his cigarette. 'Very well, how do you propose to catch this Nolan fellow? You said yourself the area around Richmond Assizes is ideal for a sniper.'

'Quite.' Prasad nodded.

'With our own snipers, Comrade Director,' said Fairburn.

'I'm sorry?' said Prasad, sitting up in his seat. 'Snipers?'

Fairburn checked his watch. '10th Directorate snipers. The best in the world. Their flight touches down at Biggin Hill tonight.'

There were six passengers on the Ilyushin that landed at the aerodrome just south of London: five men and a woman, joking about the weather as they disembarked into the wet October evening. 'Comrades,' said

Nikolai Sechkin, smiling as he held up a dripping umbrella. 'It's England. What did you expect?'

'I never expect much. That way I'm seldom disappointed,' said the first of the men. He was stocky, with a flat, windburned face and deep-set eyes. 'Anyway, it's good to see you, Comrade Colonel.'

Sechkin turned to Fairburn. 'You've met Comrade Captain Fairburn, I understand?'

'Yes,' said the Russian, 'in North Africa. That was a good operation, Tommy.'

'I aim to please, Vasily Grigoryevich.'

Captain Vasily Grigoryevich Zaitsev, Hero of the Soviet Union and the USSR's most accomplished sniper, smiled. 'I aim to kill. I find it's easier than pleasing people.'

'Well, this job's a little different,' said Fairburn.

'How so?'

'We need you to capture someone, not kill them.'

Zaitsev shrugged. 'We can spot your shooter, of course. But catch him? That's down to you.'

'We'll have men ready,' Fairburn replied. 'I just need you to identify his position and, if necessary, keep him pinned down.'

'Dogs,' said Zaitsev, rain dripping off the end of his nose. 'You need dogs or artillery, both are good for flushing out snipers. Especially artillery – mortars are good but howitzers are better. Then again, this isn't Hungary or Poland, is it?'

Sechkin pulled a face. Few people knew the full extent of how the Polish rebellion was crushed. 'Tell me, Vasily Grigoryevich, how are things with our Basque friends? The struggle goes well?'

'I've learned to keep my nose out of politics, Comrade Colonel, especially Spanish politics. The Basques find targets and we shoot them.'

During the Stalin years, and a return to civilian life, Zaitsev had found himself out of favour. After the dictator's death, he'd been offered a way back into the Party's good books by working for the 10th Directorate.

'At least the food's good, Vasily,' said the woman, stepping forward. She was in her mid-forties, Fairburn guessed, with a snub-nose and reddish braided hair.

Fairburn nodded politely and took her hand. 'I don't think we've met, Comrade.'

'Senior Lieutenant Raisa Tarasov. I'm Comrade Zaitsev's second-in-command.'

'Welcome to Great Britain, Comrade,' said Fairburn. 'I'm not sure we can compete with French or Spanish food, though.'

'Hopefully we won't be here long enough to mind,' Tarasov replied, looking at the rain-heavy clouds. 'When's the job?'

'Three days,' said Sechkin.

'Not long,' Zaitsev replied, sucking on a tooth. He turned to his team. 'Get your stuff, boys. We'll go and take a look at the site now.' The men nodded and began unloading equipment from the transport plane.

'Don't you want to eat first?' asked Sechkin.

Zaitsev shook his head. 'Later, Comrade Colonel. I'd like to see the terrain while it's dark and wet.'

'Then it will be easy when it's dry and light,' Tarasov added, hefting a rucksack onto her shoulder.

'Dry?' Sechkin grumbled, raising his umbrella. 'Fat chance, Comrade.'

Fairburn waved at a Bedford RL truck parked at the airfield's edge. Its headlights flashed once as the engine fired, Sid Ross at the wheel. He drove along the runway and wound down the window. 'Where we goin'? The barracks?' Ross had arranged accommodation at a nearby CSS base, where a team of Russians would draw little attention.

Fairburn climbed up into the cab. 'No, they want to go to Richmond first.'

'They don't waste their time, do they?'

The Russians loaded their gear onto the Bedford while Zaitsev conferred with Sechkin and Tarasov. Finally, Sechkin got into the cab next to Fairburn. 'Right, Comrade Sergeant,' he said to Ross. 'Richmond Assizes, quickly as you can.'

'Right you are, Comrade Colonel,' Ross replied, lighting two cigarettes and passing one to Sechkin. The journey to Richmond took less than an hour, Ross driving fast along the rain-slicked streets. There was little traffic – a 21.00 curfew had been announced for the duration of the Liberation commemorations. Ross snorted when he saw two rain-caped militiamen huddling beneath an umbrella. 'Stopping kids putting up posters? It's all those fuckers are good for.'

Sechkin laughed. 'You really hate the *musors*, don't you?'

'A man needs a hobby,' Ross replied, turning to Fairburn. 'Anyway, what if you've dragged these snipers all the way from Spain for nothing? How d'you know Nolan's gonna turn up?'

Fairburn wrinkled his nose at the cigarette smoke. Reaching across Sechkin, he wound down the window. 'It's how the Americans operate. They play mind games and assume we won't expect them to try the same thing twice.'

'And where'd you learn that?' asked Ross.

'Hungary and Poland. The best terrorist groups were organised by CIA paramilitary officers. Their field men were ruthless, always prepared to lose agents in order to succeed.'

'I thought the Yanks were soft.'

'A common misconception,' said Sechkin. 'If they think Frayne poses a risk to their wider network, the Americans will eliminate him.'

'Well you two are the experts, I s'pose,' said Ross. 'Now, Comrade Captain?'

'Yes, Comrade Sergeant?'

'Can you shut that fucking window? It's freezing.'

The Richmond Assizes were housed in a stately home on the edge of Richmond Park. Originally known as White Lodge, the Ministry of Justice commandeered the place shortly after the war. As political prosecutions surged during the Stalin years, the building was repurposed as a court complex. From the handsome Palladian mansion, thousands of class traitors were sentenced to death, imprisonment or labour service.

The lorry stopped at a checkpoint at the end of a long, straight driveway. Ross showed the Ministry of Justice troops his identity card and they opened the barrier, rain splashing on their capes while guard dogs growled and strained at their leashes. 'This is it,' he said, the Bedford's headlights slicing into the trees flanking the drive. 'Vehicles and court visitors get checked at the perimeter, but the rest of the park's public. Anyone on foot could get close to the wire easily enough.'

'You are to be commended,' said Sechkin, slapping Ross on the back. 'It's why we need an officer with local knowledge.'

They drove to the holding facility, a squat building to the rear of the manor house. Ross parked and opened the back of the truck. 'This is it,' he said in Russian to the 10th Directorate snipers lounging in the back. 'The target will be looking to shoot a prisoner from a vehicle parked where we are now.'

Zaitsev and Tarasov jumped down from the truck first, followed by the rest of their team. Fairburn and Sechkin appeared, each carrying two bottles of Stolichnaya. The Russians grinned as Sechkin opened one, took a swig, and passed it around. Zaitsev sniffed the air awhile, torch in hand. 'Tell me about the target,' he said finally.

'Michael Nolan is a self-taught sniper,' Fairburn replied. 'He learned his trade in the Resistance, killing fascists during the war. Afterwards, he joined the Militia as a marksmanship instructor.'

'He's good,' Ross added. 'He could've killed us both when he shot McGrouther, but he didn't. He put one bullet in his head and another in his heart: a three hundred metre shot with a Mauser 98k.'

Zaitsev shrugged. 'A decent shot, but hardly exceptional. He was a partisan, you say?'

'Yes,' Fairburn replied.

Zaitsev looked at Tarasov. 'That means he's unpredictable. Not a conventional soldier. How would you do this, Raisa?'

Arms folded across her chest, Tarasov studied the parking lot and outbuildings. 'There's no elevated position for a shot into the compound, apart from the trees to the east,' she replied. 'And the ground has only shallow elevation. Tricky to take a long shot – I'd say he'd have to get closer than three hundred metres.'

Ross rubbed his chin. 'So we've chosen the wrong location?'

'*Nyet*, Comrade.' Tarasov smiled. 'You're simply guilty of assuming because your man's a sniper, he'll always snipe.'

'Exactly,' said Zaitsev, accepting the bottle of Stolichnaya and taking a swig. 'The man's a killer. The rifle is simply a tool at his disposal. Please, Raisa, continue.'

Tarasov pointed at the holding facility. 'Do you see? The prison truck has only one route from the checkpoint to the courthouse. If I was a partisan, I'd blow it up with a roadside bomb, or machine gun it from the scrubland to the south. Why wait for it to get to the courthouse? There are several good escape routes, especially for a someone on a motorcycle.'

'Yes, a bomb or maybe an RPG-2,' Zaitsev added. 'A rocket-propelled grenade.'

'Yes, like that job we did in Andorra,' Tarasov replied.

'Precisely. Tell me, Comrade, do your terrorists have access to such weapons?'

Ross shook his head. 'Never seen anythin' like that, but the British Action Front have used German stuff left over from the war. Panzerfausts, mainly.'

'Panzerfaust?' said Tarasov, eyes sweeping the floodlit drive. 'Primitive weapon. Fifty-five metre range. Sixty at most.'

Zaitsev nodded his agreement. 'Very close. You'd have to be a madman, or have other shooters covering you.'

One of the snipers, a weaselly looking fellow, shrugged. 'I think Raisa's correct, Vasily. If it was me, I'd just take out the vehicle. But blowing up a prison truck ain't a one-man job, they would need a team. And Comrade Captain Fairburn wants prisoners, too?'

Shooting Fairburn a sour look, Sechkin lit another cigarette. 'Then I fear we've wasted your time, comrades.'

Zaitsev licked his teeth, breathing in the damp evening air. A smile spread across his face. 'On the contrary, Comrade Colonel. You have a photograph of your man for us?'

'Of course.'

'Excellent, now we know who *not* to kill,' the master sniper replied. Then, he ran a finger across his throat. 'But anyone else? *Kak yagnyata dlya Volkov. Like lambs for the wolves.*'

Chapter 18

'Comrade Captain Fairburn? It's Renton.'

'Yes, Renton?'

'I have the results as requested. The trace on a telephone call from a kiosk in Stockwell?'

Fairburn pulled his notebook from his pocket. 'Excellent. Please, go ahead.'

Renton read out a London telephone number. 'You were correct, there was a security operation on the day the call was made. There's no voice recording, but the post office did trace the number the caller dialled. It belongs to a café in Vauxhall called *Fratelli's*.'

'Any security traces?'

'Nothing much on Fratelli's, Comrade Captain. Some antisocial activity with young men, quite normal for that part of town.'

'I'm grateful. Was there anything else?'

The technician sounded hesitant. 'There is something.'

'Please, speak freely.'

'Director Philby ordered the monthly audit of our telephone checks to be brought forward.'

'*Audit?*'

'Yes,' Renton replied. 'CSS internal security check to see if anyone's abusing the system. Y'know, officers looking up their neighbours for personal reasons. That sort of thing.'

'That makes sense,' said Fairburn. 'Besides, isn't that Director Philby's prerogative?'

'He's never brought it forward before,' the technician sniffed. 'It's as if my office isn't trusted.'

'We're working on a sensitive case,' said Fairburn. 'I'd expect extra scrutiny, and I'm sure it isn't personal. Think nothing of it.'

'I'm grateful for your confidence, Comrade Captain.'

'You're welcome, Renton. I'll see you in the morning.'

It was before dawn when Fairburn was escorted to Philby's office by a tired-looking secretary. Sitting with the Director were Nikolai Sechkin, Ash Prasad, a fair-haired CSS officer in battledress and a smartly dressed woman. The desk was littered with maps, aerial photographs of Richmond Park, empty coffee cups and an ashtray full of cigarette ends. 'Good morning, comrades,' said Philby, his voice raspy. 'It's quite the show you've arranged, Tommy.'

Prasad, dressed in a three-piece suit, peered up from his notebook like an accountant scrying a rounding error. 'Yes, I think *show* is a good word. Or circus, perhaps? I note Captain Fairburn flew a team of KGB assassins into Britain without authorisation, then commandeered a battalion of CSS troops. Is this based on cogent intelligence, I wonder? Or a hunch?'

Sechkin scowled. 'Get out of the wrong side of the bed this morning, Comrade? Or was there a pea under your mattress?'

'My job is to protect the Director and the CSS,' Prasad replied. 'I make no apology for scrutinising high-risk operations.'

'Really, chaps, it's too early for bickering,' said Philby, gently patting Prasad's hand. He gestured at the man and the woman. 'Tommy, this is Tony Hodges and Alison King.'

The CSS officer cleared his throat. He was wiry and well spoken, the stem of a pipe sticking from his battledress pocket. 'Comrade, I'm Colonel Hodges, officer commanding the CSS Special Action Group. My men will support your operation at Richmond Assizes.'

King was ruddy faced with sandy hair. 'Captain Alison King, Bureau 6.' Huskily voiced, she spoke with a South African accent.

'I've asked Alison to interrogate any prisoners taken during the operation,' Prasad explained. 'I thought it might be helpful for her to sit in on the briefing.'

Fairburn nodded and took a seat. 'It's good to meet you, comrades. What's your view of our proposal?'

Hodges took his pipe from his pocket and pointed the stem at the map. With his watery eyes and weathered face, Fairburn thought he'd the look of an angler or a birdwatcher. 'The job looks straightforward enough. We maintain a discreet cordon around the park until you call us forward. Then we sweep for terrorists. I've got a section of dog-handlers for that. I'll need to visit the site later this morning, but looking at the map I think three companies will be sufficient. That's 240 men plus my HQ platoon. We've also access to a helicopter if we need it.'

Prasad nodded. 'Colonel Hodges, what d'you think of Captain Zaitsev's theory the terrorists might use explosives or rockets? There'll be members of the judiciary onsite, after all. Plus journalists, jurors and legal staff. *Civilians*.'

Hodges began packing his pipe. 'Well, you have six extremely accomplished snipers covering the area. I imagine they'll neutralise any immediate threats. Then, once the suspects are located, we'll quickly flood the area with troops. We'll do everything possible to take this Nolan fellow prisoner.'

'It's imperative he's taken alive,' said Fairburn.

Hodges raised an eyebrow. 'As I said, Comrade Captain, we'll do everything possible. Nothing's certain on an operation like this.'

Sechkin tapped a cigarette from a soft pack and lit it. 'If your men kill Nolan, Comrade Colonel Hodges, you'll find yourself on my shit-list. That's a terrible place for a man to find himself. Do you understand?'

Hodges looked at Philby. 'Comrade Director?'

Philby smiled sympathetically. 'What can I say, Hodges? I hate to sound like an arse, but Comrade Sechkin's entirely correct. *Cometh the hour, cometh the man*, eh?'

King smiled and patted Hodges on the back. 'Besides, Colonel, it would be good if I had someone to interrogate afterwards.'

Hodges lit his pipe and puffed on it. Seeing King grimace at the cloud of tobacco smoke, he smiled. 'Then I suppose we'll be taking this Nolan fellow prisoner, won't we?'

'Excellent,' Philby replied. Then there was a knock on the door. 'Ah, that will be the stewards with breakfast.'

'An English breakfast?' asked Sechkin, patting his belly.

'Well, Anglo-Russian,' Philby replied. 'There's vodka to go with the bacon and eggs.'

After breakfast, Sechkin and Fairburn walked across the parade square. Fairburn shook his head. 'Why was King there? A Bureau 6 officer?'

'Maybe she's Prasad's mistress?' Sechkin chuckled. 'I didn't think he had it in him. Anyway, a good interrogator is a good interrogator. It makes sense to have one available, especially if we arrest Nolan.'

'Yes, I suppose you're right.'

'How much sleep did you get?'

'Two hours,' Tommy replied.

'Not enough. Get some rest, I'll deal with Zaitsev and the CSS. Call me later this evening.'

'Nikolai—'

'That's an order, Comrade Captain,' Sechkin interrupted, gripping Tommy's shoulder. 'Prasad was right about one thing, this is a high-risk operation. If it goes wrong, General Teplyakov will fuck me over like a dockside whore. I won't have it go wrong because my best officer was tired.'

Tommy nodded. 'May I stand Sergeant Ross down too? He's worked hard.'

'Yes of course.'

Fairburn found Ross smoking with a coven of CSS sergeants in the underground car park. Seeing Fairburn, he stubbed out his cigarette and got in his car. 'You need a lift back to your digs, Comrade?' he said.

'Yes please. Then go home and sleep. The next couple of days are going to be hard.'

'You don't need to tell me twice,' Ross replied. 'How did it go with the guvnors?'

'Prasad seemed unhappy.'

'Arrest operations ain't his area of expertise, are they? The Director relies on him too much.'

'I'm told Prasad was an excellent field agent during the war. Why wouldn't Comrade Philby rely on him?'

'There are two sides to CSS,' said Ross. 'You've got the intelligence officers, people like Prasad and Philby. Then there's the policemen, fellas like me and Colonel Hodges. The intelligence types are usually in charge.'

'And the problem is?'

Ross nosed the GAZ onto the King's Road. 'Well, if you ask me, sometimes the intelligence types are too clever for their own good.'

'So you think Prasad's playing games by raising doubts? Hedging his bets?'

''Course he is. If we catch Nolan, it'll be because he okayed the plan.'

'And if we don't?'

'You won't see his arse for dust and I'll be digging up beetroots in Vladivostok.'

Fairburn's smile was tight. 'Well, Comrade Sergeant, perhaps it's for the best we take Nolan alive.'

Chapter 19

Fairburn woke mid-morning, dusty light filtering through a gap in the curtains. He got up, dressed in casual clothes and took a bus to Vauxhall. In his notebook was the address Renton had provided for the café called Fratelli's. Why had Aunt Maggie telephoned the place straight after his visit? And why for only ten seconds? It had to be something to do with the ex-SS man she'd spoken of. Fairburn's fingers brushed the grips of the Makarov in his shoulder holster. Wasn't hunting and killing fascists a sworn duty for a Spartan of the KGB's 10th Directorate?

Fratelli's was a greasy spoon café near Vauxhall Park. Fairburn studied two young men standing by the door smoking roll-up cigarettes. Both wore heavy crepe-soled shoes and velvet-collared jackets, their hair worn in oily pompadours. 'Teddy Boys', they called themselves, self-styled rebels who enjoyed American music. Why weren't the Militia here, moving them on? Taking their names? He stepped inside the café and studied the menu chalked on the board behind the counter. There was the usual selection of soup and stews, plus overpriced pies and sandwiches. Ordering a cheese roll and a cup of coffee, he sat down behind a corner table. The waitress quickly brought his food, nodding along to the music playing on an old Dansette player. 'Who sings this song?' Fairburn asked.

'Where've you been hiding?' the waitress replied. 'It's Elvis Presley.'

'Ah, the American singer?'

'Yeah.'

Fairburn sipped his coffee, which was awful. 'Where d'you get American records around here?'

'They ain't illegal, if that's what you're askin'.'

'Of course not. I was thinking of buying my sister a birthday present.' Fairburn smiled. 'She likes this stuff.'

The waitress smiled back. 'The sailors bring 'em over. They cost a few bob, though, maybe try Brixton market?' When the waitress left, Fairburn pulled a copy of *The Daily Mirror* from his pocket and started the crossword, getting a feel for the café and its customers. Most looked like municipal workers, older men with ruddy faces and cropped hair, grumbling as they chopped at powdery sausage and oily bubble and squeak. Eventually, Elvis Presley was replaced by another musician he didn't recognise. The music was furious and crass. 'Can I get you anything else?' said the waitress, pulling a pencil out of her hair as she tapped a foot to the music. 'Before you ask, this one's Jerry Lee Lewis.'

'I'll have some pie, if you have any.'

'We've got apple crumble today.'

'That's fine. And another coffee? By the way, I was looking for a friend of my auntie's who comes here. I can't remember his name though.'

The waitress cocked her head. 'And what's your auntie called?'

'Margaret Young. Maggie.'

'Oh, the old lady from the Stockwell Park estate?'

'Yes, that's her.'

The waitress dabbed the corner of her mouth with a finger, catching a stray piece of lipstick. 'You know her boys, then?'

'Robbie and Clive are my cousins,' said Fairburn. 'It's terrible what happened, getting sent to Russia like that.'

'Okay, what does her friend look like?' the waitress replied, her tone softening. 'The fella who's name you can't remember?'

Fairburn gestured at the girl to come closer. He lowered his voice. 'He had a rough time in the war, if you know what I mean?'

'Wait a minute,' the waitress replied. 'It's my dad you need to speak to.'

The waitress disappeared. A few minutes later a jowly man wearing a greasy chef's jacket appeared. He put a bowl of apple crumble and custard in front of Fairburn and scowled. 'So you're the nosy fucker. Who you lookin' for?'

'A friend of my—'

'Look, mate, I don't know who you are but there's a phone box down the road. Why not call your auntie and ask her for this fella's name?'

'I can't.' Fairburn took a spoonful of the crumble and nodded. 'She doesn't know I'm here. She wouldn't be happy if she knew, either.'

'Why?'

Fairburn put something inside his newspaper and passed it to the chef. 'I've got a bit of work he can help me with and it isn't buying Yank records from sailors.'

The chef opened it and saw two neatly folded five pound notes – more than a fortnight's pay for most workers. 'A tenner? What for?' he whispered.

'To show I'm not messing around,' Fairburn replied. 'The man I'm looking for was abroad during the war, right?'

The chef nodded towards the front door. 'Him and Maggie have lunch together now and then. They always have the spaghetti.'

'Who is he? Tell me and the tenner's yours.'

'His name's Ronnie Todmorden.'

'Address?'

'He lives next door to the butcher's on Fentiman Road,' the chef replied uneasily, his eyes fixed on the big white banknotes. 'I dunno the number, but the front door's red. It's only ten minutes away, but for fuck's sake don't mention my name.'

'He'll never know, but if he did he'd thank you,' Fairburn said with an easy lie, eating another spoonful of crumble. 'Right, I'll be on my way. Here, I'm done with my newspaper. Do you want it?'

'Thanks, I think I will,' the chef replied, watching Fairburn head for the door.

Fentiman Road was quiet except for shabbily dressed locals queuing for soup outside a church. The houses were battle-damaged but people had cheered them up with flowerboxes. Faded posters plastered to the walls promised a future of playgrounds and seaside holidays. Fairburn found the butcher's shop, the windows bare apart from a few sad-looking chops. It was shutting up for the day, two men in bloodstained aprons scrubbing the counter while a third swept the pavement outside. The house next door was a dilapidated terrace, its windows boarded. When the man with the broom went back inside, Fairburn pulled a lockpick from his pocket and disengaged the mortice. Sliding the Makarov from his shoulder holster, he crept inside. The ground floor parlour and kitchen empty, Fairburn made his way up the stairs. The floorboards creaked beneath his shoes, warped and damp.

Then, a noise.

Metal on metal.

The sound of a weapon being made ready. 'Put your gun down,' said a London-accented voice. 'Slowly, so I can see what you're doing.'

'Of course,' Fairburn replied, placing the Makarov on the step in front of him.

'Right, now fold your hands on top of your head. No sudden moves, there's a Schmeisser aimed at your back.'

Fairburn complied. 'Can I turn around, Mister Todmorden? I came to talk, nothing else.'

'With a gun?'

'Force of habit.'

'Okay, but slowly. Else I'll shoot you dead.'

Fairburn turned to see a balding man with greyish skin, his face cratered with old acne scars. He was armed with a German MP40 machine pistol, the muzzle only a yard from Fairburn's belly. 'I'm Tommy Fairburn. Maggie Young's nephew.'

'You're the fucker who joined the KGB.'

Glancing into the parlour, Fairburn saw an open trapdoor. Todmorden had been in the cellar. 'And you're the fucker who joined the SS.'

Ronnie Todmorden smirked. 'Cocky little shit, ain't you? Why shouldn't I kill you?'

'Because I need your assistance. I'm willing to pay.'

'Why?'

'That's my business. Now, can I take my hands off my head?'

Todd's finger rested on the MP40's trigger guard. He lowered the weapon a fraction. 'Just watch yourself. Now, step into the parlour and sit your arse down.'

Fairburn obeyed. Despite his graveyard pallor, the ex-SS man looked fit and alert. He moved with an economy of effort, a person who considered every move. A veteran, without doubt. A survivor. 'I'm here, Mister Todmorden, because Maggie said you knew the identity of the person who informed on my parents during the war.'

'She gave you my name?'

'No, she refused.'

'Then how'd you find me?'

'I'm a Captain in the 10th Directorate of the KGB,' Fairburn replied. There was nothing boastful in his voice. 'It's my job to find people who'd prefer not to be found.'

'And killing 'em?'

'Sometimes. Then again, you were an SS man. People in glass houses, eh?'

Todmorden lowered the MP40. 'I was a soldier, nothing more. You don't know a thing about the Free Corps or why people like me joined.'

'You were fascists. What else is there to know?'

'I ain't gonna waste my breath,' Todmorden said. 'You said you'd pay me. How much dough are we talking about? I'm gonna have to move house now and my work's important.'

'Important? How?'

'I'm collecting information on you Red bastards. Stuff you don't want people to know. Stuff that'll get folk out on the streets.'

'Such as?'

'The truth.'

Fairburn laughed. 'The fascist truth? How many truths are there?'

'I asked how much?' said Todmorden, jabbing the MP40 at Fairburn.

Fairburn settled into a lumpy sofa. There was two hundred pounds cash left in his operations fund. 'Seventy pounds,' he said easily. 'Cash, of course.'

'I want a hundred.'

'Very well,' said Fairburn. He cared little for money. 'In return, I want the identity of the person who betrayed my parents.'

Todmorden licked his lips. 'It's a deal,' he said, laying the MP40 on the table.

Fairburn pulled an envelope from his jacket pocket. 'Here's thirty. I'll pay you the rest later.'

The ex-SS man took the money, checked it, and stuffed it in his trouser pocket. 'If you fuck me over, I'll kill you.'

'I've no doubt, Mister Todmorden.'

'In which case I'll put the kettle on. Tea?'

'Just water, please.'

Todmorden led Fairburn into the tiny kitchen and put a kettle on the range. He lit the gas with a petrol lighter and reached for a teapot. 'Suit yourself. Now, where do I begin?'

'My parents, Mister Todd. I want to know who informed on them to the Gestapo.'

'I first met your old man in 1938,' said Todd, sipping tea from a mug decorated with the faded likeness of King Edward VIII. 'Your aunt Maggie asked me to get him a bottle of gin for his birthday. I was a warehouseman at the Beefeater distillery in Vauxhall.'

'And you were a fascist? A BUF man?'

Todmorden looked at the long-dead king on the side of his mug. 'I'd been in the BUF, but I fell out with the bloke in charge of our section. I knew your dad was a Red, but I never talked politics in front of your aunt. Maggie wasn't interested in that stuff.'

'My father was a shop steward with the Amalgamated Engineering Union,' said Fairburn. 'I know he represented machinists at a plant in Croydon. They made aircraft parts.'

'Yeah, I remember,' Todmorden replied. 'Anyhow, I was called-up for the army just after they signed the Halifax-Ribbentrop pact. Then, when Moseley took power, some of us ex-BUF lads volunteered for the Free Corps instead. The pay was better, and we knew we'd see action.'

'The SS?'

'We were attached to the SS. We only ever fought Soviets. That was the deal when we signed up.'

'We were talking about my father.'

'Sure. I was back on leave just after the Kiev offensive. That would've been Christmas '44. Anyhow, I met some old BUF pals for a drink. Turned out one of the fellas worked in the same factory as your old man. He told me your mum and dad were pinched by the Gestapo. Word was your old man was grassed on by one of his union mates. Apparently he was trying to get the blokes at his plant to sabotage machinery.'

Fairburn sat up. 'Who was the informer?'

'The fella's name was Benedict O'Brien. I only remember because of the irony.'

'Irony?'

'O'Brien was meant to be a Gestapo grass, right? But guess what? All along he was working for the Russian NKVD. We found out after the war when the Reds gave him a fucking medal.' Todmorden slapped his knee, a grin on his pockmarked face. 'Trust me, there's nobody as ruthless as a fucking Soviet. But I don't need to tell you, eh, *Comrade*?'

Fairburn felt his stomach churn. 'O'Brien was a double agent?'

'Yeah, we reckon he gave up your parents to impress the Germans. You know, work his way deeper into the Gestapo's good books? His NKVD handlers would've given him the order to do it.'

'Where's O'Brien now?'

Todmorden pulled up the sleeve of his shirt and scratched his arm. It was covered with a shiny sleeve of burn tissue. 'O'Brien died of cancer in 1952. Peacefully, I'm told, in a nice clean Party-run hospice in Barnet. They even buried him in the Patriot's plot in Highgate Cemetery. War, eh, Tommy? It's a funny old thing.'

Fairburn balled his fists. 'O'Brien was playing a bigger game. *He* didn't kill my parents,' he said finally. 'It was the fascists who executed them both.'

Todmorden shook his head. 'You really don't get it, do you, Tommy?'

'What d'you mean?'

'Who said the *Germans* killed your parents?'

'What the hell are you talking about?'

'You asked me what information I was collecting?'

'Yes.'

Todmorden smiled. 'Follow me. I promise you'll be getting your money's worth.'

Chapter 20

'I didn't get back home until 1949,' said Todmorden, leading Fairburn into the cellar. 'I passed through Sweden on the way. People there told me stories about British POWs being sent to Russia as slave labour.'

'They weren't *slave* labour. They were war criminals serving sentences for crimes against the Soviet Union,' Fairburn replied.

Todmorden chuckled. 'Jesus, what did they wash your brains with? Fucking bleach?'

Fairburn ignored the insult. 'How did you escape justice?'

'There's no shortage of anti-communists in Scandinavia,' said Todmorden, flicking a switch. A lightbulb flickered into life, yellowy-white. The cellar's walls were covered in a muddle of diagrams and photographs. 'Anyhow, wherever I went, I kept hearing the same rumours about missing people. Not just POWs, either.'

'Most prisoners were murdered by the Germans, not the Russians.'

Todmorden nodded. 'Yes, that's true. Towards the end of the war, the Jerries exterminated prisoners at a fair old clip: Jews, Reds, Homosexuals. They couldn't have killed 'em all, though, the Russian advance was too quick.'

'Let's talk about Britain. The Germans couldn't murder anyone without *British* fascists,' said Fairburn, studying a map stuck to the wall. Pins marked the location of the main Nazi concentration camps in Great Britain. 'People like you, Mister Todmorden.'

'You ain't listening, are you?' Todmorden scowled. 'At the end of the war I was fighting rear-guard actions on the Baltic coast. The only people I killed were Russian soldiers.'

'Then why are you so interested in the British camps?'

'Cuz I hate the Soviets. They didn't liberate anyone. They made people slaves.'

Fairburn sighed. 'In Russia, they have special hospitals for people like you.'

'For what? Telling the truth? You've just proved my point,' Todmorden replied with a sneer.

Fairburn pulled Sechkin's letter from his pocket. 'Your fantasies are immaterial. I'm interested in what happened to my parents. I want facts. *Evidence.*'

'I'll show you evidence,' Todmorden replied, prising opening a dog-eared scrapbook. Inside, the pages were covered with official-looking papers, diagrams and reports. 'I've spent years talking to people, visiting what's left of the camps and gathering details. It's like a jigsaw.'

Fairburn double-checked Sechkin's letter. 'In 1943, my mother was sent to Cadmore End concentration camp in High Wycombe. My father was at Dungeness. The only available records indicate both were executed by the Germans in 1946.'

Todmorden opened a drawer and pulled out an index card. 'Yes, Cadmore End was a proper death camp. Sorry, Tommy, your old lady probably died there.'

'I don't doubt it. And my father?'

'Well, Dungeness is a different story,' Todmorden replied, pulling a water-stained piece of paper from his scrapbook. 'I spoke to a fella who worked as a handyman at the Soviet military port in Hythe. He says back in '47 at least a thousand British prisoners from Dungeness passed through Hythe on their way across the Channel.'

Fairburn shook his head. 'The official record shows the prisoners were murdered by the Germans. The SS men responsible were executed by the Red Army in 1947. There are names, unit designations – everything.'

'Of course that's what the official record says,' Todmorden chuckled, pulling a packet of Russian cigarettes from his pocket and lighting one. 'They ain't gonna admit they sent a bunch of British *communists* to work in Siberia as slave labour, are they?'

Fairburn shook his head. 'Why would they do that?'

Todmorden blew a plume of smoke at the cobwebbed ceiling. 'Look, we all know the Reds lost millions of people in the war. Manpower's the only resource they don't have. I suppose they thought it was their due. I mean, someone had to rebuild the Motherland, right?'

'The official record versus the word of a... *handyman*?' said Fairburn sourly. 'It's hardly compelling evidence.'

'You're quite right, Tommy. I might be an amateur, but I've learned a thing or two about this sleuthing lark. You need more than one person's say-so to prove something,' he said, pulling a photograph from the scrapbook. 'Have a butcher's at this *evidence*. That's what this is. Proper evidence.'

Fairburn studied the photo of three young Soviet soldiers posing by a harbour wall. One, wearing a traditional *shapka* fur hat on the back of his head, was smiling and pretending to play a banjo. Behind them was an army truck full of wretched-looking men. Faces pinched, they wore distinctive striped uniforms and caps. Turning the photo over he saw, written in Russian, *Sasha and the boys, Hythe, England, May 1947*. 'Where'd you find this?' he asked, focussing on the men in the truck. Could his father have been one of them?

'*Sasha and the boys* were killed by British Action Front patriots in 1948,' Todmorden replied. 'The photograph was found in one of their pockets and handed to a BAF intelligence officer. Years later, he gave it to me.'

'The BAF? You admit to associating with terrorists?'

'I wouldn't be much use to you if I didn't, would I?'

'Do you have the names of these prisoners? The men from Dungeness?'

Todmorden shook his head. 'I've got names from some of the other camps, but not from Dungeness. I reckon the official record's a mixture of lies and guesswork. Most of the witnesses I've spoken to – including a few Jerries, as it happens – said the first thing they did was burn all their paperwork.'

Todmorden's investigation was a political crime of the highest order. It would be easy to overpower him. But witnesses from the café might identify Todmorden as a friend of his aunt's. 'There's a possibility my father lived?'

'I dunno.' Todmorden shrugged. 'Maybe?'

Fairburn passed Sechkin's letter to Todd. 'Can you read Russian?'

'Enough to get by.'

'Here are the details I was given. Copy them down, I want you to see if your contacts know anything.'

A smile. 'You want me to work for you, Tommy?'

'You've taken my money, haven't you?' Fairburn replied. 'I have more.'

'I'll think about it.'

Fairburn's smile was cold. '*Agents* live, but terrorists die Mister Todmorden. Which would you rather be?'

The ex-SS man studied the tip of his cigarette. 'I'll see what I can do. I look forward to seeing the rest of my money soon, eh?'

'Of course,' said Fairburn, making for the stairs. 'If I need you, I'll leave a message at Fratelli's.'

'Sure, I'll swing by,' Todmorden replied. 'Take care, Tommy, and have a little think about what your Russian friends are doing to this country. And what they did to your parents.'

Fairburn reached the top of the stairs. He turned, his lip curling. 'I won't have that, not from a fascist like you.'

Todmorden stubbed out his cigarette. 'I don't see any difference between my lot and yours anymore, truth be told,' he said with a shrug. 'In fact, I think the Yanks have got the right idea – they don't believe in anything much, do they?'

'Only money,' said Fairburn, heading for the door. 'I think you'd fit right in.'

'Sleep well?' asked Ross, driving up Richmond Hill.

'So-so,' Fairburn said, lying. After his encounter with Todmorden, Fairburn had returned to his apartment and took a long, hot shower. His gut told him some of the ex-SS man's story rang true. The informer, Benedict O'Brien, betraying his parents as part of a Soviet infiltration operation sounded familiar. He'd seen the KGB use similar tactics in Poland and Hungary.

'You look knackered,' said Ross, winding down the car window to let in a blast of fresh air. 'After we've finished the briefing, why not go home? It's gonna be a long day tomorrow.'

'I need to be here.'

Ross patted Fairburn's shoulder with a brawny hand. 'You're a good officer. We wouldn't have got this far without you. Don't mess it up now, eh?'

'Thanks, Sid. What will you do?'

'I'll hang around and see what the bosses are sayin'. Just in case they try and change the plan. You know what bosses are like, always fucking things up.'

'I doubt Zaitsev will let them,' Fairburn replied. 'He's too shrewd. Would you want to argue with him?'

Ross ran a red light and honked his horn at a startled pedestrian. 'When all's said and done, Zaitsev's a shooter. He ain't got any political clout, not like Ash Prasad. Besides, won't Zaitsev and his boys be hiding on a roof or in some bushes?'

'And the Director?'

'Comrade Philby's a hands-off sort when it comes to ops. He'll trust Sechkin to get on with it. If he needs a bulletproof vest? Well, that's Prasad's job.'

'Prasad's too shrewd.'

Ross looked uncomfortable. 'Like I said, spies can be too clever for their own good.'

They crossed Richmond Park, the trees orange and brown, deer scattering before them. Signs warned poachers would be shot on sight. 'It's scenic,' said Tommy, taking in the views across London.

'They keep it nice and tidy. Lots of high-ups live out here,' Ross replied. 'You know what they say: the Politburo think everything smells of fresh paint.'

Fairburn smiled. 'Now it's daylight, I wonder where Colonel Hodges is going to hide three companies of troops?' he asked. White Lodge lay on a gentle apron of parkland flanked by a scattering of outbuildings. Beyond was scrubbier ground surrounded by trees.

Ross twisted in his seat. 'Back that way,' he said, pointing at the parkland. 'They've got field cars and motorbikes. They'll make up ground quick enough.'

'You sound unusually optimistic, Sid.'

'There's strength in numbers when it comes to counter-ambushes,' said Ross. 'The terrorists can be as sneaky as they like, but they can't outrun cars, tracker dogs and a bloody helicopter.' They stopped at a security checkpoint, where cars full of KGB men waited. In front of them was a Mercedes, its coachwork gleaming and black like a beetle's carapace.

'Colonel Sechkin's here,' said Fairburn, nodding at the dark GAZ nearest the checkpoint. 'Whose is the Mercedes?'

Ross smiled. 'That's Ash Prasad's motor. I hope he's brought his galoshes.'

Again, Fairburn found himself chuckling. He suddenly found the idea of Prasad wandering around a muddy field in his brogues amusing. 'Let me do the talking, Sid.'

'You're welcome,' Ross replied, showing his ID card to a sentry. 'If this thing goes pear-shaped, nobody will remember me if I keep my trap shut, eh?'

Chapter 21

The CSS and KGB officers gathered in a draughty workshop. Smoking and laughing, they stamped their feet against the cold while a stony-faced Captain Vasily Zaitsev waited for them to quieten down. At his shoulder was his deputy, Raisa Tarasov. She looked relaxed, as if she were about to enjoy a countryside ramble. Both snipers wore waxed jackets with oversized hoods, woollen britches and hiking boots, their Mosin–Nagant rifles lying on a groundsheet by their feet. Before them, fashioned from children's wooden playing blocks, was a crude model of the Richmond Assizes and the surrounding area. The woods were represented by clumps of moss. 'This operation is called '*Fallow*',' said Zaitsev in heavily accented English.

'Yes, it's one of the varieties of deer you find in Richmond Park,' said Colonel Hodges, packing his pipe with tobacco. The CSS colonel wore battledress and a camouflaged smock, a holstered pistol on his webbing belt.

'Ah, but we're hunting wolves, not deer,' Zaitsev replied, pointing at the model of the courthouse. 'We shall use a tactic we call *Sixes*. Three teams, each consisting of a marksman and a spotter. Three rifles, six people. Our role is to triangulate and contain.'

'We have identified suitable counter-sniper positions,' Tarasov added, pointing at clumps of moss surrounding the complex. 'Comrade Captain Zaitsev and his spotter will take position in a hide we've established on the courthouse roof. I will be in the woodland to the east. The third team will cover the west.'

'Between us, we can cover all of the open ground across the site,' Zaitsev said, nodding. 'We will spot and report any movement, but we won't fire unless we can confirm the target *isn't* your man Nolan.'

'We have photographs of the target,' said Tarasov. 'We've familiarised ourselves with his features.'

Zaitsev pointed at the checkpoint at the end of the road, represented by a yellow playing brick. 'The prison van will stop here for exactly ninety seconds, giving any attacker an ideal opportunity to make their move,' he explained. 'Especially if they have a panzerfaust or an RPG.'

Ash Prasad stood to one side of the uniformed scrum with the Bureau 6 interrogator, Captain King. The political officer wore a cashmere overcoat and a maroon tie, his blue-black hair neatly parted. 'If the other side are armed with anti-tank rockets, Comrade Captain, won't it be too late to save Frayne? I'd rather like to see both him and Nolan charged and convicted.'

Zaitsev studied Prasad for a moment, as if the political officer was the source of a bad smell. 'Frayne won't be in the van, Comrade Prasad. A team of KGB officers smuggled him inside last night. He's safely locked up.'

Prasad nodded, but Fairburn could see his shoulders tense. 'I see. Who authorised that without my oversight?'

Sechkin, standing on the opposite side of the garage, held up a hand and smiled. 'I did, Comrade. Naturally, I asked Director Philby for his opinion.'

'I'm sure it's a masterful piece of deception,' Prasad replied silkily. 'Is General Teplyakov aware too?'

Sechkin wrinkled his nose. 'That's KGB business. Let me worry about Comrade Teplyakov, I have his full confidence.'

Prasad smiled. 'Very well. Please, Comrade Captain Zaitsev, do continue.'

Zaitsev turned to Tarasov. 'Raisa?'

Tarasov stepped closer to the model, casting a shadow over the courthouse. 'We have liaised with Comrade Colonel Hodges,' she said, nodding at the pipe-smoking CSS man. 'We'll communicate via radio-telephone and act as his eyes, ears and – if necessary – fire support.'

'I can't think of a more capable source of support, Comrade,' Hodges replied smoothly.

'I am grateful for your kind words,' said Tarasov. 'The CSS will hold their position until the enemy reveal themselves. With troops in vehicles, our observations *and* the benefit of radios we have the advantage.'

'I agree entirely,' Hodges replied, pointing at the diorama with his swagger stick. 'We've a concealed harbour area on Sawyer's Hill and the Isabella Plantation – two hundred men in total with motorcycles, Saracen armoured cars and utility vehicles. We'll flood the area in minutes. If that fails, I'd like to see this Nolan fellow outrun our dogs.' Smiling, Hodges plugged his pipe into his mouth and took a puff.

'Plus, we have a helicopter if we need it. *Vishenka na torte*,' said Tarasov. 'The cherry on the cake.'

'A question, if I may?' asked Prasad, stroking his chin with a leather-gloved hand. 'What happens if the assassin decides to wait until Frayne *leaves* the prison van, as he did with McGrouther? Won't he realise it's a trap and not take a shot?'

'Another excellent question, Comrade,' Raisa Tarasov replied, pointing to the blocks representing the cells on the eastern side of the complex. 'We've considered this possibility. There's a prisoner in the van of the same age, and of similar appearance, to Frayne. A decoy. The men driving the van are also convicts.'

'I take it these tethered goats were authorised by Director Philby too?'

'Yes,' said Sechkin, clearly enjoying Prasad's discomfort. 'I kept it secret for security reasons. Although the original idea was Captain Fairburn's.'

Finally, Fairburn spoke. 'I ran a similar operation in Hungary.'

'Did it work?' asked Prasad.

'Yes, Comrade Deputy Director.'

Prasad nodded, his eyes locked onto Fairburn's. 'And who is this prisoner? Has their transfer been authorised by our judicial authorities?'

Fairburn shrugged. 'They are KGB prisoners, held under Soviet jurisdiction. There's no need for any permissions on behalf of the British authorities.'

'I take it these men are aware they might take a bullet in the head?'

Sechkin smiled. 'This is an arrangement between them and the KGB, Comrade. Trust me, they're volunteers. The alternative, for them, is considerably worse.'

'Of course, Comrade Colonel Sechkin.' Prasad smiled. 'The KGB is famous for persuasion.'

Zaitsev sighed and clapped his hands. 'Right, there's nothing worse than a long briefing, is there? I'm sure we all need a cup of coffee, a smoke and a piss. Unless there are any more questions we should take our positions.'

'Already?' asked Prasad, checking his wristwatch.

Puffing out his ruddy cheeks, the sniper picked up his rifle. 'If *I* were looking to kill Frayne, Comrade, I'd already be out there. We have less than thirty-six hours before we bait the trap.'

'He's right,' said Hodges. 'Although I doubt British Action Front terrorists are as thorough as Captain Zaitsev. Nonetheless, my men will take their positions at dusk.'

'Then I'd better get back to Burgess House,' Prasad announced, nodding at his bodyguards. 'Our operations room will be open from 1800 hours. Captain Fairburn, you're more than welcome to join the Director and I if you wish?'

Fairburn shook his head. 'I'll stay with Colonel Sechkin and Sergeant Ross. This was my idea, it's only right I remain here.'

'You're quite sure?'

'Yes, Comrade Deputy Director.'

Prasad smiled. 'Of course. I would wish you luck, but given the impressive amount of preparation you've put in I'm sure it's entirely unnecessary.'

Sechkin chuckled. 'Really? Experience teaches me no plan survives first contact with the enemy.'

Zaitsev nodded. 'Indeed, Comrade Colonel. All the talking in the world is no substitute for getting on the ground. Rifle ready, eyes sharp!'

Prasad was already at the door, followed by Captain King and a troupe of CSS bodyguards. 'I'll let Director Philby know how swimmingly everything's going,' he said airily. Then he was gone.

'Jumped up prick,' Sechkin half-whispered. He turned to Tommy. 'Have you decided where you want to take up position?'

'In the courthouse,' Fairburn replied. 'I want to be near Frayne.'

'Why?'

Fairburn frowned. 'As you said, Nikolai, no plan survives first contact with the enemy.'

The sun was hidden by porridge-coloured clouds, the trees obscured by mist. Fairburn, standing in an office above the courthouse, checked his watch. He stood back from the yellowed net curtains. 'No movement. Why?'

'It's three hours before the prison van's due,' said a rumpled-looking Sid Ross. He wore a pair of binoculars around his neck, held a radio-telephone set and had a Kalashnikov rifle lying by his feet. He lit another cigarette. 'There ain't nothing like observation duty, is there?'

'You must be mad,' said Sechkin, accepting a roll-up cigarette from the CSS man. 'Surveillance is the dullest duty of all. I've always hated it.'

Ross wrinkled his boxer's nose. 'With the greatest respect, Comrade Colonel, you ain't lookin' at it the right way.'

'How so?'

'Bureau 5 pay a special allowance for overnight duty. That means I'm getting extra for just sitting on my arse, smoking and drinking tea.'

'You'll earn your pay when the BAF turn up,' Sechkin replied. Unshaven, dressed in a leather jacket and a roll-neck sweater, he looked more like a Baltic sea captain than a KGB Colonel.

'Nah, your snipers'll take care of 'em. I reckon the most I'll be doin' is photographing dead men and taking fingerprints. There's an allowance for that too. Five shillings.'

'You British are too generous,' said Sechkin. 'Service is its own reward.'

Ross chuckled and reached for his flask of tea. 'Did you see that, Tommy?' he guffawed. 'The Colonel even kept a straight face.'

Sechkin laughed. 'Is there vodka in that tea, Sid?'

'Only whiskey, Comrade.'

'That will do.'

Fairburn scanned the parkland beyond the window. Zaitsev had warned it would be possible for someone to crawl into position overnight without the snipers spotting them. The night before had been cloudy and moonless. 'When's the next update?'

Ross checked his watch. 'Twenty minutes. Can you see anything?'

'No, it's quiet.' Fairburn replied. They waited, comfortable in their silence, Ross and Zaitsev sipping their whiskey-laced tea.

Finally, they heard Raisa Tarasov's voice on the radio. 'Heron Two, all Heron call-signs,' she said in English. 'We have movement: Red Zero, ten yards east. Repeat – Red Zero, one-zero yards east. Confirm male target in trees. He's carrying binoculars.'

'Heron One, all received,' Zaitsev replied gruffly. 'You will cover Red Zero.'

'Affirmative,' said Tarasov. 'Yelena call-signs confirm?'

Ross keyed his handset. 'Received by Yelena One,' he replied.

'Received by Yelena Two,' said Colonel Hodges. The CSS officer and his men were half a kilometre away. Trained and equipped by the Soviets, the Special Assault Group enjoyed a reputation for discipline and aggression.

Leafing through his notebook, Fairburn found the diagram he'd sketched during the briefing. The snipers had divided the parkland into sectors using code-named vantage points; *Red Zero* was a gentle slope leading to the easternmost woods, marked by a fallen tree. Then, raising his binoculars, he saw something else – a flash of pale skin against the foliage? 'I think I see him,' he said.

'Has the fella got a book about the local wildlife, by any chance? Be a shame if they blew a birdwatcher's brains out, wouldn't it?' Ross chuckled. 'Don't ask me to write that one up.'

'Then the idiots shouldn't watch animals near a high-security facility,' Sechkin replied. He got up and joined Fairburn. 'What do you think, Tommy?'

'I'm not sure, Nikolai. We don't know if Nolan's a loner, or if he'll bring support.'

'It's a big area to cover,' Sechkin sighed. 'I'd bring as many people as I could. Maybe someone to create a distraction?'

'Well, he's gonna be a dead distraction soon, ain't he?' said Sid, snapping open his copy of *The Daily Mirror*. 'Relax. We've got another three hours before the prison wagon arrives.' They waited another ninety minutes, watching cars and military vehicles – both British and Russian – pass through the security checkpoint. A selected group of reporters, politicians and officials were invited to witness the proceedings against Francis Frayne, as well as the British Politburo's Chairman for Public Justice.

Finally, Heron One – Vasily Zaitsev – spoke. 'All call-signs, movement on Green Four. Subject in hooded jacket in trees. *On poshyol otlit'* – he's taking a piss.' Green Four was a track leading to the woods south of the courtroom, only two hundred yards from the main complex.

'All received,' Tarasov replied. 'We have two possible subjects, one east, one south.'

'Then I'd keep an eye on the westernmost side,' said Ross, ambling towards the window with his binoculars. 'If Nolan's brought company, it wouldn't surprise me if he copies Zaitsev's tactics. Three shooters, spread out to cover the plot.'

'That makes sense.' Sechkin nodded. 'Tommy?'

'Something's not right,' Fairburn replied. 'A sniper standing at the end of a lightly wooded track and pissing in plain sight? What if he *wants* to be seen?'

Ross squinted into his binoculars. 'Well, he's gone now. Besides, you need to meet some of the clowns who join the BAF nowadays. Thugs and petty criminals.'

Fairburn focussed his binoculars on Green Four. There was no movement, except for the breeze stirring the orange-brown leaves. 'Perhaps, but Nolan's a professional. Consider the possibility we're seeing what he wants us to see.'

'If you say so,' said Ross. 'We've got two hundred troops, the best snipers in the world and a dozen hungry Alsatians.'

Sechkin finished his tea and reached for the flask. 'I applaud your caution, Tommy, but I agree with Sid.'

'Yes, you're probably right,' Fairburn replied, but he still felt a tightness in his belly.

The radio-telephone rang. Ross answered, speaking in his plodding Russian. 'It's for you, Comrade Captain. Frankie Frayne's asked to speak with you.'

'Did he say why?'

'No.'

'Just go and see what the man wants, Tommy,' Sechkin grumbled. 'He might have something important to say. You're like a tiger pacing a cage up here.'

'He's down in the cells,' said Ross. 'Bortnik and Yakunin are with him.'

'Very well,' said Fairburn, heading for the door. 'I'll see you in a moment.'

'Good,' Ross replied. The CSS sergeant kept his binoculars trained on the parkland to the south, a cigarette glued to his lower lip, 'because it's catching.'

'What is?' Fairburn asked.

Ross frowned. 'Your bloody paranoia, that's what.'

Chapter 22

Dressed in a suit and tie, Fairburn blended in with the lawyers, legal clerks and reporters mingling in the atrium outside Court Number One. Someone with a keen eye might have noticed Fairburn's stubble, his semi-blackened eye and the bulge of the Makarov pistol under his jacket. He found the State Prosecutor's office and showed his identity card. 'Captain Fairburn, KGB. Frayne's asked to speak with me.'

'Another visitor? I'll check with my boss,' the guard replied, not quite rolling his eyes. Fairburn scowled, his patience wearing thin with the British mixture of boredom, insolence and officialdom. A Russian would be petrified by a KGB officer, but this fellow seemed indifferent. The guard picked up a telephone and made a call, taking time to exchange small talk about a football match.

'While I'm waiting, can I check the visitor's log?' Fairburn asked.

The guard nodded at the ledger on the desk in front of him. 'Help yourself.' Frayne had received visits from several legal representatives, his wife and a TUC official. He'd also been visited by a delegation from the CSS, identified only by their service numbers for security reasons. The number of visitors didn't strike him as unusual; even as prisoners, Politburo members enjoyed privileges denied to ordinary convicts. 'You can go through,' the guard said, pointing at a door. Opening it, Fairburn was met by two Ministry troops with machine pistols.

'Comrade Captain Fairburn?' asked one of the soldiers. 'May I see your identity card?'

Fairburn produced his *dokumenty*. 'I'm here on Colonel Sechkin's authority.'

'Please, follow us,' the guard replied. They trooped down a flight of steps and through a dimly lit tunnel, boots echoing on concrete. Finally, they reached a sturdy metal door.

'This is it?' asked Fairburn.

'Yes, Comrade. The other entrance is controlled by Colonel Sechkin's men for today's hearing,' one of the guards replied, pressing a buzzer. There was a metallic clank as a battery of locks disengaged. The door opened slowly on well-oiled hinges.

Beyond stood a hulking man in a dark suit. KGB Sergeant Bortnik. 'Comrade Captain,' he said in Russian. 'It's good to see you.'

'You too, Bortnik. Is Yakunin here?'

Eyeing the British guards with suspicion, Bortnik lowered his voice. 'Yes, now Frayne's visits are over for the day Yakunin is guarding his cell. We've got two more men from the embassy watching outside. Don't worry, Comrade, security's as tight as a fish's arse.'

'That's good to hear. The prisoner asked to speak with me?'

'I suppose he's looking to save his skin,' Bortnik shrugged, leading Fairburn to a cell.

'Has he had many visitors?'

'A few,' Bortnik replied. 'We let them get on with it, this place is totally locked down, Comrade Captain. The British guards are terrified of us – they'll keep their mouths shut about the prisoner.'

A pale-looking Frayne sat on a metal chair with his eyes closed. He wore a blue prison uniform, his hair neatly combed. Fairburn knew the rules on beating prisoners were similar to those of a tattoo parlour: no marks below the cuffs or above the collar.

'Prisoner, on your feet!' Sergeant Yakunin barked.

Frayne stood and smiled, his hands cuffed in front of him. 'Comrade Captain Fairburn, thanks for taking the time to see me,' he said. 'I genuinely appreciate it.'

Fairburn checked his wristwatch. 'You're welcome. How can I help?'

'What I have to say isn't for these gorillas,' he said, eyes darting around the room. 'I've important information about the Americans. I'm prepared to cooperate in return for a reduction in my sentence. I'm only prepared to speak to you, though.'

Fairburn shook his head. 'These men are trusted KGB officers.'

'Well, I don't trust them,' Frayne sniffed. 'I don't trust the KGB.'

'*I'm* a KGB officer, Frayne.'

Frayne winced. A traitor, he'd lost the right to be called *Comrade*. 'You're a British KGB officer,' he said.

'And that makes a difference?'

Frayne smiled. 'You know what? I think it might.'

'This is bullshit, Comrade,' said Yakunin. 'If he knew anything, he'd have said something by now.'

'Yes, the English interrogators did a proper job,' Bortnik added. 'For a change.'

'I spent the war in a concentration camp,' Frayne replied. 'The CSS are amateurs compared to the Gestapo.'

Fairburn pulled his pistol from his pocket and handed it to Bortnik. 'Bortnik, Yakunin, may I have a moment alone with the prisoner?'

'Of course, Comrade Captain,' Bortnik replied. 'Coffee? I know you like the decent stuff.'

'Yes please,' said Fairburn, pulling up a chair. 'Now, Frayne, go on.'

The former Deputy Chairman of the Communist Party of Great Britain smiled. 'I know you recently met with a British Action Front terrorist called Ronnie Todmorden. The man's a wanted SS Free Corps volunteer.'

'Dealing with criminals and terrorists is my job.'

'You paid Todmorden a lot of money, so I'm told. KGB money. It sounds like a bit of a mystery, don't you think? A bit… dodgy?'

'The only mystery, Mister Frayne, is who gave you this information. May I ask?'

Frayne put his hands on his lap, handcuffs shining dully in the gloom. 'You may, but I'm not telling. I'm also willing to bet your meeting with Ronnie Todmorden was off-the-books.'

'I'm a 10th Directorate officer. Virtually everything I do is off-the-books. In any case, the matter was authorised by Director Philby.'

'Philby?' Frayne laughed. 'Oh well, it's not like Kim Philby to drop his colleagues in the shit when it suits him, is it?'

'Director Philby is a socialist hero.'

'Philby sent his friends to the gallows. Guy Burgess, for example. Maybe Uncle Kim will tell you the story one day, if you ask nicely?'

'Unless you've significant information, anything else you say is chaff. You're facing a firing squad.'

Frayne licked his teeth. 'What time is it?' he asked.

'Just after 09.00.'

'Not long now.'

'Your hearing isn't until 11.45.'

Frayne nodded. 'I suppose time's relative at moments like this. I know what sort of dirt Todmorden's digging up. Dangerous stuff, Fairburn. You want to be careful, son. Some of it might even be true.'

'You're running out of time,' said Fairburn, getting to his feet.

Frayne closed his eyes, mouth clamped shut, fists balled on his knees. 'Is something wrong?' he asked. 'Frayne?'

Then, he heard men bellowing orders. The growl of vehicle engines. The staccato of automatic fire – submachine guns – followed by the whipcrack of rifles. An explosion. Possibly a grenade? Frayne opened his eyes. He was smiling. 'You've been played, Tommy boy. Welcome home.'

The cellblock door burst open. Bortnik staggered inside, hands clutching his belly, blood bubbling between his fingers. Fairburn dashed to the injured KGB officer. Ripping off his jacket, he pressed his hand over the bloody wounds in Bortnik's gut. 'What happened?'

Bortnik's eyes flickered. 'They got Yakunin,' he rasped, blood bubbling on his lips. Then, silence.

Fairburn began patting Bortnik down, looking for the pistol he'd handed him for safekeeping. A figure slid into the room, back to the wall, armed with a Kalashnikov. He wore the uniform of a Red Army major, but Fairburn recognised him immediately. 'Michael Nolan.'

Nolan raised the Kalashnikov and shot Francis Frayne, the closeness of the gunshot making Fairburn's ears buzz. The Deputy Chairman's head snapped back, a ragged void where his right eye and cheek had been. 'Come with me,' the gunman growled. It was a voice used to giving orders. Fairburn gazed for a second into the Kalashnikov's barrel, his hand still inside Bortnik's jacket. He could feel the edge of his pistol's smooth wooden grips. As if reading his mind, Nolan stepped towards him, his jackboots scraping on concrete. 'You won't make it, Fairburn. You're welcome to try, though.'

'You can't get away,' Fairburn shrugged. 'It's impossible.'

Nolan nodded towards the cell block door. 'I've heard that one before, and here I am. There's an army staff car outside. Get in the back and keep your head down.'

'No,' Fairburn replied, standing his ground.

'Silly boy,' Nolan sighed, reversing his Kalashnikov and smashing the butt into Fairburn's face. The last thing the young KGB officer remembered was collapsing on top of Bortnik's body.

Chapter 23

Fairburn stirred, the salt-and-iron tang of blood on his tongue, his face aching like he'd been kicked by a horse. 'Fuck this for a laugh,' said the pasty-faced man sitting next to him. He wore Red Army uniform like Nolan, but with an infantry *Starshina's* – a sergeant-major's – crimson shoulder boards.

'Shut your mouth, Tony,' said Nolan, 'or I'll kick you out of the fucking car.'

Fairburn twisted in his seat to watch the courthouse burning behind them. His eye was caught by movement to his left – a field car, nosing from the treeline like a curious forest creature. It was followed by a skirmish line of CSS troops. 'It's Eddie,' said Tony, nodding at a figure lumbering across the parkland. 'Silly bastard.'

'He's following orders,' said Nolan, accelerating towards the checkpoint at the end of the drive. The man called Eddie wore a camouflaged outfit covered in foliage and netting. He paused to raise a rocket to his shoulder and fired, sending out a plume of orange flame. The GAZ field car rocked on its axles, engulfed in blue-grey smoke. Then the RPG gunner spun as a sniper's bullet took him in the heart, his body sinking into the bracken.

'Why ain't those snipers firing at us?' asked Tony, hunkering down in the back seat.

'Because we're in a Russian staff car, you mug,' Nolan replied. 'Just shut up and watch the prisoner.' Dead guards lay scattered around the checkpoint. The guard hut was full of bullet holes, a platoon of CSS troops lying on their bellies in a nearby culvert. Nolan drove by, picking up speed and waving urgently as he passed the CSS men. Machine-gun fire whistled from the trees beyond, a bullet whining as it struck the staff car's boot.

'Shit,' Tony hollered, eyes wide. 'That was our lads! Silly fuckers'll kill us too if they ain't careful.'

Nolan drove to the edge of the park, the gates guarded by three uniformed CSS men sitting in a GAZ. 'Get ready,' said Nolan, slowing the staff car to a crawl. 'Only shoot if I do.'

'Okay,' said Tony, hands gripping the MP40 on his lap.

Nolan rolled down his window. 'Get out of the fucking way,' he bawled at the CSS men in fluent Russian. 'I've got an important casualty onboard. A wounded KGB officer.'

'Sir, we still have to check your *dokumenty*,' a corporal replied in the same language.

'Listen to me, *debil-blya* – halfwit,' Nolan roared, flashing an identity card. 'Did you hear me? I've got a casualty in the back. He's bleeding to death. Now get out of the way or I'll shoot the fucking lot of you.'

'What did you say?' said the corporal, face flushed. Raising his Sten gun, he took a step towards the car.

'Leave it, Matthews,' said a moustachioed sergeant, hobnailed boots crashing on gravel as he marched towards the car. 'Go through, Comrade Major,' he said icily, 'but I've got your vehicle registration. This ain't conduct becoming a Soviet army officer. I'll be taking this further.'

'Fuck you,' Nolan said in Russian-accented English. It was

excellently done – Fairburn would have sworn he was a native speaker –
'Yellow bastards, the lot of you. Hiding by a gate while your comrades
fight.' Scowling, he drove away.

'I can't believe you just did that,' said Tony, pale-faced. 'You've
got some balls.'

'Just keep your eyes on the prisoner,' Nolan snapped.

'He's awake,' said Tony, jabbing the MP40s muzzle into Fairburn's
ribs. 'Ain't you, mate?'

'Then cuff him,' said Nolan, his dead-man's eyes fixed on the road.
'They said you knew what you were doing.'

'I do,' Tony replied, his voice rising an octave, 'just not this kind
of stuff.' Resting the MP40 on his lap, he pulled a pair of handcuffs
from his pocket and passed them to Fairburn. 'Put these on, eh?' he
said, not unpleasantly.

Fairburn glanced at Tony's machine pistol, realising he'd be unable
to grab and reverse the weapon in the car's cramped interior. They were
also driving too fast for him to leap out. Although he'd completed
parachute training, it assumed impact on soft ground, not a metalled
road. And, he realised, Nolan scared him. 'Of course,' said Fairburn
calmly, ratcheting the first cuff to his wrist, then the second. If the
plan was to kill him, he'd already be dead; Frayne had lured him to
the cells to be captured. His best course of action was to be compliant,
then identify a moment for action.

'Where are we now?' Tony asked.

'Don't matter,' said Nolan, driving through a village on a tree-lined
stretch of the Thames. 'Just keep your eyes on the prisoner.'

'I won't let you down, honest,' Tony replied, wrinkling his nose.
Tony was in his mid-twenties, moon-faced and pencil-necked. Fairburn
thought any operation that teamed a professional like Nolan with

such an oaf must have been hastily prepared. Nonetheless, it was clear CSS had a leak. A serious one.

'Tony, you'll end up in front of a firing squad. You do realise that?,' said Fairburn calmly.

'Now why say something like that?' Tony replied, looking hurt.

'He's KGB. He's playing mind games,' said Nolan, driving across a bridge. 'Fairburn, shut your mouth.'

'Tony, there's still a chance,' Fairburn continued, locking eyes with Nolan in the rear-view mirror. 'Shoot Nolan and let me go. You'll be quite safe, you have my word. In fact, you'll be rewarded.'

Nolan smiled back. There was something almost human in the smile. Not quite admiration. Amusement, perhaps? 'Gag him, Tony.'

'Yes, Mick,' said Tony, pulling a dirty handkerchief from his pocket and stuffing it into Fairburn's mouth.

Nolan nodded. 'Now if the fucker speaks again, shoot him in the kneecap. Got it?'

Tony smiled, like a child promised a bag of sweets. He nudged the MP40 into Fairburn's leg. 'You got it, Mick!'

Nolan drove to a warehouse. Inside was a pantechnicon, rear doors open with a ramp leading inside the cavernous vehicle. Gently revving the engine, Nolan edged the staff car inside. Two men in brown overalls appeared and closed the doors. 'Right,' said Nolan, turning in his seat. 'Tony, ungag him.'

Tony obeyed and Fairburn took in a gasp of stale, dusty air. His nose was swollen, making it difficult to breathe. 'Where are we going?'

Nolan got out of the car and began stripping off his uniform. 'Tony,' he said, ignoring Fairburn's question, 'fetch the doctor.'

'Yes, Mick,' said Tony, getting out of the car.

Shortly afterwards a small chubby man wearing a balaclava appeared. He pulled a metal case from his bag containing a large-bore hypodermic needle. 'How long do you want him out for?' he asked.

'Twelve hours,' Nolan replied. 'I need him out like a light, understand?'

The masked man jabbed the needle into Fairburn's upper arm, straight through the sleeve of his jacket. 'There you go,' he said. 'This stuff works on horses, laddie. I'm sure it'll work on you.'

Nolan pulled on a pair of workman's overalls. 'Sweet-fucking-dreams, Comrade,' he said.

Fairburn woke, his face throbbing. Still handcuffed, he lay in a bed with fresh white sheets, the semi-darkened room smelling of mothballs. He sat up, checking for exits. There was only a single window – shuttered and barred – and a stout wooden door. On the nightstand next to him was a glass of water. After taking a gulp, he swung his legs off the bed and took a moment to listen. *Seagulls. No traffic.*

He found a mirror and examined his injuries. His nose had been washed and treated with iodine, a plaster placed carefully across the wound. Then he explored the room, his feet chilly on bare wooden floorboards. Someone had dressed him in a clean pair of pyjamas and there was no trace of his old clothes. Finally, he tried the door handle. As he expected, it was locked. Putting his shoulder to the door and pushing it, he found no give. Although Fairburn was trained not to make assumptions, he suspected Nolan would have ensured the place was escape-proof. Everything else he'd planned was professional, why would this be any different? He returned to bed, finished the glass of water, and waited.

Finally the door opened and two tough-looking men appeared. 'Get up,' said the first. 'Come with us and keep quiet. Do anything stupid and we'll give you a kicking. Understand?' Fairburn nodded. They led the KGB officer down a flight of stairs and into a hallway decorated with stuffed animal heads and hunting trophies. The floors were well polished, a crystal chandelier hanging from the ceiling. It felt like one of the stuffy British clubs in Cairo he used to frequent.

Nolan stood in the hallway, hands on hips. 'I'm going to ask that you behave yourself. Trust me, there's nowhere to run.'

'Very well,' Fairburn replied. 'In which case, could you remove my handcuffs? And get me some proper clothes?'

Nolan nodded. 'I don't see why not. Harry, go and fetch Mister Fairburn some clobber.'

'Yes, Mick,' one of the men replied, heading back up the stairs. He returned with a pair of slacks, a shirt and a dark knitted sweater. Fairburn's own shoes and a clean pair of socks lay on top.

Nolan unlocked Fairburn's handcuffs and put them in his pocket. 'Now get dressed,' he ordered. When Fairburn was done, he nodded and opened a door. 'There's someone waiting to see you.'

Chapter 24

'Good afternoon, Mister Fairburn,' said the woman sitting by a fireplace, logs smouldering orange in the grate. Her accent was that of the English upper-middle class, clipped and precise. Dark-haired and pale-skinned, she wore a tweed skirt and a pink woollen twinset. 'Please, take a seat.'

'Thank you,' Fairburn replied. 'It was a pleasant surprise to wake up in a clean bed.'

'You're welcome. I must say, you're less hot-headed than your file suggests. I imagined there would've been at least one escape attempt by now. Perhaps a gunshot or two?'

'My file?'

The woman smiled. 'Of course we have a file. It describes a feral orphan groomed into a monstrous killer. You're the *Butcher of Budapest*, aren't you?'

'The Hungarians gave as good as they got.' Fairburn replied quietly. 'I lost many comrades there. May I ask who you are?'

'They were defending their country. You were invading it.'

'I asked who you were.'

'Where are my manners? Please, call me Katherine.'

Fairburn warmed his hands by the fire. 'Well, Katherine, I'll admit your attack on the Richmond Assizes was impressive. It must have taken a lot of planning at very short notice.'

'You see, Mick?' Katherine said to Nolan, who stood guard

by the door. 'He's trying to elicit information already. A true professional.'

Nolan's lip twitched. Not quite a sneer. 'He weren't too professional when I smacked him in the mug with my rifle butt. He went down like a sack of shit.'

'You're a force of nature, Mick,' Katherine chuckled, turning to Fairburn. 'May I call you Tommy?'

'Of course.' Katherine got up and walked across the room to a shuttered window. The tasteful décor, Turkish rugs and book-lined walls reminded Fairburn of McGrouther's Wiltshire dacha. She opened the shutters, revealing a view across a choppy sea. The room was filled with light, pearlescent grey, bright enough to make him squint. 'Where are we?' Fairburn asked.

'Somewhere quiet,' she replied. 'It's amazing how little of England the Russians have explored, given the size of their country compared to ours. They're an incurious bunch.'

Fairburn stood and joined Katherine by the window, studying the lonely coastline. 'I imagine this is a good place for a submarine to launch a dinghy.'

Katherine, her shoulder nearly touching Fairburn's, smiled. 'Perhaps. Now, let's talk, shall we?'

Nolan lay an envelope on a table and tapped it with his finger. 'You asked for this?'

Katherine smiled. 'Yes. It's for you, Tommy.'

'D'you want me to keep an eye on him?' said Nolan.

'I'm sure we'll be fine, Mick.'

Nolan folded his arms. 'If you play up, Fairburn, just know the first people I'll visit are Sechkin and his wife. I know they're like family to you.'

'There's no need for threats, Mister Nolan.'

When Nolan had gone, Katherine shook her head. 'He's a troubled soul, that one. War does that to people, doesn't it?'

'Does what?'

Katherine smiled sadly. 'Hardens their hearts.'

'From what I've seen of his record, Nolan's always enjoyed violence.'

'Violent men are a necessity in our line of work.'

'I agree, but I never knew Nolan had become a fascist,' Fairburn continued. He glanced at the envelope on the table. 'You *are* fascists?'

Katherine pulled a face. 'Absolutely not. Occasionally we're compelled to do business with the British Action Front, but needs must.'

'May I ask where you spent the war? Where was your heart hardened?'

Opening the envelope, Katherine pulled out a piece of paper. 'My family were from Hampshire. Monarchists. We escaped in 1940. I spent the war in America and Canada.'

'And then?'

'Let's talk about something else,' said Katherine, passing the envelope to Fairburn. 'We found this when we put your file together. I suspected it might come in useful.'

'We? You mean the CIA?'

A smile. A gently raised eyebrow. 'Perhaps. It's a complicated arrangement between the British government in exile and our American friends.'

Fairburn opened the envelope and took out a piece of paper. It was a facsimile of an official report, written in Russian:

* * *

Monday 7th November 1950

General Labour Facility 34, Magadan Oblast (Kolyma)

NOTIFICATION of FATALITY

A foreign guest worker died on 30/10/1950 from influenza. He was Q357 MALCOLM ARTHUR FAIRBURN (b. 28/04/1908), a British national who arrived at the facility in January 1948. No next of kin details are held in our records. Therefore, he was buried locally in the communal cemetery. Please forward to the British Labour Service Liaison Office.

Signed,

Capt. K.L. Ivanov MGB

'*Guest* worker,' said Katherine, shaking her head. 'You probably know about Kolyma. Labour Facility 34 is part of the Soviet gulag system.'

Fairburn re-read the note. 'How do I know this isn't faked?'

'We have sources inside the Kremlin, just as the KGB have spies inside our agencies. We've been investigating you for some time. Naturally, we looked into your family circumstances.'

'This is your idea of leverage?' asked Fairburn. 'You've targeted me for recruitment?'

A smile. 'Oh, absolutely.'

'I'm a loyal KGB officer with an exemplary service record. I display none of the vulnerabilities one might look for in a traitor.'

'You're already a traitor, Tommy,' Katherine replied. 'You're British, aren't you? You betrayed your country when you chose to join the KGB.'

'I'm a Socialist. We're internationalists.'

Katherine chuckled. 'I see. That's why you wear a Russian uniform?

187

It's also why the Soviet army patrols London's streets and why British *slaves* die in Russian labour camps? Is it also why the Kremlin issues orders to the British Politburo?'

Fairburn slammed a fist on the table. 'That's propaganda. The situation is more nuanced.'

'You see? You even talk like a Soviet,' Katherine replied, reaching for the packet of Lucky Strikes lying on the table. 'Didn't you learn anything in Cairo?'

'I learned how my country collaborated with the Nazis. Moseley and the King supported Hitler when they should have fought against him. That's all I need to know.'

Katherine shook her head. 'No, the Nazis did to the British what the Soviets are doing to them now. Occupying them. Exploiting them. For what it's worth, I'm glad Moseley and the King died horribly. They were a bloody disgrace.'

'I suppose you'd return to the old ways? The class system? Monarchy?'

Katherine pursed her lips. 'You can't undo the past. Maybe the British people would never accept the Queen, not after the way Edward conducted himself. On the other hand, maybe they would – she's a remarkable young woman. Her return, if it ever happens, should be their choice. None of them chose a communist politburo, after all.'

'Whatever it is you're offering, I refuse,' said Fairburn. He'd read the note in front of him six times now. The words hadn't changed.

'The Nazis murdered your mother. The Russians worked your father, a loyal communist, to death. The Soviet NKVD betrayed them both. Don't you see? Both sides are mirror images of the other.'

'I won't work for the Americans. I will not betray the Workers.'

The door opened. Quietly, on well-oiled hinges. 'Jesus Christ, you sound like a spoilt brat. Get a grip, Fairburn,' said a familiar voice.

Fairburn turned around. 'You?'

'Yes,' said Ashim Prasad, Chief Political Officer of the CSS. 'Now, let's take the sea air, shall we? It might clear some of the cotton wool out of your bloody head.'

Chapter 25

Seagulls hung on the wind, squawking angrily. 'I'll never get used to the British weather,' said Prasad, pulling up his collar. 'Give me Capetown any day of the week.'

'I couldn't stand the heat in Egypt and Libya,' Fairburn replied.

'Massachusetts has the best of both worlds,' said Katherine, skimming a stone into the sea. 'I know Eliza Crewe's happy there.'

Fairburn stopped. 'Prasad, how long have you been…'

'I was recruited by the American OSS in 1944,' he replied, watching foamy waves inch up the beach.

Fairburn stepped back from the seawater. 'Why?'

'The Soviets suspected someone in my network of spying. He was a friend of sorts. The NKVD ordered me to kill him.'

'Did you?'

'Yes.'

'Was your friend a spy?' asked Fairburn.

'I very much doubt it, although his drunkenness and sexual proclivities made him vulnerable to blackmail. After I shot him I didn't feel remotely guilty. In fact, it opened my eyes.'

'To what?'

'I usually trade information,' Prasad replied. 'A secret for a secret. But today's a day for candour, don't you think?'

Katherine laughed, the wind teasing a strand of hair free of its bun. 'Candour? You're funny, Ash.'

Prasad shrugged. 'Even I'm capable of indulging myself with the occasional moment of truth.'

Tommy watched a seagull peck at the sand. 'Which is? What did you open your eyes to.'

'I realised I was on the wrong side. The order to kill was sloppy and ill-considered. It put me at risk.'

'This made you betray the Soviet Union? The requirement to follow orders?'

Prasad continued strolling along the beach. 'Betray is such an empty word, isn't it? Especially among spies. Besides, I'm good at what I do.'

'You want to be the best traitor? Like Philby?' asked Fairburn.

Prasad shook his head. 'I plan on being significantly better. Kim's become nothing but a glorified policeman. The Soviets have his precious Bureau 6 on a short leash.'

'Philby's a true believer,' said Katherine.

Prasad frowned. 'There's nothing worse than a believer, is there?'

Fairburn watched Nolan, standing just out of earshot. The assassin carried a pistol, aimed squarely at Fairburn's chest. Fairburn shook his head. 'Do you believe in anything, Mister Prasad?'

Prasad paused. 'Yes, I suppose I do – the freedom not to believe in anything, if one so chooses. The freedom not to be told what to do, or to think. And do you know the most important of all?'

'Do tell,' said Fairburn acidly.

'The freedom not to have your intelligence insulted. It's the original sin of totalitarianism, Tommy, the lies they make you tell every day. We're all complicit, aren't we? *There are no shortages. The industrial strategy's a success. The people are happy and well fed. The justice system isn't rigged to provide slave labourers for Russia.*'

'Don't you have a Party-approved answer, Tommy?' asked Katherine with faux innocence.

A seagull locked eyes with Fairburn, squawked, and flew away. 'Whatever the answer is, it isn't America,' he replied testily, kicking the sand from his shoes.

'Who said it was? You're a talented young man, Tommy,' said Katherine, resting a hand on his shoulder. 'You're resourceful and intelligent. Ask yourself if serving Moscow is the best use of your gifts. We all know they'll start a war eventually. A war with hydrogen bombs and strategic rockets. A war nobody could ever hope to win.'

Prasad nodded, his dark eyes shining. 'All Russia sees are enemies. You could put them on Mars and they'd accuse Saturn of aggression.'

'We aren't the aggressors,' said Fairburn. 'The Americans are.'

Prasad gave Fairburn a sour look. 'I think I've a marginally better grasp of geopolitics than someone indoctrinated in the KGB's world-view. The Kremlin won't settle for simply conquering Europe. As for the Irish question? It's only a matter of time before Khrushchev goes eye to eye with the Americans over that one.'

'I've seen the B-52 bases in Egypt, Prasad. They didn't look very peaceful to me.'

Katherine went to speak, but Prasad held up his hand. 'We're going around in circles. I think we'll leave Tommy for a while. He has much to consider.'

'Such as?' asked Fairburn.

Prasad's tone was friendly. 'Well, the photographs I have of you leaving Ronnie Todmorden's house. My watchers took them, of course. Or the post office telephone records you pulled without authority? Todmorden's linked to the BAF terrorists who attacked the Richmond

Assizes, by the way. I wonder what dear old Kim will make of it? Or Nikolai Sechkin when he's returned to Moscow in disgrace?'

'Is Aunt Maggie involved? Did you arrange for her to contact me?'

A tight smile. 'You know it's bad form to discuss sources, Tommy. Although you found Todmorden quicker than I thought you would. Bravo.'

'I'll tell Philby the truth. Teplyakov too. You have more to explain than me.'

Prasad stepped back from the wave creeping up the beach, the wind tousling his hair. 'You really think they'll believe you? You're a confused young man with mixed loyalties, shocked by the terrible truth behind the death of your parents. You're emotionally scarred by the horrors of irregular warfare in Poland and Hungary. It's a script that writes itself, I'm afraid. Now, you've only a few hours to contemplate my offer.'

Katherine turned to Nolan. 'Would you escort Mister Fairburn back to the house, Mick? Get Mrs Hall to fix him breakfast.'

'Will do,' Nolan replied, putting a hand on Tommy's shoulder. 'Come on, son. You look like you could do with some grub.' They trudged back to the house; Prasad walked towards a Rover saloon parked on a road leading to the beach. The political officer got in the back and the car drove away. Nothing in Fairburn's training, he realised, had prepared him for a situation like this. Physical injuries and hardship could be endured, but a rolling barrage of revelations, offers and threats? Then he remembered General Teplyakov's dead-man's eyes. Yes, he'd enjoy humiliating Nikolai. Fairburn clenched his fists. Prasad had made a fool of him. Made him look weak. Naive. *Outplayed.* That hurt most of all. Prasad was cleverer than him, just as Nolan was more ruthless.

Perhaps the only answer was to play a similar game.

* * *

193

A blousy woman who introduced herself as Mrs Hall plonked a plate of bacon and eggs in front of Fairburn. She wore a knitted beret and, he suspected, was drunk. 'There you go,' she said, sweeping him with kohl-heavy eyes. 'I can't say I've ever cooked breakfast for a KGB pig.'

'Now then Patsy, mind your manners,' said Nolan.

'Fuck off, Mick,' she said, sashaying unsteadily away.

'Writers,' Nolan grumbled. 'The place is full of 'em. Always pissed, no self-discipline and they talk shit all day.'

Fairburn ate hungrily. The eggs were fresh and the bacon thick cut. 'I suppose they're all waiting to defect to America like Eliza Crewe?'

'Eventually,' Nolan replied. 'This is a safe house. Although it feels like a bloody lunatic asylum most of the time.'

'Why put all this effort into rescuing writers? Don't the Americans have enough of their own?'

Nolan slurped from a cup of tea, his brow furrowed. 'It's all about culture, innit? Katherine says culture's important. She says the Reds worked that out long before the Yanks did, but they're catching up now.'

'Then why are you here? You're hardly an artist.'

'I want to go to America,' Nolan replied, getting up from the table. 'I've had enough of this bloody country. It's proper fucked and I reckon my luck's running out. You can only pull so many stunts like Richmond and hope to get away with it.'

'And what will you do there?'

Nolan shrugged. 'Kill people for the Yanks I suppose. I know what I am.'

Mrs Hall reappeared with a pot of tea. 'You finished, KGB man?'

Fairburn mopped up the last of his egg with a piece of toast. 'Is there any more bread, please? And perhaps some jam?'

'You're very polite, for a pig.'

'Names don't trouble me, Mrs Hall. An empty stomach does,' Fairburn replied, nodding at someone entering the room. It was a dishevelled-looking man, unshaven and bleary, dressed in corduroy slacks and a moth-eaten cardigan.

'Good morning,' he said brightly, taking a seat at the dining table and offering his hand. 'I'm Brian Bliss. It's smashing to meet you.'

'Thomas Fairburn,' Fairburn replied, accepting the handshake.

'Ah, you must be the KGB chap Katherine mentioned,' said Bliss. 'Funny old world, eh? You wouldn't have any cigarettes by any chance, would you?'

'I don't smoke.'

'Very sensible. Bloody terrible habit,' Bliss replied, smiling as Mrs Hall brought him a plate of kippers. 'Ah, excellent. Thank you, Mrs Hall.'

'Have one of mine, Brian,' she replied, tapping a Capstan free of its pack. She took a slice of bread from her apron and tossed it on Fairburn's plate. When she'd gone, Bliss began eating.

'Are you a writer too, Mister Bliss?' asked Fairburn, taking the bread and wiping his plate clean.

'I was a writer, yes.'

'*Was?*'

Bliss looked up from his plate. 'Someone reported me to the State Committee for Publishing after I submitted my last book. They put me on a blacklist. I was even interviewed by the CSS. Can you imagine?'

'What did you write?'

'My novel was about an expedition to Mars, but the censors disap-proved. You see, *the protagonist failed to display adequate socialist vigour in his leadership of the space mission. His methods suggested bourgeois attitudes at odds with the communal values of the British people. The prose is assaultive and harmful in its depiction of the protagonist's approach to authority.'*

Fairburn took a sip of his tea. 'Were they correct?'

Bliss chuckled. 'I write escapist stories about spaceships and little green men, dear boy. I'm afraid the political dimension went straight over my head.'

'There's a political dimension to everything, Comrade.'

'Apparently so. It's a terrible bloody shame if you ask me.'

'And now you're here.'

'Yes,' said Bliss cheerily, taking a puff of his cigarette. 'I'm told Americans love science fiction. I'm quite sure I'll get published over there.'

'How many other writers are here?'

Bliss finished his kippers and reached for the teapot. 'I'm not sure that's the sort of thing I should be discussing with you. No offence, of course.'

'None taken. May I ask something else?'

'Depends what it is, I suppose.'

'Do you know Eliza Crewe?'

Bliss scratched his nose as he considered the question. 'Yes, we were acquaintances. Via a mutual friend, actually.'

'Did she persuade you to come here?'

Bliss' laugh was a throaty cackle. 'Persuade? Wild horses wouldn't have stopped me from coming, dear boy. Yes, Eliza heard I'd been blacklisted. She takes an active interest in such things.'

'And may I ask who the mutual friend was?'

'Why?'

Fairburn tilted his head and smiled, as he'd been taught in his elicitation class. *One is able to establish trust through non-verbal*

196

communication and tone of voice. 'I'm here because I've been asked to help Katherine.'

'And will you?'

'I'm considering it, but I'm trying to find out a little more about the situation before I decide. She didn't say I wasn't allowed to speak to the other guests.'

That was when Katherine appeared, her hair windblown and beaded with seawater. 'Hello Brian, how are you this morning?'

Bliss looked nervous. 'Oh, hello Katherine…'

'It's fine, Brian. Our guest is curious, which is to be expected. Isn't it, Tommy?'

'I suppose so.'

'Then come with me.'

Chapter 26

'Do you recognise this man?' asked Katherine, passing Fairburn a photograph of a young RAF officer. He looked uncomfortable in his uniform, tie twisted and eyes beady behind thick-lensed spectacles. 'He's the mutual friend Brian Bliss mentioned.'

Fairburn was good with faces. He remembered the photo he'd found tucked inside the novel seized from McGrouther's bathroom. Three students, standing by a river. 'Yes, wasn't he at Cambridge with Eliza Crewe and William McGrouther?'

Katherine nodded. 'Yes. His name's Andrew Fisk, known to his friends as Sandy. He was awarded a first-class degree from the Cavendish Laboratory at Cambridge. Afterwards, he was invited to study astrophysics at University College London. He spent the war working on advanced ground-to-air radar systems for the Luftwaffe. We believe he was also involved in elements of the V2 and V3 rocket projects.'

'Apart from Cambridge, what's the link to Crewe?'

'Eliza Crewe considers Sandy her muse, I think. He writes poetry, apparently. Eliza told me Sandy was one of the gentlest, purest souls she'd ever met. I think their relationship was physically platonic but emotionally intense.'

'Crewe was a science student at Cambridge for a term. Then she switched to English. That's how she met Fisk, I take it?'

'Yes. Well remembered, Tommy.'

Fairburn frowned. Katherine's approval was patronising. 'Fisk's a scientist. I take it he's of intelligence value?'

'You know, I'm beginning to wonder if you do this sort of thing for a living?' Katherine smiled, crossing one leg over the other. 'Yes, we want him on a submarine to America as soon as possible.'

'Has anyone asked Fisk if he wants to leave?'

'Eliza did a deal with the Americans. She'd persuade Fisk to defect, but in return the CIA would smuggle as many artists out of the country as they could.'

'And the Americans agreed?'

'Of course. Setting up this network was a small price to pay for what's inside Sandy Fisk's head.'

Fairburn suddenly realised Katherine's work wasn't about culture. It was about technology. 'How do I fit in?'

'Your friend Colonel Sechkin is responsible for all counterintelligence concerning the programme Fisk's working on. Operation *Zapad*.'

'The Russian for *West*. Is that significant?' Fairburn remembered Nikolai mentioning a project in East Anglia and how valuable Britain's scientists were.

'That's the direction where the USSR's main enemy is, right?' Katherine's accent, for a moment, sounded a little American. 'It's where they point their missiles.'

'And you've a plan to exfiltrate Fisk?'

Katherine lit a cigarette. 'Yes, it's cunning. I think you'll like it. We decided to recruit a KGB special operations officer who enjoys unique access to Nikolai Sechkin. Then, task him with springing Sandy Fisk.'

Fairburn smiled politely. 'Flattering, but I think you overestimate my influence.'

'You're a captain of the 10th Directorate of the KGB. A Spartan.

Besides, Fisk's already agreed to defect. This isn't a kidnap, it's an escort mission. All you need to do is bring him in.'

Fairburn shook his head. 'I don't even know where Fisk's being kept.'

'We'll provide the details,' Katherine replied, glancing at her wristwatch. 'In any case, we need him here by next Thursday.'

'Why?'

'Something to do with tides, apparently. Submariners are obsessed with them.'

Fairburn went to the fire and warmed his hands. 'Say I agree to help? What happens afterwards?'

'We hoped you'll continue to work for us,' said Katherine. 'You'd be part of Ash Prasad's network. Then, eventually, you'd come to America. Or Spain, we've excellent contacts there. You're a single man, Tommy. No commitments. No family. Why wouldn't you?'

'Because you're asking me to betray everything I believe in.'

Katherine reached across and touched Fairburn's hand. 'I'm asking you to betray the people who killed your parents. The people who keep your countrymen hungry.'

'We've been through this before, Katherine.'

'Besides, you don't have a choice.'

'How so?'

'Without our help, you'll be tarnished. The operation at Richmond Assizes was a disaster. Afterwards, you mysteriously disappear after meeting a BAF terrorist in suspicious circumstances? Ash wasn't joking, Tommy. He'll give you to Teplyakov and wash his hands of you. I know he'd prefer not to.'

Fairburn's stomach knotted. Katherine was right. If he was lucky, the KGB would shunt him off to a dead-end job. The alternative was the gulag, or worse. Sechkin would suffer a similar fate. 'If I agree, Prasad will smooth my way back into favour?'

'Of course. He holds you in high regard. You'd carry on with your career and, occasionally, we'd ask a small favour.'

Fairburn looked out of the window, across the choppy sea. 'And if I don't agree?'

'That's not my call,' Katherine replied. 'It depends on the CIA. I suspect it might involve you, Nolan and a walk in the woods.'

'And only Nolan will come back?'

'You're the KGB officer. What do you think?'

Fairburn felt a flush of anger. He was used to being the one making threats. 'You must know I could agree to work for you, then tell Philby that Prasad's a traitor.'

'Of course you could, although you'd be dead shortly afterwards. So would Sechkin and his wife. The CIA has a long memory, absolutely no morals and a limitless supply of dollars.'

Fairburn listened to the crackling logs in the fire. To the caw of seagulls beyond the window. To a cough from outside the door, where armed men stood guard. 'What now?'

'I take it that's a yes?'

'I suspect we'll both end up regretting it.'

Katherine stood up and smiled. 'Regrets? Those are something of a luxury in our line of work, Tommy. Wouldn't you agree?'

Nolan drove along a track, rutted and muddy. 'Where are we?' asked Fairburn.

'North Devon,' Nolan grumbled. 'It's the arse-end of nowhere, the Russians leave the place alone. Can't say I blame 'em.'

'Yes,' said Prasad, fiddling with his silk scarf, 'they've a garrison at Exeter and a naval base at Plymouth. Apart from that, they leave Devon for the Militia to deal with.'

'And what now?' asked Fairburn, looking for any landmarks that might be useful later. All he could see were fields dotted with under-nourished-looking cows.

'Your escape must look convincing,' said Prasad. 'You have to bounce back from this disaster with your reputation intact. Enhanced, even.'

'If the boy's got it in him,' said Nolan.

Fairburn sighed. 'What do you want me to do?'

Nolan stopped outside an old farmhouse. Prasad pointed at the front door. 'There are three BAF men inside. They've been told we're bringing you for interrogation before we kill you. As you can imagine, they're quite excited at the prospect.'

'I don't understand.'

Nolan guffawed. 'You're gonna kill *them*, Tommy. It'll make your escape look real. Then steal their car. Just follow the road signs to Barnstaple, it ain't too far away.'

'There's a militia barracks on the main road into town,' said Prasad, pulling a Walther PPK from his pocket and pressing it into Fairburn's hand. 'Tell them you were held hostage, but managed to escape. The Militia will call the CSS, they'll pick you up and arrange for transport back to Burgess House. I'll lead your debriefing, of course. You'll be fine.'

'You're letting me kill three of your men?' asked Fairburn, taking the pistol and checking the action.

'They're not *our* men,' Prasad replied. 'The BAF are allies of convenience. In any case, we've little time for fascists either.'

'They're a bunch of arseholes,' Nolan added. 'You'll be doing the country a favour.'

'In any case, the BAF hierarchy will keep their mouths shut. They rely on us for funding,' Prasad explained, opening the car door. 'Now, off you go. Your identity card's inside the farmhouse, along with your wallet.'

Fairburn got out of the car. The air was cold and smelled of dung. 'I just kill them?'

'I thought you said he was clever, Mister Prasad,' Nolan sighed. 'Yes, you just fucking kill them. Then nick their car. One more thing, though.'

'What?'

Nolan punched Fairburn in the eye. 'There you go. Along with your busted nose, it'll look like you were properly turned over.'

'Yes, very convincing,' Prasad chuckled from the back of the car. 'You've got Fisk's details?'

'Yes,' Tommy replied.

'Then toddle along now. I've got a plane to catch if I'm going to beat you back to London.'

Fairburn touched his puffy eye, the Walther cold in his other hand. Why not shoot them both? Have done with the whole thing? He looked at Nolan, knowing the assassin was thinking the same thing. With a nod, he winked and drove away.

The farmhouse lay on the slopes of a shallow hill, a miserable hovel with cobwebbed windows. Parked outside was a rusting Austin Cambridge motorcar. Picking up a stone, Fairburn knelt behind the engine block and threw it at the nearest window. Moments later, the front door swung open. A skinny man wearing a string vest appeared, illuminated by dim electric light. Cradled in his arms was a shotgun. He stepped outside and shouldered the weapon. 'It might be kids messing about,' he called back inside. 'Ain't nobody here.' He spoke with a London accent.

A second man appeared, crop-headed and lean. He carried a revolver in one hand and a pocket torch in the other. 'It won't be kids, you mug. Not out in the sticks.'

Fairburn popped up from behind the car, holding the Walther in a single-handed grip. He squeezed the trigger twice, the men illuminated in the doorway like targets on the pistol range at Yurlovo. Both fell, eyes wide, a dark hole drilled into their foreheads.

Then, footsteps. 'John? Fred?' said a reedy voice. A scrawny lad stood in the doorway. He was a teenager, no more than seventeen or eighteen. He saw Fairburn, his eyes fixed on the pistol in his hand. 'Don't shoot,' he said. 'I ain't got no gun, I swear.'

'Give me the keys,' Fairburn ordered, nodding at the Austin.

The lad was wild-eyed. 'I'll get 'em, mister.'

'I need to take a look inside.'

The teenager nodded. 'Whatever you want.'

Fairburn stepped into the farmhouse. The BAF men were prepared for a prisoner; a pair of handcuffs and a blindfold lay on the kitchen table next to a blowtorch. Nearby lay his red KGB identity card, wallet and Vostok wristwatch. Taking his things, he searched the squalid bedrooms. The only item of interest was a copy of Hitler's *Mein Kampf.* Possessing a copy carried a twenty-year prison sentence. 'That ain't mine,' the kid whined. 'I ain't never seen it before. I can't even read.'

'So how do you know what it is?'

'The others told me.'

'Shut up and give me the keys.'

The boy opened a drawer and put a car key on the table. 'The tank's full,' he said eagerly. 'It's all yours. The clutch is a bit stiff, but apart from that…'

Fairburn shot the boy in the forehead. He slumped drunkenly to the floor, groaning and flailing. Fairburn frowned. He'd little time for the PPK, finding its .32 calibre round lacking punch. He shot the kid just left of his sternum and into his heart, pulling the trigger until the Walther's magazine was empty. Then, taking the car key, the KGB officer left the house. Pausing a moment to smooth his hair, he settled himself into the Austin and drove away.

Chapter 27

Senior Sergeant of Militia Fitzjohn was an officious young man, hair neatly parted and boots highly polished. When he spoke, it was with a broad Devonian accent. 'You say you were kidnapped by the British Action Front, Comrade Captain?' he said, snapping open his notebook and licking the nib of a pencil. 'Nasty business. Where are these fascists now?'

'They're dead,' Fairburn replied.

'How?'

Fairburn placed the Walther on the desk. 'I overpowered one, took his pistol and shot him. Then I shot two more.'

Fitzjohn raised an eyebrow. 'Where exactly is this farmhouse?'

'I'd say about ten miles to the west of here, but I'm not familiar with the area. I was blindfolded when I was kidnapped in London.'

'I'll get a map. I'm sure we'll find the place. Then we can confirm your story.'

Fairburn's eye throbbed from Nolan's punch. 'Are you *questioning* me, Comrade?'

'I'll need a full account of what happened for my report,' Fitzjohn replied primly. 'It's only proper.'

'I'll tell you what's proper, Comrade Sergeant. Get on the telephone to the CSS and the KGB. I need to get back to London. Immediately.'

Fitzjohn held up a hand. 'All in good time, Comrade.'

Fairburn's eyes narrowed. 'Give me the bloody telephone. I'll ring Gerry Scanlon myself and tell him what an arse you are. You'll be mixing cement in the fucking Urals by Thursday.'

Fitzjohn's face turned grey. 'Comrade General Scanlon?'

'We had drinks last week. He asked me to call him personally if I required Militia assistance.'

Fitzjohn, fingers trembling, put his notebook back in his pocket. 'Please, feel free to use the telephone.'

Fairburn connected to an operator and asked to be put through to the KGB reserve room at the Soviet embassy. 'I need to speak with Colonel Nikolai Sechkin,' he said in Russian. 'Tell him it's Captain Fairburn of the 10th Directorate. It's urgent.'

'Yes, Comrade Captain,' the operator replied. 'I have your number. Your message will be passed on immediately.'

Fairburn put the telephone down and took the chair behind Fitzjohn's desk. 'I'd appreciate a cup of coffee,' he snapped. 'You do have coffee?'

'Of course,' the militiaman replied, smiling obsequiously. 'Comrade Fenton!' he bawled at a passing militiaman. 'Coffee and biscuits. The chocolate ones.'

Soon afterwards, Corporal Fenton drove Fairburn to Exeter in a militia car, sirens wailing. He passed Fairburn the radio-telephone handset. 'It's Colonel Sechkin for you.'

Fairburn nodded his thanks. 'Nikolai?' he said, switching to Russian.

'Tommy are you okay?'

'I'm alive.'

'I've arranged a flight from Exeter to London. I'll meet you at the airport.'

'What's the situation there?'

Sechkin lowered his voice. 'Not good. Philby's convinced the compromise comes from inside the Militia. I had to talk him out of having Gerry Scanlon arrested. It would spark a fucking riot. Teplyakov went crazy, he called Chairman Serov to complain about my conduct. We need to debrief you as soon as possible, Tommy. They're talking about cancelling Comrade Khrushchev's visit.'

Fairburn knew there was no going back now. He had to lie to Nikolai. 'Yes, there's a leak. Nolan knew about our ambush.'

'There's a spy hunt underway, Tommy. Be prepared for difficult questions.'

'Someone got to Frayne at the Richmond Assizes, someone on the inside. It's why he asked to see me. I've been set up, Nikolai. There's something else I need to tell you…'

'Not over the R/T,' Sechkin replied.

'Take care, Nikolai.'

'Forget *care*, Tommy. We need luck.'

A Soviet transport plane flew Fairburn to London, a crewman plying him with coffee and slices of fruitcake. The flight took just over an hour, a car pulling up as they taxied onto the military section of the airport. 'Look what the cat threw up, eh?' called Sid Ross from the driver's seat. The CSS man had a field dressing stuck across his forehead.

'Been in the wars, Sid?' said Fairburn, climbing down from the Antonov.

'Just a touch of shrapnel.' Ross shrugged. 'Lots of rockets flying about. Anyhow, you look worse.'

Fairburn touched his nose and winced. 'The British Action Front are old-fashioned when it comes to interrogation. They hit me in the face with a rifle butt.'

'Sounds about right. What did you tell 'em?'

'The chaff I keep memorised for such occasions,' Fairburn replied. 'They seemed happy enough, until they weren't.'

Ross smiled. 'They said you did for three of 'em.'

'News travels fast.'

'Shame you didn't get Nolan.'

Fairburn got into the car. 'Nolan's a special case. Now, there's a man who knows his business.'

Ross started the engine. 'He's thrown his hand in with the BAF?'

'I think it's more complicated, Sid.'

'How?'

'I think he might be a link between the Americans and the BAF.'

Ross drove out of the military terminal and onto the Great West Road. 'I've been told not to discuss the balls-up at Richmond Assizes,' he said finally. 'Everyone's under suspicion. Me, you... even Sechkin.'

'How convenient for the real traitors,' Fairburn replied. He took strange comfort in that he was, to a certain extent, telling the truth. Prasad was safe after all.

'Traitors? You reckon there's more'n one?' asked Ross.

'We'll speak later, Sid. Can I ask a favour?'

'No problem, boss.'

'I need you to get hold of the visitor's log from the courthouse. We need to find out exactly who saw Frayne on the morning of the ambush.'

'Why?'

'Someone told him to make sure I was there at a certain time. I want to know who.'

'The log – did you check it?'

'Of course I did. There was his wife and legal representative, I think. And a TUC official?'

'Anyone else?'

'Yes, a group of CSS officers. They signed in using their service numbers, not names.'

'Careful,' Ross replied. 'I see where you're going with this.'

Fairburn put his hand on the CSS man's shoulder. 'You said it, not me.'

'I'll find out, Comrade Captain. You have my word.'

At the Soviet embassy an armed guard escorted Fairburn to an interrogation room. 'Sidearm and identity card, Comrade Captain,' he demanded.

'It's just a formality, Tommy,' said Sechkin, sitting behind a steel table.

'Of course,' Fairburn replied, handing over his *dokumenty*. 'I have no weapons. Nolan took my pistol at the Richmond Assizes. May I ask who's leading my questioning? KGB or CSS?'

'General Teplyakov agreed your debriefing should be a joint effort,' said a familiar voice. 'Hello, Tommy. I'm glad to see you made it.'

'Comrade Deputy Director Prasad,' Fairburn replied. 'I hope you're well?'

'I'm more concerned about you, old chap,' said Prasad, peeling off his overcoat. Taking his journal from his briefcase, he sat down. 'Colonel Sechkin, may I have a moment alone with Captain Fairburn?'

Sechkin wrinkled his nose. 'Tommy?'

'It's fine,' Fairburn replied.

When Sechkin left the room, Prasad leaned across the table. 'Don't worry, this room isn't bugged,' he said quietly. 'Things are moving quickly, Tommy. Too quickly.'

'How?'

'I thought Teplyakov would be keen to downplay the incident at Richmond ahead of Khrushchev's visit. There's only so much blame he can deflect.'

'I presume it's had the opposite effect?'

'Rather. He's spooked Philby.'

'What does that mean?'

Prasad looked troubled. 'You have to act quickly. If Teplyakov puts enough pressure on Moscow, he can have you withdrawn. Sechkin, too.'

Fairburn sighed. He was growing sympathetic to Sid's theory about spies being too clever for their own good. 'What now?'

'Fisk's expecting you to call. He's been told your name's Mister Wenlock. Got that?'

'Wenlock. I understand.'

'Excellent,' Prasad replied. Raising his voice, he called for Sechkin to come back into the room. 'Thanks for your patience, Nikolai. You'll observe for the time being.'

'For now, Comrade,' Sechkin snapped. 'However, if I have to speak to the ambassador or General Teplyakov, I will. Tread carefully, Comrade.'

Prasad's voice was cold. 'I'm afraid I must tread as heavily as necessary. After all, we're dealing with an egregious security breach.'

'Just get on with it,' Sechkin replied, pulling up a chair. 'For the record, though, I think you need to be looking a little closer to home.'

Prasad made a note with his fountain pen. 'I assure you, Comrade Colonel, we are. Now, Comrade Captain Fairburn, let's discuss the events leading to the attack on the Richmond Assizes...'

* * *

'How did it go?' asked Ross, rolling a cigarette. He'd removed the field dressing from his forehead, revealing a neatly stitched cut running from his ear to his eyebrow.

'It could've been worse,' Fairburn replied, pocketing his ID card. Prasad played the part of inquisitor well, just stopping short of accusing him of betrayal. The intimation, however, was clear. *Why weren't you more badly beaten? You expect us to believe you established no rapport with your captors? Did you really tell them nothing of operational significance? Did you meet any Americans? You didn't? I find that hard to believe… let's go over that again, shall we?*

'Some of his allegations were outrageous,' Sechkin said, fuming. The three men sat in Sechkin's office, drinking vodka. 'He more or less suggested my team is full of CIA spies!'

Fairburn nodded. 'I think Prasad knows there's a rat in his house. And he knows it's not me, either.'

Gulping his drink, Sechkin motioned for Ross to pour another. 'Why d'you think that, Tommy?'

Fairburn took a moment. Telling a lie, especially to Sechkin, was walking in virgin snow. Every untruth would leave an indelible footprint. 'The BAF men who took me prisoner were respectful of Nolan, but I felt their orders came from elsewhere.'

'You said Nolan was working for the Americans?' said Sechkin.

'The BAF men intimated as much. They couldn't help but boast. They thought they were going to kill me.'

Ross shrugged. 'That doesn't answer the question – who's the leak inside the CSS? Who got Frayne to ask you to see him in his cell?'

'The officers concerned only used their service numbers when they signed in. And those are probably false.'

Ross rubbed his face and sighed. 'Well, Agnes Muir might know. I'll identify the other visitors and ask if they saw any CSS people. Or the guard, if he survived the attack. It's just detective work, Tommy. Nothin' complicated.'

Fairburn suspected it was Prasad, or one of his people, who'd visited Frayne. 'I agree, Sid.'

'Yes, time for you to play Sherlock Holmes,' said Sechkin. The joke was as weak as the Russian's smile.

Ross laughed anyway. 'Right, Tommy, let's go along with your theory. Why would the BAF or the Americans go to the effort of kidnapping you?'

Sechkin tapped the table with a quick-bitten finger. 'From an intelligence officer's perspective, the answer is self-evident: to make us suspect Tommy of treachery. To throw suspicion on the KGB. To poison British relations with Russia. Classic wrecking tactics.'

Fairburn nodded. 'I think the CIA knew their network was compromised when we arrested McGrouther and Frayne. So they decided to kill them *and* muddy the waters as part of an exit strategy. It's actually quite clever.'

'It would also protect any spies inside the CSS,' said Ross. 'Yeah, it sounds like the sort of complicated bollocks spies think up, ain't it?'

Sechkin shrugged. 'It's espionage.'

'Still, the more complicated the plan, the more chance there is of something going wrong,' Ross replied.

'Then find the visitor's log,' said Tommy, pouring himself another drink. 'I want to know who set me up.'

'I'll get it tonight.'

They drank some more. When Sechkin was suitably drunk, Fairburn lay a hand on his shoulder. If his first lie was one footprint in the snow, this was a hundred. 'Nikolai, there's something I didn't mention to Prasad.'

'What?'

'Nolan had a visitor at the farmhouse, a woman. I heard her when they thought I was sleeping. She mentioned something about a project with a Russian name: *Zapad*.'

Sechkin's eyes narrowed. 'Dammit, Tommy. What did she say?'

'The woman ordered Nolan to find someone working on the project somewhere in Cambridge. I didn't catch the name.' Katherine had told him Sandy Fisk lived in a KGB-guarded hotel in Suffolk but was often relocated for security reasons. Mentioning Cambridge would hopefully divert attention away from his target.

'Why didn't you mention this to Prasad?'

The lies tasted like ashes in his mouth. This was Nikolai Sechkin. Surely he'd know he was lying? 'I don't trust the bastard, that's why.'

Sechkin reached for his jacket. 'We need to make a secure call to Moscow. Now. Sid, would you excuse us?'

'Of course, Comrade Colonel,' Ross replied, making for the door. 'I'll make myself scarce, eh?'

Fairburn stood up and put on his jacket. 'Moscow? Who are we calling?'

'Comrade Chairman Serov,' the KGB Colonel replied. '*Poneslos*, my friend – it's kicking off now.'

Chapter 28

Colonel Nikolai Sechkin swept into the embassy's communications centre, red-faced and angry. 'Get out,' he bawled at the clerks. 'I want the senior radio operator. The rest of you can go!'

'Comrade Colonel,' said a skinny man wearing a yellowish shirt and a black tie. 'I'm the duty radio operator.'

'Your name?'

'Dmitri Ilyin, Comrade Colonel.'

'Right, Ilyin, I need a secure call to Comrade Chairman Serov in Moscow.'

Ilyin licked his teeth. 'I'll put the request through immediately.' Straightening his tie, Ilyin picked up a handset and began operating a series of switches on a control panel.

'We don't have much to tell Serov, do we?' said Fairburn. 'Shouldn't we find out more?'

'The fact the Americans even know the codename *Zapad* is enough,' Sechkin replied, shaking his head. 'We're compromised.'

'Why is this so important?'

'Have you ever seen Khrushchev in a bad mood?' Sechkin growled, ignoring the question. He was drunk. 'People forget what he was like at Stalingrad. Not to mention the fucking Ukraine. He'll be furious.'

'Is there anything I can do?'

, Tommy, can you fetch coffee? And maybe bread and sausage? aven't eaten all day.'

'I'll ask the clerks.'

'Good lad. Hey, Ilyin, when's my fucking call?'

Fairburn entered the office next to the radio room. A handful of clerks sat in a huddle, talking quietly among themselves. 'Comrades, is there any coffee? And something for the Colonel to eat?'

'Yes, Comrade Captain,' said a dark-haired woman. 'I will fetch something. Is there anything else?'

Fairburn saw an opportunity. 'Colonel Sechkin needs me to check the cipher logs for a project called *Zapad*.'

The woman pointed at a fair-haired man with glasses. 'Boris, can you get the cipher logs? Make yourself useful for a change.'

Boris, muttering something under his breath, walked towards a green-painted safe. 'You'll have to sign for them, Comrade Captain,' he said, working the combination.

'It's okay, I'm not taking them anywhere,' Fairburn replied, pulling his notebook from his pocket. He gripped it tightly to stop his fingers trembling. 'I just need to cross-reference a few details.'

'As you wish,' Boris yawned, checking the office's twin wall clocks. It was the graveyard shift for the London station, 03.00; 06.00 in Moscow. The clerk pulled out a wad of papers. 'Here are the *Zapad* signals logs. How far back do you need, Comrade Captain?'

Fairburn honestly didn't know, so chose the period around Crewe's defection. 'The beginning of September,' he said.

'Well, there isn't much,' Boris replied, opening the file and passing Fairburn a sheet of waxy teleprinter paper. 'Most *Zapad* traffic goes through the air force communications centre, mainly technical data. We only deal with security and counterintelligence.'

'That's fine,' said Fairburn, scanning the notes. Most concerned routine inspections and personnel matters, including reports of employees' ideological weaknesses. However, one signal, to the headquarters of the 1st Directorate of the KGB in Moscow, was of interest:

<u>Subject: Dr. Andrew FISK</u>

Doctor Andrew FISK is a senior technical officer within Project ZAPAD and former associate of the defector Eliza CREWE. British CSS (Bureau 5) were tasked to investigate the nature of their relationship and identify any security risks. They reported no adverse intelligence; it appears FISK attended Cambridge university with CREWE in the 1930s. FISK is reportedly a conscientious worker of sound political convictions.

I interviewed FISK at his workplace. I found him to be a quiet, thoughtful man preoccupied with his scientific research. He admitted to a historic friendship with CREWE but insisted they were no longer in contact. FISK agreed to contact me directly if he receives any communications from anyone concerning CREWE in the future. He was suitably counselled regarding the penalties for non-compliance with security protocols.

For the time being I will review FISK'S security clearance on a monthly basis. FISK currently resides at KGB-approved accommodation at The Regal Hotel, Mildenhall, Suffolk. Hotel management reports directly to my officers concerning all ZAPAD-assigned

```
personnel. He is due to move to new accommodation
in the New Year of 1958.
   Signed,
   Col. N.A. Sechkin
```

'Thank you, Comrade,' said Fairburn, handing back the report.

The female clerk appeared with a flask of coffee and a plate of bread and ham. 'We have vodka if Colonel Sechkin's thirsty.'

'I think he's had enough,' Fairburn replied, taking the food. 'Thanks for this, Comrade.' He returned to the signals room to find Sechkin on the telephone. The KGB colonel nodded his thanks and waved him away. 'Get some sleep, Tommy,' he said, covering the mouthpiece with his hand. 'We'll speak later.'

'Of course,' Fairburn replied, getting up and leaving the room. Sechkin would usually let him sit in on telephone calls? Wouldn't he? The fear was like a maggot gnawing at his brain. Willing it to stop – forcing it – he headed for the stairs.

'Tommy?' said Sid, waiting in the corridor outside. 'Are you okay? You look a bit peaky.'

'I think the last few days are catching up with me.'

'Look, I'll drive you back to your place. Get some sleep, eh?'

'Thanks, Sid, but we need to find the visitor logs from the Richmond Assizes.'

'Will you rest afterwards?'

'Yes, I promise.'

'Right,' Ross replied, 'let's go.'

'The storeman will be asleep on duty, I s'pose,' said Ross, knocking on the door. 'Lazy bastard.'

'Who is it?' said a bleary-sounding voice.

'Senior Sergeant Ross, Bureau 5. Is Arthur around?'

'Arthur's on day shift.'

'I need to book out some property.'

'At this time in the fucking morning?'

'Yes, at this time of the fucking morning.'

'Alright then,' the voice grumbled. The door was opened by a young, ginger-haired man. 'What do you want?' he said sleepily.

Fairburn cleared his throat. 'I think what you meant to say was, *how may I assist you, Comrade Captain?*'

'This is Captain Fairburn,' said Ross. 'He's from the KGB.'

'Well you should have said so before. How may I assist you, Comrade Captain?' the ginger-haired man replied.

'I need a piece of evidence, Comrade. The prisoner visitor's ledger from the Richmond Assizes.'

The storeman opened a register and leafed through pages of hand-written entries. 'I'm sorry, Comrade Captain, that item was booked out yesterday. Arthur was on duty.'

Sid stepped into the storeroom. 'Who took it?'

Watkins read aloud. 'Comrade Captain King. Says here she's a Bureau 6 officer.'

'King?' asked Fairburn. 'That's Prasad's colleague. The interrogator.' *And a member of Prasad's network.*

Sid motioned him into the corridor, out of the storeman's earshot. 'Why would she need that, Tommy?'

'I don't know.'

Ross grimaced. 'Well, she's either looking for traitors, or—'

'She's looking to destroy any incriminating evidence,' Fairburn interrupted, tapping his foot on the linoleum floor. 'We need to find her.'

'Tommy, you need to take it easy,' said Ross, putting a hand on Fairburn's shoulder. 'You've had a rough time. Let's not go off half-cocked, eh?'

'I'm absolutely fine,' Fairburn snapped.

'No you ain't. Look, I'm gonna find out what happened to the ledger and you're gonna get some kip. Colonel Sechkin won't thank you for barging around like a bull in a china shop.'

Fairburn closed his eyes. *I'm out of my depth.* 'You're right, Sid. I'm sorry.'

'Look, there's a folding cot in my office. Why don't you get your head down for a couple of hours, eh? I'll wake you if anything important happens.'

'I will, but there's one more thing.'

'There always is with you. What is it?'

'Can you go and see Comrade Renton?'

Sid raised an eyebrow. 'Why?'

'I need the Protona Minifon. The one we planted in Scanlon's car.'

'A micro-recorder? Why?'

Fairburn shrugged. 'Insurance.'

'Okay,' he replied. 'I just hope you know what you're doing.'

'Yes, Sid. So do I.'

Chapter 29

Fairburn slept fitfully. He woke just before dawn, mouth dry, and returned to his office. Lying on his desk was a parcel wrapped in brown paper. Opening it, he found the grey plastic Protona micro-recorder. He watched as a janitor mopped the corridor outside, whistling as he worked. Fairburn poured a cup of coffee, drank two cups and felt better. Straightening his tie and smoothing his hair, he tried to brush the creases from his suit. Then, turning to the large-scale CSS map of the British Isles on the wall, he found the county of Suffolk. The map showed locations of confidential military and security establishments, Mildenhall marked with the roundel of the British Peoples' Air Force. The aerodrome was only twenty miles north-east of Cambridge and enjoyed decent road and rail links. Beneath the map was a shelf full of reference books and telephone directories. He took the directory for East Anglia and found the entry for the Regal Hotel, where Sandy Fisk was billeted. Memorising the address, Fairburn replaced the directory.

The janitor reappeared in the doorway, half-heartedly mopping the floor. He was bearded and grey, his eyes fixed on his mop. 'Comrade, I think you dropped this,' he said quietly, passing Fairburn a slip of paper. Before Fairburn could reply, he hurried away.

Fairburn unfolded the note, written in Russian: YOU HAVE UNTIL NEXT THURSDAY TO DELIVER OUR FRIEND. YOU WILL FIND COMRADES AT 25a ALDERNEY STREET, VICTORIA.

Then footsteps outside. 'Comrade Captain?' said a voice.

Fairburn tucked the note and the micro-recorder into his jacket pocket. 'Yes?'

The voice belonged to a barrel-chested CSS major in full uniform, his cap tucked under his arm. 'I'm Major Hobson. Director Philby's asked to see you.'

Fairburn checked his watch. 'Now, Comrade Major?'

A curt nod. 'Yes.'

Five minutes later Fairburn and Hobson stood in the lobby outside Director Philby's office. Hobson put on his cap and knocked once. 'In you go,' he said. 'I'll wait for you here.'

Fairburn stepped inside. The shutters were closed, the room lit by a single Anglepoise lamp. Philby, wearing a homely looking cardigan, sat reading from an open file on his desk. 'Take a seat, Tommy,' he said easily.

'Yes, Comrade Director.'

Philby studied Fairburn with pale blue eyes. 'I've just been reading Ash's report into your disappearance. I must say, you've been in the wars.'

'Yes, Comrade Director.'

'The thing is, of course, the affair at Richmond Assizes was a disappointment. I was rather hoping your reappearance might bring with it a dividend of some sort.'

'A dividend?'

'Something to give me traction with the Politburo, most of whom have been on the telephone to Moscow demanding my head on a spike.' Philby smiled. 'Preposterous, of course, but you know what politicians are like when their backs are up.'

Fairburn squinted. The lamp was positioned deliberately in his field of vision. 'I'm sorry, Kim, I told Comrade Prasad everything I know.'

222

'It's clear we have a traitor, Tommy. Not some loose-lipped cretin from the Politburo, but someone inside CSS. Or even the KGB. Chairman Serov agrees, so does General Teplyakov.'

'Yes, I think so too. As you can see from my report, Nolan was well prepared for the operation at Richmond. He was tipped off.'

Philby made a temple with his fingers, his tone measured. 'Tell me, why do you think Francis Frayne asked to see you before the ambush?'

'I think I was set up to look like the source of the leak. I've sent Sergeant Ross to retrieve the prisoner visitor's log. Whoever saw Frayne may have ordered him to ask to see me. I think I was targeted for kidnapping.'

Philby raised an eyebrow. 'An interesting theory. Tell me, why would they go to all that trouble?'

'I don't know. A wrecking tactic? I saw an opportunity to escape before I was able to find out. I hope I can't be blamed for taking it.'

'Of course not,' Philby sighed. 'I suppose it's like that fellow Churchill once said about Russia: it's *a riddle, wrapped in a mystery, inside an enigma.* I'll get to the bottom of it, Tommy. Until then, I've come to an arrangement with General Teplyakov.'

'An arrangement?'

'Yes, I intend to deal with this in-house, before things get out of hand. The KGB has agreed to step back in order to steady the horses with our Politburo before Chairman Khrushchev's visit. I'm sure you understand? It's politics, dear boy.'

Fairburn felt a stab of anger. 'I'm not sure I do. What about Scanlon?'

'I've had to bury the evidence you gathered against General Scanlon. For now, at least. If we arrest him, there'll be workers on the streets. I'm not entirely sure the Militia will stop them, either. The cult of personality around the man is too strong. I appreciate the effort you've put in, but it's time to accept your operation was a failure.'

'And now?'

'You'll be confined to the embassy while decisions are made. We've made all the necessary arrangements.'

Tommy shook his head. 'Kim, I must follow this lead. The visitor's log…'

Philby held up a finger. 'Senior Sergeant Ross will report directly to me about this mysterious register. Now, Major Hobson will escort you back to the Soviet Embassy.'

'This is a mistake.'

Philby returned to his papers. 'Perhaps. We all make them, Tommy. Now, good day to you.'

Hobson walked with Fairburn across the parade square, where a black ZIS saloon waited. 'Get in, lad,' the CSS officer ordered, opening the rear door. An angry-looking Nikolai Sechkin sat in the back, dressed in full KGB uniform.

'Nikolai, what's happening?' asked Fairburn.

'Not now, Tommy,' he replied wearily. There were bags under his eyes and he still smelled of booze. 'Let these pricks have their moment of glory, escorting KGB officers off the premises.'

Hobson got in next to the driver. 'Right, let's go,' he announced, slapping the dashboard with a leather-gloved hand. 'Kensington Palace Gardens and don't hold the horses.'

As the car pulled onto the King's Road, Sechkin leaned in close to Fairburn. Close enough for the big KGB man's lips to brush his ear. 'Teplyakov's on manoeuvres,' he whispered in Russian. 'He's told Serov that Khrushchev's visit should go ahead, but only if we declare martial law for the duration.'

'What will the Militia do if Serov agrees?'

'That depends on Philby. If he arrests Scanlon, it strengthens Teplyakov's hand. If he doesn't, Scanlon gets stronger and weakens Philby's hand.'

'Philby's going to bury the evidence against Scanlon for now.'

'That makes sense,' Sechkin replied. 'He's fucked either way.'

'What's going to happen to us?'

Sechkin finally smiled. 'I've heard Teplyakov's wants to send me on a punishment posting to Chukotsky. What will I do there, spy on polar bears? Irina will go crazy.'

'I'm sorry, Nikolai.'

'I'm more worried about you. I've got Serov arguing my case, after all. You, on the other hand, seem to have got under Teplyakov's skin.'

'Why?'

'He wants to use you as leverage against Serov, maybe? Or because you're English? He's no admirer of the 10th Directorate either. Who knows what goes on inside the mind of a snake?'

Fairburn watched a convoy of Soviet army trucks rumbling along Gloucester Road, youthful conscripts crammed in the back. Wearing steel helmets, Kalashnikovs clutched to their chests, they looked as if they were patrolling bandit country. Not London. 'Maybe I'll be joining you in Chukotsky?'

'That's an old man's punishment,' Sechkin replied. 'I'm sure they'll be more imaginative with you.'

The driver turned onto Queens Gate, red banners hanging limply from flagpoles. Fairburn was a tiny cog, easily replaced if malfunctioned. Were there not fresh Spartans passing out of the academy every year? He was disposable. A strange feeling for someone who'd only known success. 'Driver, can you pull over please?' he asked. 'I think I'm going to be sick.'

'Do as he says,' said Hobson. 'Comrade Colonel, please keep an eye on the lad. No silliness, please?'

'I will,' said Sechkin, a look of concern on his ruddy face. 'Tommy, are you okay?'

'No,' Fairburn groaned, clutching his gut. 'Please, pull over.'

The driver stopped near Kensington Gore. Fairburn opened the door and retched, swinging his legs onto the pavement. Putting a hand on his shoulder, Sechkin whispered in his ear. 'I hope you know what you're doing, Tommy.'

'So do I,' Fairburn replied. Then, he ran.

Chapter 30

Fairburn found himself in a park adjoining a university building, where he mingled with a crowd of fresh-faced students. They were only a few years younger than him, dressed in heavy duffel coats and long woollen scarves. Even the young women smoked roll-up cigarettes. The black CSS car cruised by, Major Hobson scanning the crowd through an open window. The students sneered. 'Pigs,' said one, spitting into the straggly grass. Fairburn stepped from behind a tree and watched the car drive slowly away.

It was only a short walk to Knightsbridge. The famous shopping district was popular with diplomats, civil servants, academics and military officers. The pavements bustled with Russians and Yugoslavs visiting Party-only shops. Smart ladies chatted outside cafes and white-capped militiamen directed traffic. Fairburn walked to a taxi rank. 'Where to?' asked the driver.

Fairburn pulled the note the janitor had given him from his pocket. 'Alderney Street, Victoria,' he replied in a thick Russian accent.

The drive only took ten minutes, the cabbie weaving in and out of the potholed streets. 'Here you go, Comrade,' he said, nodding at a row of neglected-looking townhouses. The flat 25a was a basement flat with a rusty bicycle chained to the railings outside. Fairburn waited until the cab was gone and knocked on the door.

A dark-haired young woman answered, dressed in an old fisherman's jumper and a long woollen skirt. 'And who are you?' she asked in a Northern Irish accent.

'My name's Tommy,' he replied, passing her the note. 'I was told there were friends at this address.'

The young woman nodded. 'Best you come in then. I'll put the kettle on.'

'Do you have vodka?'

'They said you were like a Russian.'

'Who did?'

The young woman laughed. 'That's a secret. There's no vodka here, Tommy. Take a seat and I'll make us a cup of tea.'

'I don't take milk,' Tommy replied.

'That'll be fine, there isn't any.'

The apartment was cosy, with a smouldering coal fire and sofas covered with tartan blankets. A radio sat on a sideboard, next to a bookcase full of paperback novels. A small window let in a sliver of light. Fairburn took a seat. 'Who are you?' he called into the kitchen.

'All in good time,' said a gravelly voice. Ronnie Todmorden appeared from another room, his pockmarked face drawn into a scowl. 'How are you keeping, Tommy?'

'Todmorden? You set me up.'

The ex-SS man laughed. 'You set yourself up. You ain't as clever as you think.'

'He really isn't, Ronnie,' the girl called from the kitchen. 'He thinks there's milk in the shops.'

Todmorden sat down opposite Tommy, his knees cracking like an old man's. 'Welcome to the real Britain. Rationing and empty stomachs. We're on the same side now, ain't we?'

Fairburn laughed. 'You think the Americans are on the BAF's side?'

'I'm on the side of anyone fighting the Reds, Tommy. I don't care if they're Yanks or BAF or Monarchists. Or even KGB men. Makes no difference to me.'

Fairburn scanned the room. He decided the glass ashtray on the table would make for a weapon if he needed one. 'I'm here for a reason, Todmorden. How can you help me?'

The ex-SS man rifled in his coat pocket. He pulled out a packet of cigarettes and lit one. 'Just tell me what you need.'

The young woman nodded. 'Vehicles? Papers? Weapons? Messages sent up the chain of command? Stuff like that.'

'I need to smuggle a man out of a hotel in Suffolk. He needs to get to the West Country.'

The young woman nodded. 'Okay. Is your man willing to come with you? Or is it a kidnap?'

'He wants to defect.'

'Well that's a relief, eh Ronnie?'

'Kidnaps can be messy,' Todmorden agreed.

'The KGB are interested in this man. The hotel's protected by them.'

'Which is why they got you involved,' the girl replied. 'You just walk in and wave your *dokumenty*, right?'

'I'm on the run. I was about to be confined to the Soviet embassy.'

Todmorden laughed, revealing a mouthful of stumpy yellow teeth. 'So you ain't the golden boy anymore? That's fucking marvellous, Tommy. Just fucking marvellous.'

Fairburn shrugged. 'We play with the hand we're dealt. I presume you're under orders to assist me anyway? As you say, we're on the same side.'

Todmorden stood and buttoned his coat. 'You can stay here as long as you like, Suzie will give you a key,' he said, avoiding the question. 'We've got a telephone if you need one. And you can kip on the sofa.'

'You'll be needing new clothes,' Suzie added. 'You look like a KGB man in that suit.'

'Find him some gear, will you?' said Todmorden, heading for the door. 'I'll call by later.'

'Will you be wanting something to eat, Ronnie?' asked Suzie.

'Save your food for yourself, Suzie. I'll get something down the pub.' With that, Todmorden gave Tommy a wink and left.

The kettle boiled. Suzie disappeared into the kitchen, returning with a cup of black tea in a mug. 'There you go,' she said.

'Thanks,' Tommy replied, taking a sip. 'I have ration coupons, if that helps?'

'They've got serial numbers. They can be traced. Anyway, it will look suspicious if I go into a Party shop. Do you have cash?'

Tommy opened his wallet and pulled out a five pound note. 'I don't have anything smaller, I'm afraid.'

Suzie laughed and snatched the banknote away. 'Made of money, are you? We'll be eating properly tonight. There's always food if you've got a fiver and know where to look.'

Tommy pulled his notebook from his pocket. 'To begin with, we need a map of Suffolk. And transport and weapons. Pistols and SMGs, nothing too big.'

Suzie nodded and reached for her coat. 'No problem.'

'Thank you.'

'It's nothing,' she replied, carefully folding the five pound note and putting it in her purse. 'I'll get us something decent for dinner too.'

'And coffee, perhaps? I like decent coffee.'

'I'll try,' she said. 'It's not easy to get hold of though, even on the black market.'

Tommy sipped his tea. It wasn't too bad, although he preferred Russian green tea. Then, slipping off his shoes, he lay on the sofa and fell asleep.

Suzie cooked thick pork sausages, mashed potatoes and runner beans. She poured light ale into two glasses and lit a candle. 'There's butter in the mash,' she said proudly. 'It cost a fortune, but it's Russian money so who cares?'

Tommy was hungry and the buttery mash was delicious. 'This is good. Are food shortages really that bad?'

'Bloody awful. My aunt in Coleraine said folk over there were eating dogs last winter.'

Fairburn felt guilty but ate anyway. The sausages were good, better than the gritty *Merguez* he'd got used to in North Africa. 'I was at a drinks party at Harry Pollitt House recently. There was lots of champagne and food.'

Suzie scowled. 'I'd love to blow that feckin' place up, especially with that bastard Scanlon inside.'

'And people like me too?'

'You've changed sides, haven't you?'

Fairburn shook his head. 'I'm not sure what that even means. I'm a victim of circumstance.'

'Well, watch yourself. Circumstances change, but ballistics don't. And I've got a gun on my lap.'

'Ballistics? Where did you learn about weapons?'

Suzie sipped her beer. 'Belfast, although I'm more of a demolitions girl than small arms. Anyway, when the Russians came, we fought 'em.'

'We?'

'Everyone. Catholics and Protestants. My father was an Orangeman, but he fought the Russians shoulder to shoulder with Republicans. Now the Republic's neutral and Ulster's occupied, so nobody got what they wanted. That's Ireland for you, I suppose.'

'And you, Suzie?'

'I blow up Reds,' she said proudly. 'Those old battles? A waste of time and feckin' ammo. Besides, it's only a matter of time before De Valera has to roll over for the Soviets. He can't play the neutrality game forever, hiding behind the Americans. Then the whole island will go up in smoke, mark my words.'

'Is that why you're in London?'

Suzie opened a second bottle of beer. 'Partly. It was getting hot in Belfast if you know what I mean? And the Monarchists needed someone who knew their way around explosives.' She chuckled. 'God Save the Queen, eh?'

Fairburn finished his food and beer long after Suzie, who ate quickly and licked her plate clean when she'd finished. The girl was waiflike, with a pinched face, skinny wrists peeping from the sleeves of her jumper. 'Thank you, the food was excellent,' he said.

'Do you want seconds?' she asked, putting a small Beretta pistol on the table in front of her. 'There's plenty left.'

'No, thank you. I'm full.'

'I'll save some for Ronnie then,' she said, getting up and clearing away the plates. 'He says he'll eat down the pub, but what he really means is he'll neck six pints and have a bag of pork scratchings.'

Fairburn looked at the pistol. 'You know Todmorden was in the SS, don't you? He's a war criminal.'

Suzie disappeared into the kitchen. When she returned, there was a half-empty bottle of Scotch in her hand. She took the pistol off the table and tucked it in the waistband of her skirt. 'Will you stop talking about the bloody past? You sound like an Ulsterman. All that matters is *now*.'

'That's naive,' Tommy replied.

'Don't patronise me, Mister KGB,' she replied, putting the bottle on the table. 'Are you saying you never shot a man in the back of the head?'

'Yes, I have. Too many.'

Suzie poured two glasses of Scotch and pushed one towards Fairburn. 'Sure you did, just like I blew up a bus full of Protestants on their way to repair Russian frigates at Harland and Wolff.' She took a gulp, winced, and poured more. 'It's like it says in the Bible, we've all got feet of clay.' There was a knock at the door. Then two more in quick succession. 'That'll be Ronnie,' she said, reaching for a third glass from the sideboard.

Ronnie Todmorden stepped inside the flat, smelling of beer. 'What's that?' he growled, sniffing the air like a truffle hound. 'It smells good.'

'Sausages and mash,' Suzie replied. 'There's butter in the mash, too.'

'Butter? You're a bloody angel,' Todmorden cooed, shrugging off his coat.

'Catch yourself on,' she laughed. 'You can thank Tommy, he gave me a five pound note.'

'Yeah he gave me some money an' all,' Todmorden replied. 'I've found he's very generous with the KGB's dough. He still owes me, in fact.'

Fairburn studied his Scotch and took a sip. He didn't like the stuff usually, but it would have to do. 'What did you spend my KGB *dough* on, Todmorden?'

'Things that go bang, my son. Now, tell me your plan.'

Chapter 31

Fairburn walked to the row of public telephones at Victoria railway station, using the crowds of commuters as cover. He wore a black donkey jacket and a tweed cap pulled low over his eyes. The militiamen standing by the ticket office paid him no attention. He dialled a number and a woman answered. 'Good morning, Regal Hotel Mildenhall. How can I help?'

'I'd like to speak with one of your residents, please. Doctor Andrew Fisk.'

'May I ask who's calling?'

'Can you tell him it's Mister Wenlock,' Fairburn replied.

'Of course, Comrade. Let me see if he's available.' The line went quiet for a few minutes. Fairburn listened the line crackle, wondering if the KGB officer monitoring the call had been briefed about a rogue 10th Directorate officer. Would such information be shared, or hushed-up? It was almost certain Sechkin had been relieved of responsibility for Operation Zapad.

'Hello, this is Fisk,' said a voice.

'Ah, hello, Sandy. It's Wenlock,' said Fairburn cheerfully, adopting the upper-class accent he'd honed in Egypt. 'How the devil are you?'

'Oh, I'm fine. I can't be too long I'm afraid, my car will be here any minute. Duty calls, eh?'

Fairburn checked his watch: 08.15. That was useful to know. 'I won't take too long. Look, I'm up your way early next week on business. Would you be free for a spot of lunch?'

'That would be marvellous. Let me look at my diary, we've a lot on our plates at the moment.'

'Of course. Shall I call tomorrow?'

'Yes, wonderful. Same time would suit.'

'Well, think of somewhere you'd like to go. It's my treat,' Fairburn replied. 'It's the least I can do.'

'I will, Wenlock old boy. I look forward to speaking tomorrow.'

'Goodbye, Sandy,' Fairburn replied, ending the call. Then, following a fresh counter-surveillance route, he returned to the flat on Alderney Street.

'Do you have a better map of the aerodrome?' asked Fairburn.

Todmorden shook his head. 'This one's from 1955, it's the best I can do. The Russians don't let cartographers add any details of military facilities.'

'Then we need take a look for ourselves,' said Suzie. 'If it's anything like the Red naval base at Londonderry, it'll be massive. More like a factory, really.'

'There's no time,' Fairburn replied.

Todmorden traced a route on the map with his finger. 'Your man Fisk's hotel is two miles away from Mildenhall aerodrome. There's no need to go anywhere near the place. It'll be crawling with Soviets.'

Fairburn smiled. 'We need a distraction.'

'Such as?'

'Suzie, how do you feel about blowing something up?'

The bombmaker laughed. 'You're touched in the head, ain't you?'

'I'm completely serious. I'm thinking of a car bomb. A big one. Something they'll hear for miles.'

Todmorden stroked his chin. 'While everyone's running around like blue-arsed flies, we snatch Fisk?'

'Not snatch,' Fairburn replied. 'It'll look like we're rescuing him.'

'Rescue?'

'I'm still a KGB officer,' Fairburn replied. 'It's a risk worth taking. Besides, who'll be checking my background while bombs are going off?'

'It could work,' said Suzie, rubbing her hands together. 'You said bombs? I've got thirty kilos of plastic. Fifteen will blow a London bus in the air easily.'

Fairburn stood up from the table. 'How often do you get car bombs outside of the big cities?'

'Not as often as I'd like,' said Todmorden. 'Only half of 'em go off, though. The BAF struggle to get the right people. Fuck knows how they pulled off that job at Richmond.'

'It doesn't matter, we have Suzie. She has the necessary expertise, I'm sure.'

'I do,' Suzie said. 'Alright, what happens now?'

Fairburn pulled a piece of paper from his pocket. 'I'll need everything on this list. Now, I'm going out for a while.'

Todmorden licked his teeth. 'Where?'

'You're going to have to trust me when I say you don't need to know.'

'I suppose so,' Todmorden replied. His fingers brushed the grips on the P38 tucked in his waistband. 'I'll give you the benefit of the doubt. For now.'

Fairburn reached for his donkey jacket. 'How gracious of you, Ronnie. I'll be back soon. If you're lucky, I might even pick up some more sausages.'

* * *

Fairburn took the tube to Fulham Broadway. Next door to the Underground station was the Hibernian club, which Ross said was the favoured watering hole for off-duty Bureau 5 men. He went to a telephone kiosk, found the club's number in the directory and dialled the number. 'I'm after Sid Ross,' he said. 'Don't tell me he isn't there. Not on a Friday.'

'Who's calling?' asked a man with a strong Irish accent.

'Tell him it's someone from Burgess House. It's important.'

'Right you are. Hold on a moment.'

A minute later, a familiar voice came on the line. 'Ross. Who is it?'

'Tommy.'

'Fuck me, what happened? I've heard all sorts of stuff.'

'I think the less you know the better.'

'I reckon you're right. They said you were gonna be banged up at the embassy.'

'Is this line monitored, Sid?'

'Nah, the bloke who writes up the paperwork for the phone taps drinks in here.'

'Look, I had to run. Philby's lost confidence in me.'

'What? Are you a fucking lunatic? They kept that quiet.'

Fairburn had prepared his script carefully. He just hoped the wily CSS man wouldn't see through it. 'Look, did you get hold of the visitor's log?'

'I had a chat with Captain King, all innocent like. The toffee-nosed cow said it was classified. Then she more or less told me to fuck off.'

'What did you do?'

Ross chuckled. 'I broke into her office last night. If what you say is true, that there's a CIA grass, Philby'll have my back for doing it.'

'So you've got the log?'

'Yeah.'

'Who visited Frayne on the morning of the ambush?'

Sid made a slurping sound. 'Sorry, I'm just finishing my pint. You won't be surprised to learn Alison King's number was on the list. The only other visitors were Frayne's legal counsel, his missus and a bloke from the Trade Unions Congress called Jack McMahon. McMahon was an old pal of Frayne's, so I swung by his office for a chat. McMahon remembers seeing a woman just as he was leaving. According to the log, that was half an hour before you saw Frayne.'

'She was the last visitor to see Frayne before me?'

'Yes. It gets better,' Sid replied.

'He described Alison King?'

'Yeah, McMahon had her down to a tee. Even her South African accent.'

'Excellent work, Sid.'

'What now?'

Fairburn fed another coin into the telephone, his eyes sweeping the street for watchers. 'Just keep hold of the visitor's log. That's enough for now.'

'You know I want to help, Tommy. I think you've been fitted-up. It ain't right.'

Fairburn wondered if he was being played. Was Sid trying to find out where he was? 'There is something you can do. Can you keep an eye on King? She might panic when she realises the log's missing. She might incriminate herself.'

'I was going to report it to Philby.'

'Not yet,' said Fairburn. 'The traitor might be close to him. She might have any number of excuses why she needed to see Frayne – she was his original interrogator, after all.'

'Close to Philby? As high as that?'

'Yes.'

'Look, Tommy, I can't keep this quiet for long. Khrushchev will arrive in just over a week.'

'It's Friday now. Can you give me until Wednesday?'

'No, more like end of play Tuesday. Wednesdays are when Philby sometimes calls me in for a chat. Sometimes I think the bloke can read my bloody mind.'

'Tuesday it is. I'm grateful.'

'Take care, Tommy.'

'I will. And Sid?'

'Yeah?'

Fairburn closed his eyes. He promised himself the big CSS man would come out of this alive. 'Have a drink for me, will you?'

Chapter 32

'Sandy? How are you this morning?'

'I'm very well, Wenlock. No peace for the wicked, though. I'm working today.'

'On a Saturday? How wretched.'

'It's for the greater good, Comrade. I'm free tomorrow, though.'

'Excellent. Does Sunday lunch suit?'

'Yes, there's a pub called the Moon and Stars in Little Shadwell, just off the Newmarket Road. They do decent enough food if you've got coupons.'

'That's perfect, Sandy. What time?'

Fisk chuckled. 'Twelve noon? How dramatic, it sounds like one of those Western films doesn't it? *High Noon*.'

'High noon indeed,' Fairburn replied. He'd seen the American cowboy movie in a Cairo picture house. All he remembered was a very beautiful actress called Grace Kelly.

'Well, take care old chap.'

'You too, Wenlock. I'll see you Sunday.'

Fairburn, Suzie and Todmorden stood in a garage beneath a railway arch. 'We've got three motors,' said Todmorden, pointing at the vehicles parked inside. The ex-SS man wore oil-stained coveralls and a black woollen hat. 'The Bedford breakdown van has one bomb inside and the Wolseley has the other.'

Suzie ran a hand along the bonnet of an oxblood Jaguar Mark XII. 'The Jag's fast. We'll use it as the getaway car.'

Fairburn checked his appearance in the Jaguar's wing mirror; he wore a freshly laundered double-breasted suit, spit-shined Oxfords and a neatly knotted tie. His only other equipment was his KGB identity card, cash, a Makarov and the Protona micro-recorder. Unless there was a quartermaster capable of issuing a large quantity of luck, Fairburn had everything he needed. 'Now, Suzie, tell me about your bombs,' he said, smoothing his hair with his palm.

The Ulsterwoman lit a cigarette. 'Again?' she sighed.

'Again.'

'You've got twenty kilos of explosive in the Bedford. Another ten in the Wolseley. It's hidden as best I could, unless there's a thorough search, we'll be fine. I'm using C2 plastique, it'll make a big old bang.'

Todmorden pointed at three German machine pistols lying on a groundsheet. 'There won't be any thorough searches.'

'And your papers?' Fairburn asked. 'I'd like to see them.'

'I supposed you're used to checking papers, ain't you?' Todmorden replied, pulling his *dokumenty* from his pocket.

'I'm a 10th Directorate agent, not a border guard. I've used more fake papers than I've ever checked,' Fairburn replied matter-of-factly. He studied Todmorden's identity card and driving licence, then Suzie's. They were very good, both with a mauve stripe denoting them as essential workers. That meant priority for fuel rations and curfew exemptions. 'These are good,' he said.

'I've got these too,' said Todmorden, handing an envelope to Fairburn.

Fairburn opened it. Inside was a full set of identity papers, including a passport, in the name of James Hamilton. The photographs were of Sandy Fisk. 'Where did these come from?'

'A friend,' the ex-SS man said.

Ash Prasad's people, no doubt. 'Suzie, take us through the plan again.'

Suzie spread a map across the Jaguar's bonnet. 'We'll drive to Mildenhall separately. At eleven hundred hours I'll park the Wolseley on the aerodrome perimeter road near Thistley Green. I'll pretend to have broken down, which is when Ronnie will pick me up in his recovery van. Then we'll drive to the old church on the northern side of the base for 11.15.'

Todmorden nodded. 'I called our people in East Anglia. They say the churchyard's the aerodrome's emergency RV if there's a fire or a bomb threat at the base. That way we'll blow up any fuckers running from the first bomb. Every Red in a fifty-mile radius will head there like flies around shit.'

Suzie didn't look up from the map. 'See the line marked through the church symbol? It means the place is closed. There'll be no services or congregation.'

'We're only blowing up godless Reds,' Todmorden chuckled.

'Carry on, Suzie,' Fairburn replied curtly. He'd have refused to bomb a church with civilians inside.

'Tommy, at 11.20 you'll pick us up and drop us near Little Shadwell,' Suzie continued. 'Then we'll go to the pub and cover your meeting with Fisk.'

'If we have to, we'll take out any KGB men,' Todmorden added. 'He might be followed.'

'Yes, that's likely. Let me deal with them,' said Fairburn, checking his watch. 'What time will the bombs detonate?'

Suzie looked up from the map. 'I'll set the Wolseley's timer for 11.55 and the Bedford's for 12.05. Then we take Fisk, stick him in the Jag and drive like buggery.'

'Then our instructions are to take him to Alderney Street and wait,' said Todmorden.

'And afterwards?' asked Tommy. 'Have you been given instructions about me?'

The ex-SS man studied Fairburn with heavy-lidded eyes. 'You and Fisk will be collected by our people. Then Suzie will go her way and I'll go mine.'

Fairburn suspected the pick-up would be the moment of danger. Now he was compromised in the eyes of the KGB, would Prasad have him killed? He felt the Makarov close to his ribcage, wondering if he'd have to shoot Todmorden and Suzie. They were, after all, terrorists. 'Very well,' he said, opening the door of the Jaguar. 'Shall we get on with it?'

Fairburn took the north-eastern route out of London. It began raining as he gunned the Jaguar through the Hertfordshire and Essex countryside, occasionally glancing at the map on the passenger seat next to him. The fields were flat and grey, low concrete buildings marking collective farms. He passed a blue militia car idling by the side of the road, but the driver paid him no attention. Finally he saw the sign for Little Shadwell. He checked his watch – it was just after ten am. A little early, but that was no bad thing. The pub where he was due to meet Fisk, the Moon and Stars, sat on a crossroads next to a pond. Like everywhere else in Britain, it had seen better days, the pub's walls water stained and the beer garden muddy. Satisfied with his survey, he drove to the next village, parked and went into a tobacconist's.

He bought a copy of *The Sunday Times*, a bag of mints and a pack of Capstan cigarettes. Although he loathed smoking, almost everyone else smoked. Anything he could do to not stand out was welcome. Then, sitting in the Jaguar, he read his newspaper and waited.

At 11.20, he drove to the northern side of the aerodrome, following the signs in English and Russian for military traffic. As Suzie predicted, Mildenhall looked more like an industrial facility than an aerodrome – a sprawling complex of factories, smokestacks and workshops. Hangars lined a network of runways, the tails of grey-green military aircraft visible above barbed wire fences. Todmorden stood by the old church with Suzie. Both had changed into smarter clothes, suitable for Sunday lunch. The snub-nosed Bedford van was parked next to the gate leading into the overgrown churchyard, the gravestones crooked and furred with moss. 'Blimey,' said Todmorden, looking at his watch. 'Would you look at that? Everything's going to plan.'

'Don't say that, Ronnie,' Suzie chided. 'It's bad luck.'

'Get in the car,' said Fairburn. He drove back to the Moon and Stars, dropping them at the edge of the village.

'Good luck,' said Suzie.

Todmorden nodded, hefting the holdall containing the submachine guns over his shoulder. 'Let's get on with it,' he grunted.

Fairburn drove back to the pub, parking outside at exactly 11.45. A black Austin idled near the duck pond, two brawny-looking men crammed in the front. *KGB.* They watched Fairburn get out of the Jaguar, the passenger writing something in a notebook. They looked like typical 3rd Main Directorate goons – military counterintelligence – crop-headed heavies, not given to subtlety. Fairburn checked his watch as he walked inside the bar. The first bomb was due to go off in nine minutes. 'I'm just opening up,' said the landlord, a pudgy man wearing a gingham shirt. There were no other customers, the only sound the ticking of a clock.

'I was hoping to get some lunch,' Fairburn replied. 'I'm meeting a friend here.'

'Do you have any ration coupons? We take cash too, of course.'

Fairburn produced a sheaf of Party vouchers from his pocket. 'Will these do?'

The landlord smiled. 'Oh yes, those'll be fine. Would you like a drink while you wait for your friend, Comrade?'

'Just a light ale, I think,' Fairburn replied. A few minutes later Todmorden walked in, a swagger in his step, and ordered two drinks. A pint of bitter, and a port and lemon. He paid and went back outside to the beer garden. Fairburn sat facing the door, pretending to read his newspaper. At 11.54, Sandy Fisk arrived. He was a slightly built man, dressed in corduroys and a navy blue sweater. He was carrying a satchel and a rolled-up newspaper as he shuffled into the bar. 'Ah, Sandy,' said Fairburn, standing up and offering his hand. 'It's lovely to see you again.'

'It is, Wenlock,' Fisk replied, eyes screwed up behind his glasses. 'I see you have a drink…' Then the two KGB men walked into the bar, scowling.

Which was when the first bomb went off.

Chapter 33

The explosion rattled the pub's windows. 'What on earth was that?' said Fisk, clutching his satchel to his chest.

'Maybe it came from the aerodrome?' said the landlord, half-crouching behind the bar.

'Professor Fisk, come with us,' ordered one of the KGB men in English, showing his red ID card. 'We are with project security. It's not safe here.'

'He's perfectly fine,' said Fairburn in Russian, producing his own *dokumenty*. 'I'm Captain Fairburn, of the 10th Directorate.'

'Nobody told us anything about you,' the KGB man replied stonily.

Fairburn studied the KGB man's ID. 'No, I don't suppose they did, Comrade *Sergeant*. I report directly to Colonel Sechkin in London.'

'There's no time to argue, Comrade Captain,' said the second KGB man, a gorilla with bushy eyebrows. He had one hand on the shoulder holster beneath his jacket. 'Let's get Doctor Fisk away from here, then we can talk.'

'I agree,' said Fairburn. 'Let's go.'

'I estimate the explosion was two kilometres north-west of us,' said Fisk. 'I think we're quite safe, gentlemen. And I am rather hungry.'

'Unless there's another bomb nearby, Professor,' said the KGB gorilla, grabbing Fisk's arm. He dragged the scientist outside, followed by Fairburn and the second Russian. Outside, a neat column of black smoke pointed skywards. Todmorden stood up and pulled something from a bag. 'Put your hands up,' he growled in Russian, pointing an MP40 at the KGB men. 'Or I'll shoot the fucking lot of you.'

The gorilla pulled his gun and Todmorden fired, a burst ripping into the KGB man's chest. The second Russian threw his hands in the air, but Todmorden fired again, bullets knocking him off his feet. 'Suzie, go and read the landlord his fortune, will you?' said Todmorden. 'Tell him he saw nothing.' The young Ulsterwoman gulped her port and lemon, nodded and darted inside the pub.

'That was unnecessary,' said Fairburn, wrinkling his nose as he stepped over the dead KGB men.

'They saw my face,' Todmorden replied, sliding a new magazine into the MP40. 'Now move!' Fairburn got into the Jaguar and started the ignition, Todmorden bundling Fisk into the back of the car.

Leaving the pub, Suzie jumped into the passenger's seat next to Fairburn. 'What are you waiting for?' she said, eyes bright. 'Let's go.'

Fairburn drove fast. He didn't hear the second explosion but saw emergency vehicles speeding north: an ambulance, a fire engine. Then a militia van, its klaxon wailing. 'Slow down,' said Todmorden. 'We'll look suspicious if you hammer it.'

'Not speeding in a Jaguar like this? I'd say that's more suspicious,' Fairburn replied, selecting fourth gear and gunning the engine.

Suzie covered the MP40 on her lap with her coat. 'There'll be militia roadblocks on the main roads. Tommy, we need to take a back route.'

'Take the next left,' said Fisk. 'There's a shortcut to Bury St. Edmunds. I imagine it'll be quieter on a Sunday.'

'He's right,' said Todmorden, studying a map. 'We'll go via Colchester.'

Fisk shook his head. 'Why did you set off a bomb? Was that entirely necessary?'

'You're an expert ain't you, Doctor?' said Todmorden. 'What's your thing?'

'Astronautics.'

'Mine's killing Reds and blowing stuff up.'

'Shut up will you, Ronnie?' said Suzie. 'The wee fella's terrified.'

The drive back to London was quiet. Fairburn grudgingly accepted Todmorden was right to kill the two Russians; it had bought them precious time. It was 15.00 when they arrived back at the railway arch. 'We'll split up,' said Fairburn, straightening his tie. 'Meet back at Alderney Street. Professor Fisk, please come with me.'

Todmorden shook his meaty head. 'No, he comes with me.'

'My instructions were clear. Besides, where else do I have to go?'

'Tommy's right,' said Suzie, pulling a tarpaulin off a bicycle. 'Him and the doctor look like they might go for a walk together. You look like you're about to mug him.'

Todmorden pulled the bag containing weapons from the back of the car. 'All right. I'll stash our kit and tidy up. I'll see you back at the flat.'

Fairburn gave Fisk the envelope containing his new papers. 'Put your old papers in there,' he said, pointing to a metal dustbin.

'I'll burn 'em,' said Todmorden, pulling a petrol lighter from his pocket. 'Now bugger off, the pair of you.'

Fisk studied his new identity card. 'They used the name I asked for,' he said approvingly. '*James Hamilton*. He was a friend from Cambridge.'

'Just remember it if we're stopped,' said Fairburn, stepping outside. 'It can feel strange using a false name.' He led Fisk through an alleyway leading to Albert Embankment. A company of Russian soldiers in greatcoats and fur hats marched towards Vauxhall Bridge, their jack-boots crashing on tarmac. 'They're rehearsing for Khrushchev's visit,' said Tommy. 'It's fine.'

'I'm sorry,' Fisk replied. 'I'm rather shaken up.'

'We're not far from the flat. You'll be safe there.' The walk to Alderney Street took half an hour. The city was near deserted as dusk fell, smoke creeping from chimneys as families settled in for the evening.

'Come in,' said Suzie, waiting at the front door. 'I've made us a pot of tea.'

'Is Todmorden here yet?'

'No, he'll take his time. His tradecraft's good. Here, Doctor, take a seat.'

Fisk nodded his thanks and took off his coat and hat. He sat on the couch, his satchel on his lap. 'Thank you, Miss. May I ask how long I'll be here?'

'Ronnie will know,' Suzie replied, disappearing into the kitchen.

'And you?' the scientist asked, turning to Fairburn. 'I saw your identity card. I heard you speak fluent Russian. Are you really a KGB officer?'

Fairburn stood by the window, his hand resting on the Makarov's grips. 'The less you know the better, Doctor Fisk. I hope you understand.'

'Of course. I'm grateful. The risks you've taken are immeasurable.'

'We all take risks. You have too. From now on, you're a marked man as long as you remain in Britain.'

'Actually, my work here's more or less finished.'

Fairburn was tempted to ask exactly why Fisk was so important. Something stopped him; hadn't Prasad – almost certainly the most important US asset in Britain – broken cover to help rescue the scientist? 'I think we should enjoy what's called a companionable silence,' he said finally. 'I think it's safer for us both.'

'Very well,' Fisk replied. He began humming gently under his breath, eyes scrunched up behind his glasses.

Finally, Todmorden arrived. 'We're all good,' he said, looking pleased with himself. 'I called my contact.'

'And?' Fairburn asked.

'He'll be here to collect Fisk soon. He'll have instructions for you too, Tommy.'

'Very well,' Fairburn replied. At least Todmorden hadn't tried to disarm him. If they were planning on betraying him, wouldn't they take his gun?

'Tea,' said Suzie, carrying a tray of mugs. 'There's milk and sugar too. Would you like a biscuit, Doctor Fisk?'

'I think I would,' Fisk replied. 'Someone interrupted my lunch.'

There was a knock on the door. Suzie opened it, the Beretta held behind her back. 'Suzie,' said a familiar voice. Fairburn realised it was Nolan. 'Can I come in?'

'Of course, Mick,' she said. 'The Professor's here.'

Nolan saw Fisk and offered his hand. 'I'm taking you to see Katherine, Doctor,' he said, nodding at Fairburn. 'Everything's arranged.'

'Thank you,' Fisk replied. 'I'm very grateful.'

'And what happens to me?' Fairburn asked.

Todmorden's lip curled. 'Will you let Fisk get out of the door? You're a selfish little shit, ain't you?'

'It's alright, Ronnie,' said Nolan. 'Tommy's taken risks. Big risks.'

'What a shame.' Todmorden smirked. 'Now you'll have to sleep with one eye open just like the rest of us.'

Nolan, expressionless, pulled something from inside his coat. It was a black handgun, fitted with a suppressor. The weapon made a metallic sigh as a subsonic bullet slammed into the back of Todmorden's head. Suzie gasped as Nolan aimed and fired again, the inside of her skull spattering the wall behind her. Fisk's hands fluttered in his lap like dying birds. Nolan turned to find himself looking down the muzzle of Fairburn's Makarov. 'Put the shooter away, Tommy.'

Fairburn glanced at the bodies. Why?'

'Prasad calls it *disinfection*. Todmorden's too wrapped around the BAF for Prasad's liking. The girl, too. Loose lips sink ships and all that, eh?'

'Prasad? It was you who pulled the trigger.'

'I only shoot who I'm told. You know how that works, Tommy. Come on Doctor Fisk, let's be havin' you.'

Fairburn kept his pistol trained on the assassin. 'Where are you taking us?'

Nolan shook his head. 'I'll tell you one more time, put the bloody gun away. You won't need it where we're going.'

'You trust me with a gun?'

Nolan nodded. 'Yeah, I do as it happens. You're clever. You know shooting me solves nothing.'

'Then tell me where we're going.'

'Somewhere safe,' Nolan replied. Then, a smile. 'Besides, it ain't like you've got much choice.'

A black Mercedes was parked outside, the driver smartly dressed in a suit and tie. They got in, Nolan sitting in the back next to Fisk. They drove west, crossing the river at Putney, the Thames as flat and black as a coffin lid. Fisk fidgeted in his seat. 'Am I going to see Katherine now?'

'You'll spend tonight somewhere safe,' said Nolan. 'You'll see her tomorrow.'

Fairburn turned in his seat. 'Nolan, how's Colonel Sechkin?'

A shrug. 'As far as we know he's at the embassy. He hasn't left the country if that's what you're asking.'

'I need to speak to Prasad.'

'You will soon,' Nolan replied. The Mercedes parked outside a handsome-looking house on the edge of Putney Heath. Nolan led Fisk inside, Fairburn following close behind. 'Go straight upstairs, Doctor. Mrs Anderson has new clothes for you. She'll also dye your hair.'

'Very well,' Fisk replied, traipsing up a flight of stairs.

Nolan nodded to a white-painted door. 'Mister Prasad's waiting. Now I want your gun.'

'You said…'

'Gimme the gun,' Nolan repeated. 'It ain't nothing personal. You'll get it back soon enough.'

Taking off his overcoat, Fairburn unholstered his pistol and handed it to Nolan. 'I've no other weapons.'

'Show me.'

Fairburn opened his jacket. 'Nothing. Not even a knife.'

'Okay, you can go in.'

'That's very gracious,' Fairburn replied.

Nolan shrugged and opened the door. 'I've got nothing against you, son. A word to the wise: why not keep it that way?'

Chapter 34

Prasad sat by an open fire, cradling a tumbler of Scotch. 'Well done, Tommy. Please, why don't you help yourself to a drink?'

Fairburn went to a well-stocked cabinet and poured a glass of vodka. 'Thank you, Ash,' he said, taking a seat opposite the spy.

'I have to say, it's a shame you've made yourself persona non grata with your Soviet masters.'

'Really? It feels like I was set up.'

'Yes, I can see why you might think that,' Prasad replied, his eyes creasing with amusement. 'The problem with our job is one tends to see bad faith behind everything. Even when it's just damned bad luck.'

'Was it bad luck?'

'Of course. I wanted you to work for us. You had a bright future ahead of you. I know Katherine will be disappointed.'

'Are you disappointed, Ash?'

Prasad's eyes turned to the logs burning in the fireplace. 'You're a professional, Tommy. I shan't insult your intelligence. Fisk was the prize – your recruitment was simply a bonus.'

'What happens now?'

'If you have any sense you'll defect. Admittedly, your friend Sechkin will be sent back to Moscow in disgrace. It's a shame, but not the end of the world. Nikolai's well connected, he'll survive one way or the other.'

'I'm not hanging Nikolai out to dry,' Fairburn replied, finishing his vodka. He got up and poured another. 'It's non-negotiable.'

Prasad smiled his Cheshire cat smile. 'Loyalty is commendable, of course. There's another possibility, but it's not without risk.'

'What's one more? This country is full of risks.'

'Quite,' said Prasad. 'The fringes of empires can be dangerous places. It's where they tend to unravel.'

Fairburn sat back down. 'What do you propose?'

Prasad leaned forward conspiratorially. He was a good actor, Fairburn thought. *This was his preferred option all along.* 'Consider this scenario, Tommy; after your kidnap ordeal you suffered a form of psychiatric shock. This explains your erratic behaviour when you ran. You finally see sense and hand yourself in to the CSS.'

'Go on,' said Fairburn.

'I'll suggest to Director Philby you attend our special facility in Kent, a clinic for officers requiring rest and recuperation. After Khrushchev's visit is over, I'll have our psychiatrist proclaim you fit for duty. I'll persuade Philby to smooth things over with Teplyakov and we'll take things from there.'

'I can assure you, General Teplyakov is unlikely to be sympathetic to the idea of *psychiatric shock.*'

'He lost Sandy Fisk on his watch,' Prasad replied. He smiled, like a chess player watching an opponent make an ill-chosen move. 'Teplyakov's in no position to argue. And, of course, you'll be saving Sechkin too.' *Check and mate.*

'I suppose it might work,' said Fairburn without enthusiasm.

'There's only one fly in the ointment.'

'Yes?'

'Sergeant Ross. He's been badgering one of my Bureau 6 officers,

Captain King. She's my most trusted agent inside Burgess House. Ross even found a witness prepared to implicate her in the skulduggery around Frayne at the Richmond Assizes.'

'Ross is a good officer.' Fairburn shrugged. He wasn't going to admit to asking Ross to hunt down the CSS mole. 'He's simply doing his job.'

'Yes, but Ross has Philby's ear. What happens when he fills the Director's head with theories about King's loyalty? About CIA penetration inside CSS? The trail leads back to me. I recruited King, after all. So Ross has to die. It would be easier if you did the honours, given your obvious rapport with the man. It would also demonstrate your commitment to our new relationship.'

Fairburn finished his vodka. 'I'd like another drink, if I may.'

'Of course, old boy. I know, this is distasteful stuff. I take little satisfaction from it either.'

'It's the game we play. We don't have to enjoy it.'

'Precisely,' Prasad replied. 'I'm glad you understand. Would you pour me a Scotch please?'

Fairburn poured drinks and sat back down. 'I'll do it, but it's the last time.'

'How so?'

'I'll work for you, Prasad, but I won't kill for you again.'

Prasad looked surprised. '10th Directorate Spartans are killers, Tommy. Isn't it part of your job description?'

'Oh, I'll kill for the 10th Directorate. Just not for you. I think it's safer for both of us that way.'

'Why?'

'Because I think you've developed a taste for ordering people killed. I think you should go back to doing it yourself.'

'Why? Mister Nolan fills that role admirably. My talents don't extend to violence. The only time I killed someone, I discovered it wasn't for me.'

'In which case Mister Nolan will be even busier. I agree, he's an exceptional killer.'

'I think Nolan likes you, Tommy. He sees a kindred spirit, perhaps?' Prasad replied, switching to Russian. 'Now, a toast, Comrade Captain?'

'Yes, I have one,' Fairburn replied, finishing his vodka and tossing the glass into the fire. The glass shattered, making Prasad flinch. 'It's very Russian. *If you're scared of wolves, don't go into the woods.*'

'Quite so,' said Prasad.

'Then I suppose I should go,' Fairburn replied, shrugging on his raincoat. Reaching inside his jacket pocket, he switched off Renton's Minifon recorder. 'Take care, Ash.'

'Thank you, Tommy. I shall.'

'I wanted to say goodbye, Doctor Fisk,' said Fairburn. 'I hope America suits you.'

'I hope so too,' Fisk replied. He sat in a chair with a towel around his neck, a matronly looking woman cutting his newly dyed hair. 'It's not as if I can change my mind now.'

'In any case, I wanted to say I'm sorry about the violence. This business we're in…'

'It's horrible,' said Fisk. 'I can't pretend to understand how it works. I think, on the whole, I prefer physics.'

'Send my regards to Katherine, please? I'd like it if she could contact me sometime.'

'Katherine's a lovely girl. Eliza trusts her, and she's a shrewd judge of character. Eliza always was.'

'Well, Eliza Crewe speaks highly of you, so I'm told. You're a poet too, aren't you?'

'I was.' Fisk blushed. 'You're quite charming, Mister Fairburn.'

'That's not something I hear very often.'

'I've become accustomed to threats, I'm afraid. I've spent too much time surrounded by bloody Soviets.'

'So have I. Take care, Doctor Fisk.'

'You too, Mister Fairburn. Please, stay safe.'

Fairburn stepped towards the door. 'Now, there's something else I don't hear very often.'

'Come on,' said Nolan, waiting in the corridor outside. 'There's a car waiting.'

'What about the curfew?'

'It's a CSS car driven by a CSS officer. You'll be fine.'

'Very well.'

Nolan took something from his pocket. A notebook. He tore out a page. 'There's a contact number if you need anything. Just stay away from Alison King, right?'

'Thanks.'

'And you'll be needing this,' he said, returning Fairburn's Makarov.

'Thank you, Nolan,' Fairburn replied, sliding the pistol into its shoulder holster.

'Just remember something, Tommy.'

'Yes?'

'I'll be watching. Please behave yourself, alright?'

Fairburn patted the big man's shoulder. 'Thanks for the warning. If it comes to it, I think it will be interesting.'

'What?'

'The day you try to kill me, Comrade. Now, good night.'

The CSS man parked outside a mansion block in South Kensington. 'The safehouse is flat 6a,' he said, handing Fairburn a key. 'When Sid Ross is dead, call the number Nolan provided. You'll be given further instructions.'

'Understood.'

The driver's eyes swept the street. 'Mister Prasad asked me to remind you he's got eyes and ears everywhere. No fucking about, Fairburn.'

'I said I understood.'

'I'm telling you again.'

Fairburn shrugged. He was a Spartan. A wolf. And wolves cared little for threats made by sheep.

Chapter 35

Gerry Scanlon lived in an art deco villa near Hampstead Heath. Fairburn checked his wristwatch – 05.15. The CSS surveillance report noted Scanlon walked his dog every morning at 05.30. He waited in the trees on the edge of the heath, his collar turned up against the morning chill. At 05.25 exactly, Scanlon appeared and nodded at the militiaman standing guard outside his door. He wore a waxed jacket and a tweed cap like a country squire, but his dog was a fluffy little thing. Scanlon walked to the end of the road, pausing to let the dog pee against a lamp post, before turning onto the path leading to the heath. 'Good morning, Comrade,' said Fairburn, stepping from behind a tree. Scanlon's hand disappeared into his coat, but Fairburn beat him to the draw. He aimed his Makarov at Scanlon's belly. 'I'm going to put my gun away, Comrade. I need to talk, that's all.'

'Then why not come to my office, you silly bastard?' Scanlon replied, crouching down to placate the dog. 'Or telephones? You've got those in Russia, ain't you?'

'It's a long story.'

'Well, you've got twenty minutes before my driver picks me up. What do you want, Comrade Captain?'

Fairburn lowered his pistol. 'Let's walk.'

'Come on then, it's my favourite time of day. No other fucker about. Well, apart from you.'

They crossed the heath, the little dog sniffing and snuffling. 'I bugged your car on the evening of the reception at Harry Pollitt House,' said Fairburn. 'I have a recording of you confessing to helping Michael Nolan fake his own death. You arranged counterfeit papers for a CIA-linked terrorist. That's a death penalty offence.'

Scanlon sounded amused. '*Kompromat*? Nice try, son. You think I ain't been threatened before? You reckon I ain't got a safe full of shit on Philby and his CSS wankers?'

Fairburn studied Scanlon's face, as blue as woad in the half-light. 'I'm sure you have, but it's not Philby you need to worry about. I'll play the recording to General Teplyakov. He'll have you in front of a firing squad by lunchtime and there'll be tanks on Whitehall by dusk.'

Scowling, the Militia General licked his teeth. He reminded Fairburn of the feral dogs in Cairo, vicious when cornered. 'Teplyakov? He could always try, the weaselly little cunt. Does he want a war?'

'Nervous, Comrade? I would be too.' Fairburn smiled. 'Nolan's implicated in the attack on Richmond Assizes. Furthermore, I can prove he's working for the Americans.' They stopped outside Kenwood House. The stately home, overlooking the heath, had been turned into a library dedicated to Karl Marx. A floodlit statue of the great man stood outside, a copy of *Das Kapital* clutched to his breast.

'Tell me what you want or fuck off,' Scanlon growled.

'I want to stop London going the way of Budapest,' said Fairburn. 'I want you to make your peace with Philby, before Teplyakov persuades Khrushchev to order a crackdown.'

Scanlon shook his head. 'You can't make peace with Philby. His soul's fucking rotten. He's screwed so many people over he's forgotten what it's like to honour a deal.'

'He's a survivor, Comrade General, just like you. A peace of sorts is possible,' said Fairburn. 'Have you heard of something called the *Nash Equilibrium*?'

Scanlon checked his watch and sighed. 'No, I fucking well haven't.'

'Nash is an esteemed American mathematician. Soviet political scientists find his work of great interest. So much so, I attended a lecture on his work last year. Nash theorises that in any game it's possible to reach a position where neither side can win – a permanent stalemate. It occurs when both sides are intimately familiar with their opponent's strategy.'

'Like a checkmate in chess?'

'More or less. You and Philby can achieve a Nash Equilibrium. An understanding that, if neither one of you can win, the only logical choice is to coexist. Or, you can both die.'

'It probably looks fucking fantastic on a blackboard. How does it work in the real world?'

Fairburn felt a frisson of excitement. Scanlon wanted a deal. He could feel it. 'I have kompromat on Philby too – he's been duped by the Americans. There's a traitor very close to him. He'll look like a fool. He might even be forced to stand down.'

Scanlon was stony-faced. 'There's more to you than meets the eye. I had you down as just another KGB killer.'

'Oh, I am, Comrade. But I do wonder if I've had enough sometimes.'

'I know the feeling, Tommy, I did terrible things during the war. Torturing and killing. I even ended up enjoying it. It was necessary, but I wouldn't want to do it again.'

'And what about my proposal?'

Scanlon picked up his dog and ruffled its furry head. 'I can do Philby's legs and he can do mine? You think that's enough to keep the peace? For how long?'

'I'm not a politician, but with wreckers like Frayne and McGrouther out of the way, why not? Perhaps the two of you could agree a Politburo that suits you both?'

Scanlon grinned. 'Come on then, what's this precious kompromat of yours?'

Fairburn pulled a plasticky box from his pocket. 'This,' he said.

'What is it?'

'A KGB-issue Protona Minifon micro-recorder,' Fairburn replied. 'I was wearing it when I spoke to Ash Prasad last night.' Taking off the casing covering the device, he pulled the metal 'play' switch. The recording of Prasad's voice was surprisingly clear: *There's only one fly in the ointment... Sergeant Ross. He's been bothering one of my Bureau 6 officers, Alison King. She's my most trusted agent inside Burgess House. Ross even found a witness prepared to implicate her in skulduggery around Frayne at Richmond Assizes... what will happen if he fills the Director's head with theories about King's loyalty? About CIA penetration inside CSS? The trail leads back to me. So Ross has to die, I'm afraid. It would be easier if you did the honours, given your obvious rapport with the man...*

'Fuck me,' said Scanlon. Grinning, he put his dog down and pulled a cigarette case from his pocket. He lit one and inhaled deeply. 'I'd go as far as to say that's more damning than the shit you've got on me. It makes Philby look incompetent. Reliant on a sergeant? What a complete fool.'

'You've still committed a capital offence, Comrade General.'

Scanlon shrugged. 'I was doing an old friend a favour in good faith. People will realise that's human frailty, not betrayal. But Philby's been professionally humiliated. Will he play ball?'

'What choice does he have? He's agreed to suppress the recording of you for now. He needs to keep Teplyakov on his leash.'

Scanlon began walking back across the heath. Pausing to look at the statue of Marx, he shook his head. 'Can I contact you at Burgess House?'

'No,' said Fairburn. 'I told you it was a long story. It's best if I contact you.'

Scanlon laughed. 'You're in the shit too? Then I could have you arrested?'

'You could.'

'Well, good luck,' said Scanlon, walking away and not looking back. 'I reckon we'll both be needing some before today's over.'

Fairburn took an early morning bus to Kilburn. With his neat suit and overcoat, he knew he looked like a government employee. In any case, none of the other passengers would make eye contact. They passed gangs of labourers on the street, most of them elderly, filling potholes and painting walls. The younger labourers would be in Russia. He got off the bus at Kilburn High Road and found the street he was looking for. The house was easy enough to identify, a black GAZ saloon parked outside. At 06.45 the door opened and Sid Ross stepped out, dressed in his usual scruffy suit, raincoat and Homburg hat. He unlocked the GAZ and got in, Fairburn walking quickly towards him. Opening the back door, he slid inside the car. 'Sid,' he hissed. 'Just drive.'

'What the fuck?'

'I'll explain when we're on the move.'

'Are you being followed?'

'No, I'm clean. Are you?'

'I reckon so, but I reckon Bureau 6 tailed me yesterday. The cocktail squad working on a Sunday? Things must be serious.'

Tommy checked the street. It was empty. 'Drive.'

'Okay,' Ross replied, manoeuvring out of his parking space.

'Did you hear about a bombing in Suffolk?'

Ross nodded. 'Yeah, but the Russians are being tight-lipped. BAF terror attack is all they're saying. Since Sechkin was sent back to the embassy we've heard nothing else.'

'Is Nikolai okay?'

'I asked Philby in passing, he says he's fine for the moment. It all depends on Teplyakov, but word is you dropped Nikolai in the shit, Tommy. Why?'

Fairburn kneaded his face. *Damn I'm tired.* 'I'll explain, but did you get the visitor's log?'

'Yeah, and a statement from the TUC official. It puts Alison King on the scene.'

'There's something else.'

Sid shook his head. 'What now?'

'Ash Prasad's working for the CIA. He tried to blackmail me into working for him. He sent me to kill you.'

'Why?'

'To protect Alison King. She's part of his network.'

Ross shook his head. 'Last time I checked it was October, Comrade Captain, not bloody April 1st.'

'I'm not joking. I know it sounds incredible, but it's true.'

Fairburn saw Ross' eyes narrow in the rear-view mirror. 'Then show me some bloody evidence, Tommy. Not hearsay. I'm sick and tired of spy games.'

'You're right,' said Fairburn, pulling the micro-recorder from his pocket. 'I've got evidence right here.'

'What is it?'

Fairburn tapped the Protona. 'This is a recording of Prasad ordering me to kill you. Do you want to hear it?'

'Yes, I fucking well do. Now, where are we going?'

'You're going to Burgess House.'

'Now I'm proper baffled.'

'Find Renton. Get him to make a copy of the recording. Then get it back to me.'

'You've got a plan?'

'Yes, I've got a plan.'

'Fair enough,' Ross replied, switching on the car's klaxon. 'Hold on to your hat, Comrade.'

Ross dropped Fairburn on a side street near Ladbroke Grove. 'There's a café at the end of the road called Maisie's. The owner's an old friend and she's got a telephone. I'll call as soon as I've got a copy of the recording.'

'Thanks, Sid. Please, be quick.'

'I'll make sure Renton plays ball. What d'you want me to do afterwards?'

'Go and see Philby. Play him the recording. Tell him I'm pretending to go along with Prasad's plan in order to expose him. There are to be no arrests, okay?'

Ross raised an eyebrow. 'This sounds a bit moody to me, Tommy.'

'I am a Spartan,' said Fairburn coldly. 'I'm authorised to use unconventional methods. What else do you think I'm doing?'

A shrug. 'I think you'll always have Sechkin's back. That's why I'm inclined to believe you.'

'If Philby doesn't believe you, I'm a dead man. Then Prasad will have you killed too.'

Ross switched on the GAZ's ignition. 'Well, if you put it like that.'

'It's crucial you persuade Philby not to let Prasad know we're onto him.'

'How the fuck do I do that?'

'He trusts your judgement, Sid. Show me what a famous Scotland Yard detective can do,' said Fairburn, getting out of the car.

Ross pulled out into the street, smoke coughing from the GAZ's exhaust. 'And you, Tommy?' he called out of the window.

'I'll work it out after breakfast,' Fairburn replied, patting his stomach.

Chapter 36

Maisie was a chubby *babushka* with blue-rinsed hair and thick-rimmed glasses. She smiled warmly when Fairburn mentioned Sid's name. 'How is Sid?' she asked, fussing over an ageing coffee machine. Apart from a couple of road sweepers eating breakfast, the place was empty. 'He's a character, ain't he? Sid was a copper with my brother George. That was before the war, of course.'

'Sid's very well,' Fairburn replied, studying the menu. 'He said you wouldn't mind if I used your telephone.'

'It's just round the back. It's fine as long as you leave some money for the call,' Maisie replied, nodding at a jar labelled *tips*.

Fairburn put two ten shilling notes in the jar, Rosa Luxemburg's face gazing earnestly from the red-inked banknotes. 'Is that enough?'

Maisie winked. 'Very generous. That'll get you breakfast too, love.'

Fairburn sat at the back of the café. He read *The Daily Worker* and ate three fried eggs, thickly sliced ham and a hefty slab of bubble and squeak. A pile of toast appeared, drenched in margarine. There was even proper coffee. He ate with quiet efficiency, one eye on the clock on the café wall. At 08.45 he went to the telephone and dialled a number in Kensington. 'Hello?' said Irina Sechkina.

Fairburn spoke in Russian. 'It's me, Irina. I need to speak to Nikolai.'

'He's at work, I'm afraid,' she replied, using the stiff telephone manner many Russians used. That of someone who knows their calls are monitored. 'Can I help?'

'Can you give him a message?'

'Of course.'

'I need to see him soon. I have something important for him. Very important, in fact.'

'Where and when would you like to see Nikolai?'

'Tell him I'll be at the place we first met during the war at twenty-one hundred hours, okay?'

'I'll pass on your message.'

'Thank you,' Tommy replied, ending the call. He returned to find Maisie cutting cheese sandwiches. 'Can I ask a favour please?' he asked.

'What's that, love?'

'I need a new overcoat. And a hat.'

Maisie pulled a face. 'What's wrong with yours? It's very smart.'

'It is, but I'll happily swap it.'

The old woman touched the lapel of Fairburn's overcoat and rubbed the fabric between her index finger and thumb. 'That's nice *schmutter*,' she said approvingly. 'Cashmere mix? I s'pose I could get a few bob for it.'

'Exactly.'

'I've got my old fella's spare work jacket and a woolly hat.'

'Perfect,' said Fairburn, stripping off his overcoat and tie. 'There's one more thing?'

'Yes?'

'Do you have a map of London? I've been away for a while.'

'I think so, love.'

Fairburn sat back down and re-read the paper twice. Then he finished the crossword. Sid Ross rang at 10.15. 'You okay?' he asked.

'Apart from drinking too much coffee? Did you get a copy of the tape?'

'Yes, Renton's shitting himself. I told him if he mentions this to anyone I'll shoot him. Which I will, as it happens.'

'I don't doubt it. And Philby?'

'He's busy. I couldn't get an appointment until this afternoon.'

'*Busy?*' Fairburn snapped. 'Just go into his office. Put the bloody tape on his desk.'

'Hold your horses, Tommy. I'm up to my neck in shit because of your gallivanting. You told me to do this my way.'

'I'm sorry, Sid.'

'It's alright. Just take it easy on the coffee, eh? Stick to vodka. Look, after I've spoken to Philby things will get messy. What's the plan?'

'I need a copy of the recording and a cassette player.'

'Sure,' Sid replied. 'Who for?'

'Sechkin.'

'I thought you might say that. Is it a good idea? What if Teplyakov finds out?'

'Let me worry about Teplyakov.'

'Okay, meet me at the Hibernian club. One hour.'

'I will. Thank you, Sid.'

Fairburn strode along Ladbroke Grove, his hat pulled down over his ears. Turning into the streets behind Portobello Road, he found what he was looking for – a Vespa moped. He'd learned how to hot-wire Italian motorcycles in Egypt and was soon chugging towards Shepherd's Bush. Maisie had given him a dog-eared copy of a London *A-Z* map, from which he'd memorised the way to Fulham Broadway. He passed more posters of Nikita Khrushchev, red flags flying from every roof. Fairburn had never seen so many hammers and sickles, not even in Moscow. Rows of black militia vans lay parked in the side streets, helmeted men banging on tenement doors with pickaxe handles. The round-ups were beginning, antisocial elements and wreckers headed to prison for the duration of the Soviet premier's visit.

Fairburn suddenly remembered the AVO men setting up machine guns on Budapest's Republic Square. It was nearly a year ago to the day when the Hungarian secret police opened fire on the protestors. He'd watched the carnage from a balcony like a Roman emperor at the Coliseum. Fairburn knew KGB General Teplyakov would like nothing more than to stage his own version in Trafalgar Square. Then he could purge the British politburo. Ship more prisoners to Russia as 'guest workers'. Station more tanks on the border with Ireland. Strengthen the hand of his fellow hardliners in the Kremlin, men who only knew the value of obedience through fear. Fairburn suddenly felt a mixture of guilt and terror. The KGB officer breathed deeply, drawing London's polluted stink deep into his lungs. The stink of where he was born.

Leaving the moped running, Fairburn stepped into a telephone kiosk. He flipped open his notebook and dialled the number Nolan had provided. 'It's Tommy.'

'Go on,' said Nolan.

'Tell your boss I've arranged to meet Ross. This thing will be over by midnight.'

'Where?'

'Why do you want to know?'

'Because *our* boss is a details man, that's why.'

'Surrey. The old borstal in Kenley, off the Godstone Road, twenty-one thirty hours.'

'Why Surrey?' asked Nolan.

'I was there during the war,' Fairburn replied. 'I know the area well, but I doubt Sid Ross does. He thinks I'm handing myself in.'

'Okay. Contact this number when the deed's done.'

'I understand.'

'Tommy?'

'Yes?'

'Look, son, I reckon you're a good prospect. A fighter. The boss is as good as his word, he wants you onboard. You'll be safe.'

'Thanks. I don't feel like I've got many friends right now.'

Nolan's voice nearly softened. 'I can't promise I'm a friend, but I certainly ain't your enemy. Okay?'

'Then that will have to do,' Fairburn replied.

The Hibernian club had beer-sticky floors, the walls covered with peeling concert posters. Sid Ross stood at the bar, chatting to a wizened man wearing a tartan waistcoat. 'Hello Tommy,' he said, holding up a balloon-shaped glass of brandy. 'Fancy a heart-starter?'

'Why not?' Tommy replied.

'Brandy?' asked the man in the waistcoat.

'Vodka.'

'I'll find you some.'

Ross pushed a briefcase across the bar. 'There you go. Exhibit A.'

'You seem relaxed, Sid.'

The detective drained his glass. 'Come on, Tommy. We survived the war, didn't we? Fuck me, we can survive this.'

The barman placed a dusty bottle of *Bobshevskih* in front of Fairburn. 'There you go. It's the only stuff we've got.'

'That's fine, Comrade,' Fairburn replied, pouring four fingers into a glass and drinking it in one gulp. The vodka tasted fiery and old. 'That's not bad at all.'

'Shame we've got to work,' Ross sighed. 'I could spend all day here drinking and talking bollocks.'

'That's all you do anyway,' the barman chided, pouring another brandy. 'Peelers are all the feckin' same. Don't matter where you go.'

'Alright, Fergal, keep your hair on,' said Ross, putting a handful of coins on the bar. 'Now, do me a favour and give us a moment?' Fergal scooped up the coins, tut-tutted and disappeared into the beer cellar.

Fairburn checked the briefcase. Inside was a modern Nagra cassette player and a spool of tape in a halfmoon-shaped leatherette case. 'I'm meeting Sechkin tonight to hand over the recording. Oh, and I'm also going to be murdering you.'

Sid swirled brandy around his glass, sniffed it and took a gulp. 'You can always try.'

'Nolan knows where and when.'

'Then he'll show up?'

'I hope so,' said Tommy, pouring another glass of vodka.

'So it's my turn to play tethered goat?'

'Philby will put you in for the Order of Lenin, Comrade,' Fairburn replied.

Ross finished the rest of his brandy, a grin on his gargoyle-like face. 'I'll settle for a Party ration card and a cushy instructor's posting to the training school.'

Fairburn finished his second drink, then got off his bar stool. 'I've got things to do, Sid. I'll call you later.'

'Yeah, I'm gonna tell the Director of the CSS his closest ally is a CIA spy. Then I'm gonna head off to deepest darkest Surrey to get myself murdered.'

Fairburn took the briefcase and headed for the door. 'You'll miss all this excitement when you retire.'

Ross loosened his necktie and poured himself a slug of vodka. 'No, Tommy. I fucking well won't.'

Chapter 37

The old borstal had been replaced with a new school. The sign outside read ALBERT INKPIN ACADEMY FOR SOCIALIST PIONEERS. It was a modern-looking building made of concrete, steel and glass.

Parking his moped, Fairburn stood and closed his eyes for a moment, the evening air damp on his face. The surrounding area hadn't changed much, not even the woods where boy scouts once fought Soviet tanks. The crossroads outside the school was still potholed and crumbling. Some things had changed though. There was a building site opposite the school, made up of half-finished terraced houses. Craters from decade-old artillery strikes dotted the neighbouring fields, filled with rainwater and rubble. Earthmovers lay idle nearby, statue-like and strange in the darkness. Fairburn stood in the window of one of the half-built terraces, listening to the wind and distant traffic. Eventually he heard a car approach, its bug-eyed headlights dimming as it stopped outside the school. It was a shiny black ZIM limousine on Soviet diplomatic plates. Two men got out, both wearing overcoats and trilby hats. He recognised Nikolai Sechkin immediately, but not the other man. Fairburn felt a pang of anger – he imagined Nikolai would come alone. Sechkin stood by the road near the school gate and lit two cigarettes, offering one to the other man. 'Nikolai, over here,' Fairburn hissed.

'Tommy?'

Fairburn leaned out of the glassless window and waved. He saw the other man reach into his coat. 'There's no need for guns,' he said in Russian.

'That's not my decision,' Sechkin replied. He trudged across the street, followed by the second man. They stepped inside, their heavy shoes crunching on the concrete floor.

'It's good to see you,' said Tommy, studying the other man. It was General Teplyakov's driver. 'It's good to see you too Comrade Rogov.'

'Liar,' Rogov replied, smiling an oily smile.

'Comrade Rogov has General Teplyakov's confidence,' Sechkin sighed. 'He's here to represent his interests.'

'Trusted men are hard to find,' said Rogov, a Makarov in his hand. 'You're suspected of treachery, Comrade Captain. Treachery of the worst kind.'

'I can see why it looks that way.' Fairburn nudged the briefcase towards Sechkin with his foot. 'However, you'll see why I acted as I did.'

Sechkin opened the briefcase and pulled out the tape player. He cranked the lever and hit the play switch. 'Turn the sound up,' Rogov ordered.

'Watch your mouth, Rogov. I'm still a fucking colonel,' Sechkin growled.

'Of course, Comrade Colonel,' Rogov replied. 'Would you turn the sound up *please*?'

The three men listened to the secretly recorded conversation. Prasad's voice was unmistakeable. 'Incredible,' said Sechkin. 'This changes everything.'

'Prasad seems to trust you, Fairburn,' said Rogov. 'You sound like conspirators to me.'

Fairburn shrugged. 'I am a 10ᵗʰ Directorate Spartan. My job is to infiltrate traitors in order to expose them. Prasad would never have trusted a Russian. But an Englishman? He arrogantly assumed I'd work for him.'

Sechkin nodded. 'He's right, Rogov. I think General Teplyakov will understand. The recording provides significant leverage against the British.'

'I've no doubt it does,' Rogov replied, taking a drag of his cigarette. 'On the other hand, the General relies on me to be sceptical.'

'Speaking of leverage, Philby will know about Prasad's betrayal by now,' Fairburn replied. 'I made two copies of the tape.'

'What?' Rogov snapped.

'I think the British will give me time to resolve matters.'

'Then you've overstepped your authority, Comrade Captain.'

'I suppose I have, Comrade Rogov.'

Rogov shook his head. 'Now you've only made me more suspicious.'

'Oh, I've further proof of my loyalty to the KGB,' Fairburn replied.

'Such as?'

Fairburn checked his watch. 'You've just listened to me agreeing to murder a CSS officer, Sidney Ross. Well, he'll be here in about twenty minutes.'

Ross parked his car outside the school. The CSS man wore full uniform with jackboots, two pistols holstered on his Sam Browne belt. 'That's Ross?' asked Rogov.

'Yes,' said Fairburn.

'And you're going to kill him?'

'No,' Fairburn sighed.

Sechkin shook his head. 'You're a moron, Rogov.'

Rogov pulled a face. 'I don't understand. Why is Ross here?'

'Senior Sergeant Ross spoke with Director Philby earlier today,' said Fairburn. 'He played him the tape. Ross is here on his behalf.'

'And why not?' Sechkin smiled. 'You're only a sergeant yourself, aren't you Rogov?'

'I am a *Stárshiy serzhánt*,' Rogov snapped, 'a sergeant major!'

Ross appeared in the doorway, his brawny shoulders brushing each side of the frame. 'Fucking Russians. I heard you a mile away. You're like a herd of fucking elephants.'

'Hello, Sid,' said Sechkin. 'You look unusually smart.'

'Thank you, Comrade Colonel,' Ross replied, looking Rogov up and down. 'Who's this?'

'This is Rogov,' said Tommy. 'He's a sergeant major.'

'A sergeant major? Congratulations,' said Sid.

'I work for General Teplyakov,' Rogov sniffed. 'Tell me what Philby said.'

Ross raised an eyebrow. 'He's rude, ain't he?'

'Very,' said Sechkin. 'I didn't invite him, by the way.'

'Please, what did Director Philby say, Comrade Sergeant?' Rogov sighed.

Ross rested his backside on the windowsill. 'Comrade Director Philby was disappointed when he heard of Prasad's treachery, but he wasn't totally surprised. He says he's been suspicious of Prasad for a while. He says he's grateful to the KGB for confirming his doubts.'

'That's bullshit,' Rogov spat. 'Prasad's virtually running the CSS. It's common knowledge. Philby's broken. Yesterday's man.'

Fairburn unbuttoned his coat. 'Really? You of all people, Rogov, should know the official record is decided by our masters.'

Ross smiled. 'Philby's calling Comrade Chairman Khrushchev personally, to say how grateful he is to General Teplyakov for saving

Britain from a political crisis.' Shooting his cuff, he checked his watch. 'He should be making the call just about… *now*.'

Sechkin finished his cigarette and stubbed it out on the bare brick wall. 'Tommy? You didn't tell me this part.'

'I'm sorry, Nikolai, events overtook us all,' Fairburn replied, pulling his pistol. 'Ready, Sid?'

'Get on with it, Comrade Captain,' Ross sighed. Fairburn aimed his Makarov and fired once. Ross crumpled to the ground, cap tumbling from his bony skull.

'What the hell's going on?' said Rogov.

Fairburn held up a finger. 'Wait,' he whispered. They stood still for a while long moment, the wind whistling through the unfinished house.

Then, the whipcrack of a rifle shot.

Rogov flinched, but Sechkin smiled. 'I think I understand,' said the KGB Colonel. 'At least, I think I do.'

Ross sat up and dusted off his cap. 'Fucking spies. Too clever for your own good, as usual. I just hope wearing this bloody uniform worked.'

'I think it made it easier for our man to see I'd carried out my instructions,' Fairburn replied.

'What on earth are you talking about?' said Rogov.

'I missed on purpose, of course,' Fairburn replied. 'Although I think the bullet nicked your left shoulder board. I'm sorry, Sid, I'll buy you a new one.'

Two figures appeared from the trees at the edge of the playing field. They wore long coats covered in camouflage scrim, their faces streaked black and green.

Snipers.

'We got him,' said Major Vasily Zaitsev matter-of-factly, his rifle slung on his shoulder.

'I got him, actually,' said Raisa Tarasov, pulling back her hood and shaking her hair loose. 'Well spotted, though, Vasily.'

Zaitsev shrugged. 'A team kill is a team kill. Comrade Captain Fairburn, the target was hiding in a bomb crater to the south. He had a clear view into the house through the window.'

'He moved too soon after your pistol shot,' said Tarasov. 'I saw the shine off his binoculars.'

Zaitsev looked skywards. 'That's a Hunter's Moon, and no mistake. Plenty of light.'

'Comrade Zaitsev? Who ordered you here?' asked Rogov.

'Who the fuck are you?' the master sniper replied.

'He's just a jumped-up sergeant who drives Teplyakov about,' said Sechkin, offering the snipers a cigarette. 'Aren't you, Rogov?'

'Yes, Rogov, why don't you go and wait in the car?' said Fairburn. 'This is a 10th Directorate operation. Besides, you'll want to get on the R/T and call the embassy. I'm sure Philby's already spoken to your boss.'

'I'll leave you to your political point-scoring,' said Zaitsev, rolling his dark little eyes. 'Raisa, let's go and examine our kill, shall we?'

The sniper smiled and slapped her boss on the back. 'You mean *my* kill, Vasily?'

'If you say so,' Zaitsev grumbled, pulling a flask from his pocket. 'A drink, Raisa?'

Rogov scurried away to his car, eyes bright with hate. They traipsed across the bombsite. A big man wearing a trench coat lay across the lip of a muddy crater. 'Does anyone know who it is?' asked Raisa Tarasov, crouching next to the body. 'Most of his face is missing.'

'His name is Michael Nolan,' said Fairburn. 'He was our original target at the Richmond Assizes.'

Ross turned the body with his booted foot. 'Was Nolan here to keep an eye on you, or kill you?'

'To confirm I killed you. He was testing my loyalty to Prasad.'

Sechkin shook his head. 'He wasn't expecting snipers though, was he?'

'He made mistakes in the field,' said Zaitsev.

'Yes,' said Fairburn, heading back to the car. 'His biggest was trusting me.'

The next morning Sechkin told Fairburn how Kim Philby, Gerry Scanlon and General Teplyakov had spent the night carving up British politics like Victorian imperialists marking borders on a map. Philby and Scanlon agreed their truce – *a Nash Equation* – by negotiating a Politburo more to their liking. Teplyakov, Sechkin said, got everything he wanted: not only a purge of wreckers blessed by Scanlon himself, but the right to boast of crushing the CIA's British network. Khrushchev would be pleased and his visit would be a triumph. The three men sat down at midnight with six bottles of Stolichnaya and the deal was done before dawn.

Sechkin parked his car at the top of Hay's Mews in Mayfair. 'Philby was as good as his word,' said the KGB Colonel, passing Tommy a silenced Walther. 'He never alerted Prasad.'

'Prasad's still inside the house?' Fairburn asked, taking the PKK and checking the action. KGB 1st Directorate officers from the embassy had kept Prasad's London pied-a-terre under surveillance all night.

'There's been no movement, but there's a light on inside.'

'I thought he'd become suspicious if Nolan didn't call.'

'You won't know until you go through the door, will you?'

Fairburn raised an eyebrow shrugged. 'Why me?'

'You are a Spartan. *Death to spies*, eh?'

'Now Teplyakov wants to test my loyalty, you mean?'

Sechkin smiled. 'My head was on the chopping block too, Tommy. Trust me, I only get a crumb of credit.'

'At least you won't be dodging polar bears in Chukotsky, Nikolai.'

'Oh, the day is young' Sechkin said, nodding towards the mews. 'Now, go and do what you were trained to do.'

Fairburn opened the car door. 'Why not interrogate Prasad instead?'

'You haven't been paying attention, have you, Tommy? The truth's been decided. Why go and spoil it?' Sechkin opened his cigarette case. He tapped one on the lid and lit it. 'Besides, you'll be a major soon. Congratulations.'

Fairburn got out of the car and padded along the mews, his shadow cast before him by a waning moon. A KGB watcher in an alleyway nodded as he passed. Fairburn nodded and stifled a yawn. He yearned for a cup of coffee and some sleep. Reaching Prasad's front door, he slid a bobby pin into the lock and disengaged it. Pistol ready, he stepped inside the dimly lit house. Ash Prasad sat in a leather armchair, jacketless, his chin on his chest. His lips were covered in a film of dried spittle, his eyes open. Covering him with the Walther, Fairburn held two fingers to Prasad's carotid artery. He was dead. On a mahogany side table next to his chair was a half-finished glass of Scotch and a circular steel container, the sort a photographer might use to store unexposed film. Inside was a clutch of greenish ampoules. He'd seen them before, in Hungary. Potassium cyanide, CIA issue. A painful way to die.

Drawing back the curtains, Fairburn looked out of the window. Prasad would have noticed the curfew-breaking car parked at the end of the street, two men sitting inside. The shadowy figure in the alleyway. Prasad knew there was no escape and Teplyakov had expert torturers at his disposal. Fairburn imagined, in similar circumstances, he might have taken poison too. Leaving the cyanide capsules, he searched the rest of the house. There was only one bedroom, a single man's billet. In the kitchen sink he found a pyre of burnt papers, including his journal. Returning to the sitting room, he patted down Prasad's body. Taking his wallet and a leather-backed pocket diary, he returned to the car. 'He killed himself, Nikolai,' he said. 'Cyanide.'

'That was thoughtful,' Sechkin replied. 'Saves us a bullet. Now, how about some breakfast?'

'Before we go, can I ask you something, Nikolai? Something personal?'

'Of course, Tommy.'

'Do you think my father was really killed by the fascists?'

The tip of Sechkin's cigarette glowed inside the darkened car. 'What did Prasad say? More CIA lies, I suppose?'

Fairburn remembered the evidence from Todmorden's basement. 'Are they lies? Did we send British concentration camp survivors to Russia as slave labour?'

Sechkin started the ZIL's engine. 'You've seen the reports, Tommy. I choose to believe our version, not theirs.'

The truth has been decided. Why go and spoil it? 'I'm sorry, Nikolai. I'm tired.'

Sechkin slapped Tommy's back. Sechkin playing to type, the playful Russian bear, square-shouldered and beer-bellied. 'We're all tired, Tommy. Now, how about a decent breakfast, good coffee and a clean bed? Irina's made up a room for you.'

Fairburn tried to smile. 'That sounds good, Nikolai. Let's go.'

Chapter 38

Major Thomas Fairburn, *Spartan* of the KGB's 10th Directorate, stood on a flag-draped balcony overlooking Whitehall. He wore gold stars on his shoulder boards, his tunic fitted by one of Saville Row's finest military tailors. The Liberation parade was only halfway through, yet still the soldiers came: Soviets in grey-green uniforms, followed by the British in khaki. They were followed by other protectors of the state: militiamen and CSS paramilitary troops, border guards and Justice Ministry police. Armoured cars and tanks trundled by, filling the streets with the stink of diesel, followed by artillery pieces and fat atomic missiles on caterpillar-tracked launchers. Then a procession of military bands, followed by a division of Soviet Guardsmen wearing the uniforms of the Great Patriotic War, bayonets glittering, banners flying, heads turned as one towards a platform covered in banners and garlands of flowers. Crowds waved and cheered under the eyes of plainclothes CSS men.

The War Office building offered a view of the main podium, where the salute was taken by Nikita Khrushchev. Next to him sat the Chairman of the Socialist Republic of Great Britain, Oliver Weald. Weald sat huddled in a wheelchair, a blanket across his lap, flanked by stern-looking nurses. Behind him lurked General Anatoly Teplyakov and Deputy Chairman Gerry Scanlon, General of Militia, smiling like old friends. 'Ah, here come the fly-boys,' said Sechkin. A V-shaped formation of Tupolev bombers screamed overhead, escorted by a squadron of jet fighters. They gleamed like quicksilver in the dull October sky, red stars bright on their wings.

'Very impressive,' Fairburn replied, standing stiffly to attention. 'The last time I saw this much firepower was in Hungary.'

'Thanks to you the firepower's only for show,' Sechkin replied. 'Well done, Tommy.'

'I'm glad,' Fairburn replied. 'It was the best outcome we could've hoped for.'

'That's the spirit, *Major*,' said Nikolai. 'I've booked us a table at the Savoy for a late lunch, Irina's bringing some of the girls from the embassy. They're all very pretty. Maybe you'll meet someone at last? You know how the KGB likes its officers to be married.'

'Maybe I will.' Fairburn nodded. Below, someone in the crowd shook his fist at the podium. He was bundled away by burly men in raincoats. 'There's always one idiot who wants to spoil everything, isn't there?'

'Of course,' said Sechkin. 'Wreckers. They keep us in work, though.'

A uniformed CSS captain threaded his way through the crowd of KGB men and cleared his throat. 'Comrade Major Fairburn?' he asked, saluting smartly.

'Yes?'

'When you've a moment to spare, sir, Comrade Deputy Chairman Philby would like a word.'

Philby waited in a grand office the cenotaph, dressed in a smart grey suit and a black tie. No medals, apart from the Order of Lenin. He winced as he limped towards Fairburn and offered his hand. 'My back's playing up,' he said apologetically.

'Is it an old injury, Comrade Director?'

The CSS chief nodded. 'Back in '46, the Nazis accused me of espionage. I was guilty, of course, I was passing material to my NKVD contact in London every week. Anyway, the head of the German SD, a chap called Schellenberg, ordered my interrogation. You might have heard of him?'

'SS-Oberführer Walter Schellenberg. We learned about him at the Academy. He was tried and hanged after the war.'

'That's the fellow. His chaps really went to town on me,' Philby continued, his eyes fixed on a point over Fairburn's shoulder. 'They actually put me on a rack, would you believe? One of the interrogators was obsessed by medieval torture devices. I slipped a few discs, but I denied everything.'

'I'm sorry, Comrade.'

'These things happen, especially in wartime. Anyhow, afterwards, I remember Schellenberg apologising. He even took me to White's for lunch. I've met worst fascists, actually, than Walter.' There was, for a moment, an uncomfortable silence.

'You wanted to see me?' said Fairburn finally.

'I wanted to thank you personally while I still have time. There's a reception for Comrade Khrushchev, you know how it is. Bloody canapes and politics.'

'Of course, Comrade Director.'

'Call me Kim. How many times do I have to tell you?' Philby hobbled towards a drinks cabinet and produced a bottle of Dewar's white label. He poured two glasses and passed one to Fairburn. 'Not a bad view, eh? This office belongs to the Deputy Chief of the Defence Staff. We were at Westminster together.'

Fairburn took the glass. 'A toast then, Kim?'

'Why not, Tommy? Here's to *keeping secrets*.'

'Yes, to keeping secrets,' Fairburn replied, touching his glass to Philby's.

Philby finished his drink and poured another. 'I'm not sure what your role was in the Prasad affair. To tell the truth, I'm not entirely sure I want to know.'

'I've given a detailed account, Kim, but if you'd like me to clarify anything please ask.'

Philby smiled, as if enjoying a private joke. 'I'm just glad you unmasked Prasad. You've done me, and our country, a considerable favour.'

Fairburn nodded. 'I feared London might become another Budapest.'

'I'll admit to finding myself conflicted. As an Englishman, I want to see a peaceful resolution to our problems. As a Socialist? I know, in my heart, there has to be conflict.'

'Conflict?'

'Yes, of course. Class struggle. Class *warfare*. Is our revolution genuinely finished? I do wonder, though, if such wars are best fought in the shadows. We should spare the Workers any unnecessary suffering if possible.'

'I agree, Kim,' Fairburn replied, holding up his glass and swirling the golden whisky. 'Let's keep the fight in the shadows as much as we're able.'

'By the way, a sensitive Soviet research project was compromised last week. A scientist called Andrew Fisk was kidnapped by CIA-backed terrorists. Our intelligence indicates he'll soon be appearing at a press conference in Washington DC.'

'Comrade Colonel Sechkin mentioned there was a problem. I know he was involved in the project's security.'

Philby looked Fairburn up and down. He smiled. 'This, I believe, was Prasad's objective all along. It's why he tried to compromise you. It's why Eliza Crewe was so important. I think she was the CIA's conduit into Fisk. Without her reassurances I don't believe he'd have ever defected. He's a timid chap, by all accounts.'

'Prasad never mentioned Fisk. His main concern was protecting his co-conspirator inside CSS, Alison King.'

'Are you sure? King took cyanide too.'

'Yes, I'm quite sure.'

'That's a blessed relief. In any case, Fisk was taken too late to disrupt the Soviet project.'

'I'm not cleared to know the details,' said Fairburn, wondering for a moment if he sounded too formal. 'As you said, we must keep our secrets.'

'Ah, but this won't be a secret much longer.' Philby took something from a desk drawer. A newspaper. 'This is *The Times*' front page tomorrow,' he said. The headline read SOVIET UNION TRIUMPHANT! USSR WINS RACE TO LAUNCH FIRST EARTH SATELLITE.

'A space satellite? That's an incredible achievement, Kim. Fisk was involved?'

'I'm assured British scientists had a role in this so-called *Sputnik* project, yes,' said Philby proudly. 'As far as Comrade General Teplyakov's concerned, we've frustrated a brazen attempt by the CIA to compromise a historic moment for World Socialism. I spoke with Chairman Khrushchev earlier. He's delighted with our intelligence apparatus' performance. I'm putting Sergeant Ross in for an award.'

Although Fisk's knowledge was useful to the Americans, Fairburn doubted his defection changed much. It certainly never posed a threat to the launch of any rocket. 'If this is the conclusion our leaders have drawn, who are we to argue?' he replied. He felt like laughing at the ridiculousness of it all.

'Now you're beginning to sound like a professional Soviet intelligence officer,' Philby chuckled. 'Who knows what grand stratagems Comrade Khrushchev sees that we cannot? Now, would you care for one more drink?'

'Why not?' The two men sipped whisky, greyish light filtering through the high windows. Outside, passing tanks made the glass rattle.

'Well, I'll leave you to the rest of your day, *Major*,' said Philby, glancing at Fairburn's shoulder boards. 'Enjoy your lunch. The Savoy's still rather special. I recommend the Dover sole.'

'Thank you, Kim,' said Fairburn, heading for the door. 'I will.'

Chapter 39

Fairburn strolled towards Holland Park, hands in pockets. He'd been followed by Teplyakov's flat-footed KGB men for nearly a week. Sechkin assured him it was routine for operatives who'd been exposed to enemy agents. 'Besides, Tommy,' he'd chuckled, 'you always lose them.'

The first KGB tail was a bear-like goon, too imposing to be a proper surveillance operative. 'Excuse me, Comrade,' Fairburn had said, turning on his heel. 'You're following me again. I saw you twice on Argyll Road.' Scowling, the big man ambled away. The second tail was better, a skinny fellow wearing a shabby suit. He'd anticipated Fairburn's route, taking position outside a café on the junction with Earl's Court Road. Fairburn stopped outside and called a waitress. 'Can you get that gentleman another coffee? And perhaps a slice of cake?' He gave her a handful of coins, winked at the KGB man and entered the park.

Holland Park was a city farm, a Potemkin showcase for agricultural collectivization. There were rows of leafy allotments, each growing different varieties of vegetables. Pigs oinked happily while rose-cheeked women in overalls fed flocks of excitable ducks and chickens. A twee shop sold produce to specially selected visitors, including jam, meat pies and pickles. Fairburn showed his identity card and bought marmalade, tomatoes, eggs and bacon. Putting them carefully in a cloth shopping bag, he headed deeper into the park. Satisfied he wasn't being followed, he stopped at a telephone box and made a call before walking towards Ladbroke Grove. Finally, Fairburn loitered outside a pub, as if pondering whether to go inside for a pint. When he turned around, as agreed, a green Vauxhall Wyvern was waiting. The rear door opened and he got in the back. The driver was a hard-faced man wearing a leather jacket. Fairburn saw the bulge of a gun under his arm. Sitting next to him in the passenger seat was a dark-haired woman dressed in a tweed skirt and a twinset. She wore a silk scarf over her hair, her eyes shielded by sunglasses. 'Your nose looks better, Tommy,' said Katherine. 'How did you find my number?'

'Prasad's diary. It was the only thing he didn't burn before he killed himself. The code was simple enough to crack.'

'Ash knew you'd find it, perhaps?'

'Yes, I think he did.'

They drove to a shabby housing estate in North Kensington, dirty-faced children larking around on bombsites. 'If you could give us a moment, Norman?' said Katherine to her driver.

Norman shot Tommy a look. 'No problem, Katherine. I'll be back in ten minutes, okay?'

When Norman was gone, Katherine pulled a compact from her bag and flipped it open. She checked her reflection in a tiny mirror and applied a little lipstick. 'What do you want, Tommy?' she said finally. 'Why haven't we been arrested?'

'Because I helped Sandy Fisk escape, just as you ordered. I betrayed my own side.'

'You were under considerable duress.'

'I also had Nolan killed. I set him up for our snipers.'

Katherine's laugh was bitter. 'You really are a bastard, Tommy. We underestimated you.'

'It doesn't matter. There are no tanks on the streets. No bloodshed.'

'And Britain's now ruled by who? Scanlon and Philby? A policeman and a spy. Well done, Captain Fairburn.'

It was Fairburn's turn to laugh. It was also bitter. 'I'm a major now, actually.'

'Bully for you. You've destroyed the only network capable of getting people out of this godforsaken country. It'll take years to rebuild.'

'Maybe not,' Fairburn replied. 'I haven't told anyone about it.'

'How so?'

Fairburn passed Katherine a piece of paper. 'This code won't take long for your American friends to decrypt.'

'What does it say?'

'It's the details for a dead-letter drop. Here, in London.'

Katherine raised an eyebrow. 'Why?'

'I leave London in two weeks for my next assignment. I'll check the drop daily at twenty hundred hours, starting tomorrow evening.'

'Why, Tommy? Why are you helping us? It's the first thing the CIA will ask.'

Fairburn opened the car door. He smiled. 'Agent motivation? There are lots of reasons, but something Prasad said stuck in my mind. Something like, *the original sin of totalitarianism is the lies they make you tell every day.* My head's so full of lies, about so many things. Sometimes I think they'll send me crazy.'

Katherine put a hand on Fairburn's. 'You know the CIA might think you're a double agent?'

'I'd be disappointed if they didn't. Still, they won't be able to resist. We both know it.'

'Yes, that's how the game's played,' Katherine said, carefully folding the piece of paper and putting it in her purse. 'I'll pass this on.'

Fairburn nodded and got out of the car. 'Your house in Devon is safe. In fact, I liked it there. The people were different from the sort I usually meet.'

'They're free to speak their minds, Tommy. To tell the truth about what they see and feel.'

Fairburn saw a pile of autumn leaves. He felt the urge to run through them, as a child might. 'Take care, Katherine. I'll make my own way from here.'

'Yes,' she replied. 'I suspect you will.'

THE END

Afterword

My Soviet-occupied Britain was heavily influenced by Anne Applebaum's *Iron Curtain: The Crushing of Eastern Europe, 1944–1956*, an account of Soviet repression in the former German Democratic Republic, Poland and Hungary. Ms Applebaum's work is accessible, authoritative and I strongly recommend it. I'm also grateful to the *Crypto Museum* (https://www.cryptomuseum.com), an essential resource for anyone interested in the history of espionage and covert communications technology. They have functioning examples of the Protona Minifon recorder and NEVA surveillance radios featured in the book. The KGB's 10th Directorate is entirely fictional, as is the Spartan programme (although the KGB routinely trained agents from aligned regimes). However, some important characters in the story are real, or loosely based on real people:

Harold 'Kim' Philby requires little introduction. Widely tipped to be a future head of the Secret Intelligence Service (MI6), Philby was one of the USSR's most accomplished spies. A true believer in Communism, in our real-world timeline he defected to Moscow in 1963. My version of Philby remained inside MI6, working as a liaison officer with German intelligence – the Abwehr – before their replacement by the *Sicherheitsdienst* (SD) in 1944. Finally falling under suspicion and tortured by the Nazis, my Philby remains ideologically committed to Communism.

Harry Pollitt features in memoriam, with the CPGB's Kings Cross HQ named in his honour. Pollitt, General Secretary of the Communist Party of Great Britain and an unapologetic Stalinist (he served in the honour guard at the Dictator's funeral), died in 1960 of natural causes. In my timeline, he falls foul of Kim Philby and perishes in a car accident.

Vasily Zaitsev was the Red Army's most celebrated sniper, played by Jude Law in the film *Enemy at the Gates*. Originally a naval accountant, Zaitsev volunteered to join the infantry after the German invasion of the USSR. He became a sniper after impressing his superiors with marksmanship skills acquired hunting wolves in the Ural mountains. A proud, no-nonsense character, Zaitsev fell out of favour with the authorities after the war. Unlike the real Zaitsev, who led a life of quiet respectability as director of a textiles factory, my version accepts employment as a marksman with the KGB's shadowy 10th Directorate.

Andrew 'Sandy' Fisk is very loosely based on **Arthur C. Clarke**. Perhaps best known as a celebrated science fiction author, Clarke spent the Second World War in the RAF working on ground-to-air radar systems. In 1945, he published a paper on telecommunications relays and geostationary satellites. As such, Clarke is often cited as the theoretical father of the telecommunications satellite. The real Sputnik – which caused panic in Western defence circles – was launched on 4th October 1957. My Sputnik, for reasons of artistic licence, took off several weeks later. There were, to my knowledge, no British scientists involved in the real Sputnik project.

Lastly, I would like to thank Ms. Olga Kurushina for her generous assistance with all things Russian. Of course, any errors are mine. *Spasibo!*

Dominic Adler
London, August 2023